To J., *the most delicate of all flowers.*

The Sorrowful Woman

Julia Flowers' First Casebook: *The Sorrowful Woman*

Copyright © 2016 Alan M.A. Friedmann
All rights reserved.
www.alanfriedmann.com

This is a work of fiction. Any similarity between the characters and situations within its pages and places or persons, living or dead, is unintentional and co-incidental.

This edition published in 2016 by Muirhouses Partnership
Old Largoward, Fife, Scotland KY9 1JA.

First printing.
Printed in the UK by Cloc Ltd, London N17 9QU.

A CIP record for this book is available from the British Library.

ISBN: 978-1-5272-0237-5

Also available at **amazon**kindle as an e-book

Buy the paperback from **www.alanfriedmann.com**
Available from good bookshops, too.

Julia Flowers' First Casebook

The sorrowful woman

ALAN M.A. FRIEDMANN

CHAPTER 1

THE CALL

"Campbell asked you to ring Greed & Mayhem ASAP." Joan shouted along the long corridor from her receptionist's tiny office to Julia's panelled room.

"You mean Reid & McHalm?" Julia had noticed the matter-of-fact tone in Joan's voice.

"I thought Campbell said Greed & Mayhem. Sorry."

"It's fine, Joan. Will do," said Julia in her soothing voice. "Joan was new to the office, but she would get used to Campbell's feeble puns," she thought.

Thursday is sale day at Hillman Roberts and porters were busy preparing the auction hall for the usual invasion of dealers, chancers, and pensioners all looking for a bargain.

Julia hated Thursdays and was glad that she was not involved in the organized chaos of the weekly auction of household items and curios – the detritus of cleared houses and de-cluttering efforts. As a specialist in Oriental antiques her job was to seek out, value, and possibly bring to auction the bewildering array of Japanese and Chinese works of art that have mysteriously managed to end up in Scottish homes, from two-bedroom bungalows to stately mansions.

As Reid and McHalm were the solicitors who dealt with the upper end of the market, aristocrats, pseudo-aristocrats, bankers, and minor celebrities, she was not going to ignore Campbell's message, in spite of the pressing matter of rescheduling her appointment with the dentist.

"This is Julia Flowers from Hillman Roberts the auctioneers, I understand Alistair Reid is trying to reach me" – the receptionist put her through immediately.

"Julia! Long time no see. How are you? I heard you have succumbed to the lure of the East Neuk," said Alistair in his captivating tone, proceeding without a pause to the business in hand, "we need you for a rather delicate job."

"Always happy to oblige, if I can," replied Julia, knowing that the details of her recent move to a seaside village near St Andrews would be of no interest to Alistair Reid.

"Do you remember the insurance valuation you did for us quite some time ago for the property at 55 Heriot Row?" asked Alistair, expecting an immediate positive response.

"Not off hand. What was the name of the client?"

"Dr Anthony Gordon, the late Dr Anthony Gordon," stated Alistair, as if to settle the issue conclusively.

"Yes, of course. How could I forget? A most beautiful pair of Doucai bowls," replied Julia, regretting instantly her enthusiasm as she recalled the gruesome end of Dr Gordon's life.

Alistair Reid carried on unfazed: "Well, we need a valuation for probate now and," before Julia could ask what was delicate about it, "the *pòlis* may be involved."

Julia did not take on board the gist of Alistair's request as she was disorientated by the Glaswegian accent Alistair has used to pronounce "police", with an exaggerated emphasis on the first syllable – most uncharacteristic of Alistair Reid's cut-glass Edinburgh voice.

"The police?" repeated Julia, with the accent in the right place.

"Of course, you must remember Dr Gordon's murder. It was in every newspaper for days," said Alistair Reid.

"Yes, yes," Julia had recovered her composure, "it was horrendous. But why would the police be interested in a valuation? Are there problems with the inheritance?"

"No, no. No pushy heirs. No heirs at all, in fact. It is more delicate than that. And, to be precise, it is not the police as such that is interested. It's one single policeman." Alistair Reid could not hide a hint of disapproval in his voice, "Detective Bland."

"Isn't it an old case? It must have been a couple of years ago. Is Detective Bland interested in the contents of the house?" Julia felt uneasy about the whole conversation.

"All I am saying is that a Detective Bland may be in touch with you. I myself do not know why. Are you free sometime next week?" Alistair Reid was obviously keen to put an end to the awkward conversation.

"Let me just check my diary. Will have to be next Friday. Say 2pm?" Julia did not work on Fridays as a rule, but her diary was full for the rest of the week and she was not in the mood to negotiate about dates with Alistair Reid.

"Yes, excellent," Alistair Reid was glad his gambit had paid off, "Sue will get the keys to you. Usual terms. Thank you, Julia." And with that he transferred the call back to the receptionist.

Julia was left wondering what the heck was going on, but, being the curious sort, she immediately googled "Dr Anthony Gordon + murder + Detective Bland". Far fewer hits than she was expecting appeared on the screen. Just a quick skim of the newspaper clippings was enough to remind her of the gist of the case: "*Reclusive Former Diplomat Found With Skull Smashed In Botched Burglary*". Not much on Detective Bland, just a few photos with him standing next to the Chief Superintendent. "Not a memorable face," thought Julia, "good for tailing people undetected." She tried to stop herself from having a private joke along the lines "Bland by name, bland by face", but the fact was that as soon as the photos disappeared from the screen, she could not recall any of Detective Bland's features. And she was *good* at faces!

Joan came in to Julia's office with the 55 Heriot Row valuation. For some reason there was no file on the Hillman Roberts' server, but Joan had managed to find a ten-year old paper copy. As soon as Julia started leafing through the pages, her photographic memory brought all the contents of 55 Heriot Row back to life. She remembered how neatly displayed everything was and how glad she had been at the time for being able to value all the items without the hindrance of the owner following her with a running commentary on each piece to be valued. After twenty-five years in the business she should have got used to customers trying either to hype the value of items to be insured or to undervalue anything left in a will, but she still found their "help" an irritation and a waste of time.

"As I never even met Dr Gordon, Detective Bland cannot possibly be interested in me as a witness, only in the valuation," thought Julia, relieved not a little.

CHAPTER 2

INSPECTOR BLAND

For the next few days Julia could not stop thinking about Heriot Row. She had lived in Heriot Row for five unhappy years, leaving just after her divorce. Actually, most of her Heriot Row memories were happy ones – Maisie and Philip starting and finishing primary school, her friendship with Ruthie and Rupert, she eccentric and yet practical, he reserved and a dreamer. These were happy memories because they did not include any recollection of her ex, a sorry specimen of a bully, now a totally faded nightmare. Every time she drove past that beautiful row of grey stone houses she remembered the hope and trepidation that had filled her when she moved into the magnificent three-storey apartment all those years ago. Her marriage was already a shipwreck looking for a big rock to crash into, but she had stubbornly refused to admit it.

"The Enlightenment in stones", that is how Edinburgh's New Town is described in tourist guides. Well, she thought that the airy high ceilings, the beautifully proportioned windows, the sense of rational distributions of lines and volumes, could somehow restore a semblance of normality to her life, stop it from sliding into the quick sands of accepted unhappiness. She had been an idiot – she knew it now.

What had been her temporary salvation or, more accurately, her means of postponing the inevitable, was the strange inverted gated community of Heriot Row residents. What tourist guides do not mention is that, facing the neat row of Enlightenment stone houses, there are some magnificent gardens, fenced in black steel balustrades, gated, and locked – each Heriot Row resident the proud owner of a garden key.

When the weight of disappointment was unbearable, Julia would simply cross the road, unlock a gate, open it slowly and even more slowly lock it behind her and then be welcomed by the splendid reproduction of an impossibly idyllic Scottish countryside – century-old oak trees, undulating lawns, little spinneys dotted around, discreet benches beckoning her to sit down and rest. She felt secure, protected, safe.

For years, after the divorce, she had missed that sense of private space that the Heriot Row gardens had given her. Only now that she had moved to the East Neuk had she regained that very sense of inviolable personal domain, not thanks to a garden, but through leisurely walks along the Coastal Path, the reassuring sight of the Isle of May an unmoveable beacon confirming her location more accurately than any GPS device.

55 Heriot Row would be described in London as a basement flat, whereas in Edinburgh it was unmistakeably a ground-floor apartment, the few steps down at the front entrance an irrelevance compared to the back aspect of the house leading to a small but totally enchanting garden.

She was familiar with the two-lock door – A-grade listing ensures that all Heriot Row doors look remarkably similar. She enjoyed as much as ever the solid sound of a long since locked door yielding to her steady turning of the Chubb key. Automatically she reached for the light switch and was startled when the lights obligingly lit up. Sue of Reid & McHalm had warned her that the property had been vacant for over a year and therefore may be dark and cold. It was certainly cold, even in the unseasonably warm weather of early April, but it was full of light, the vestibule resplendent in the 12-light chandelier hanging from the high ceiling, the living room bathed in sunshine coming through the two full-length windows.

As soon as she stepped into the living room, she felt very uneasy – something was wrong, very wrong, but she could not say what it was. She approached swiftly the large vitrine housing the best pieces of the late Dr Gordon's collection and, just as she was about to open it, she realized why she felt so weary, as if someone was watching her. The room, indeed, as she discovered later, the entire apartment, was exactly as she had seen it over ten years ago. She was certain that, from the large Chesterfield sofa down to smallest snuff box, every single piece in the house had not been moved. It was like walking by mistake on to a movie set, left untouched from the last shoot, the cameramen and sound recordists glaring at her for disturbing the carefully arranged set.

Julia tried to shrug her uneasiness off by starting her valuation in earnest. She had decided to leave the piece de resistance, the pair of Doucai bowls, till last, – a reward for her hard work in the freezing apartment. She methodically checked every piece against the inventory in her old valuation. She loved comparing the current value of the better pieces against her ten-year old estimates, Japanese porcelain drastically under-priced today, any Chinese piece of good quality soaring in value. She proceeded much faster than she had expected mainly because she could follow her old inventory step by step, as nothing had been moved, as if it had been super-glued for posterity.

Finally, the time had arrived for her reward. As expected, the two Doucai bowls had a tiny vitrine all to themselves. She opened the glass door carefully and lifted one of the bowls slowly, turning it upside down to see again that very elusive Yongzheng mark. As she did so she nearly dropped it, as she was startled by the sound of the doorbell echoing through the empty house.

She was used to working in vacant properties and sometimes a neighbour or a delivery man would interrupt her solitary annotations of items and values, but today she was definitely unsettled by the unexpected visit. Before opening the door Julia looked through the spy-hole and was mightily relieved to see at the other end the unremarkable features of Inspector Bland.

"How can I help you?" asked Julia, not wishing to reveal that she had done some background checks on the visitor.

"Detective Chief Inspector Bland, of Police Scotland," replied Eric Bland showing his badge and his desire to gain access to the apartment as quickly as possible. Once he was inside, DCI Bland pre-empted Julia's next question: "I had asked Reid & McHalm to let me know immediately the new valuation was carried out. I meant to arrive here before you, but, you know, Edinburgh traffic."

"Nice to meet you, Mr Bland. Julia Flowers, of Hillman Roberts, the auctioneers. Forgive me if my question is out of order, but I am not sure why the police should be at all interested in my valuation."

Eric Bland could not possibly answer with the real reason. Leaving the Gordon murder unsolved was a big stumbling block to his promotion to Superintendent and, conversely, bringing a conviction home would guarantee it. He had exhausted all lines of enquiry and was clutching at straws. And if straws came in the rather lovely shape of Julia Flowers, so much the better. He reckoned she would be 50 tops, well educated, probably separated or divorced, and he found her instantly alluring.

"We checked the contents of the house against your valuation and found that nothing was missing hence the line of enquiry 'Botched Burglary' but, if I can be frank with you, it has led nowhere."

Julia relaxed and broke into one of her broad smiles, genuine, sincere, utterly charming. "Well, not quite," she said, pausing for effect.

"What do you mean 'not quite'? I double-checked myself and not a single pin was missing. I am certain." Eric Bland was thorough and he knew it.

"How much do you know about Chinese Imperial bowls, Mr Bland?" Julia surprised herself with the directness of her own question.

"I know that Dr Gordon had a pair of them of very good quality – the best pieces in his collection – and I also know that they were in their own cabinet when we released the apartment into the care of Reid & McHalm." DCI Bland did not really mean the nasty implication of his last statement, but now it was too late. He saw Julia Flowers's face tense up and her beautiful smile disappear.

"Follow me, Mr Bland," Julia walked to the vitrine housing the Doucai bowls, opened it, took the two bowls out and then asked: "You mean these?"

"Precisely." DCI Bland unaccountably and suddenly felt less secure of his case.

"To the untrained eye or even to a trained eye they *look like* the Doucai bowls, but I can assure that they are not. I can explain, if you like." Julia felt in charge and it was a warm feeling. She took Bland's silence as an invitation to carry on.

"The Yongzheng period lasted for only 22 years (1723-1735) but produced arguably the most exquisite Chinese porcelain ever. As always with Chinese pieces, the best quality bears the Imperial mark," at this point

Julia turned one of the bowls upside down to reveal some hieroglyphics, "in this case a six-character Yongzheng mark."

"I do not mean to be rude, Mrs Flowers, but if you could concentrate on essentials," interrupted Bland.

"The mark is the 'essentials', Mr Bland," continued Julia unperturbed, "probably only two or three Imperial calligraphers were entrusted with marking pieces made for the Emperor. A genuine mark is distinctive for the neatness of the strokes, and other features that I will not bore you with, Mr Bland. But I can assure you that these are *not* the Doucai Lingzhi bowls I valued ten years ago."

"I do not understand. Where are the originals? Why replace them with fakes?" DCI Bland was thinking aloud.

"I can tell you that someone went to a great deal of trouble to make these copies. These are not fakes; most probably they are 19th century replicas, with the signature added on some time later."

Now DCI Bland was angry with himself. He should have had the contents of the apartment assessed by an expert at the time. He could see it now. Too fucking late. But then what? Surely the burglars would not replace the originals with two pretty good copies that they happened to have in their swag bag and then proceed to smash Anthony Gordon's skull and leave the scene unseen. The whole business made even less sense now.

"Thank you, Mrs Flowers. I am sorry if I was a bit blunt before, but this case has been bothering me from day one. And the missing bowls make this job even harder now," DCI Bland thought best to mend bridges with Julia Flowers. As he was at it, he may as well go the whole hog and ask her for help. "Have you found anything else that may help us with our enquiries, Mrs Flowers?"

Julia realised that Bland was trying to make amends and she was happy to return to a less tense conversation: "Well, Mr Bland, I am not sure whether it may be of any help to you, but there are a couple of things …"

"Please, Mrs Flowers. Anything. Anything at all." She had not corrected his use of Mrs, he noted. Shame.

"Well, I find strange that the whole arrangement of the house has not been changed at all after ten odd years," said Julia.

"Why is it strange?"

"It is as if nobody touched anything. Ever. Every single item is *exactly* on the very same spot it was ten years ago."

Bland did not quite know what to do with this piece of information.

"And then there is the cheap Chinese puzzle box," continued Julia.

CHAPTER 3

THE CHINESE PUZZLE BOX

Before DCI Bland could ask, Julia continued:

"I find it odd that the only addition to Dr Gordon's possessions should be a relatively cheap Chinese puzzle box," and with that Julia moved swiftly to a small drawing room where on a three-legged stool with fine intaglio work sat a non-descript whitish cube. Julia picked it up and started to show to Bland the simple but ingenious mechanism.

"This is not bad quality – it is ivory for a start – but it just does not fit with the character of Dr Gordon's collection."

Bland found the notion that collections possessed "character" difficult to swallow, but he was too keen to see the contents of the box to start quibbling about semantics.

"Can you open it, Mrs Flowers? Please."

Julia was enjoying her role of teacher in antiques, a role that she would play occasionally when invited by Women's Institute clubs and the like, ostensively to give a talk on Japanese porcelain or Chinese jades but in practice to provide free valuations for the assorted items that earnest WI members and retired Army officers would inevitably bring along 'to know the history of the piece', of course.

"These boxes are made up by a series of sliding pieces, which must be pushed in and out in the correct sequence for the box to open. They were made in China in large numbers mainly for the export market especially in Victorian times, but now are out of fashion and you can pick up a decent specimen like this one for one hundred pounds or so at auction these days."

Bland was not really in the mood for an Antiques Road Show episode and his frustration must have been quite visible, because Julia stopped lecturing and started to demonstrate:

"This box's mechanism is quite primitive, you see Mr Bland, all you have to do is to slide these two pieces in opposite directions and then" – here she paused for what seemed to DCI Bland to be an unnecessarily long time – the lid is released and the box opens". Julia passed the open box on to DCI Bland without looking at what was inside it.

Bland grabbed the box firmly in his hands, peeked inside and then raised his eyes to look straight at Julia: "But it's empty." Bland could not hide his disappointment.

"Yes, most of them are; they are just curiosities, not storage devices." Julia felt sorry for DCI Bland and slightly guilty for having unwittingly raised his expectations. She took the box back from Bland's hands and started to examine it in more detail.

"This is odd," she said after a while, "See this piece, Mr Bland? It is not ivory like the others. It is ivorine."

Julia could see from Bland's expression that the significance of the detail was lost on him.

"Ivorine is poor man's ivory. In fact it is cellulose nitrate and nowadays can be manufactured to look and feel just like ivory. The question is: 'why would Dr Gordon take the trouble to replace a missing or damaged ivory piece?' Having the ivorine piece made to measure would have cost him more than the whole box is worth."

"Could I see the piece, Mrs Flowers?" DCI Bland turned the rectangular shape in his hands more in frustration than in hope. "It really looks and feels like ivory. Ah, the Chinese. They can copy anything, can't they?"

"Actually, ivorine is a European invention. Swiss, I think. It's the weight and density that gives it away."

Julia took the piece back and proceeded to tap it. "But even for ivorine, this feels far too light. Odd." Julia sounded surprised at her own little discovery. "Of course, it may be hollow. But why?"

Bland practically grabbed the piece off Julia's hands. "Do you think you can prise it open, Mrs Flowers?"

"I am not sure we should, Mr Bland. Are we allowed to damage Dr Gordon's property? Perhaps we should check with Reid & McHalm first".

"This is evidence in a murder case. I take responsibility. Please, can you open it?" Bland had a feeling about this wretched piece of fakery.

Julia took her eye-piece from her handbag and inspected the ivorine rectangular shape under magnification, looking for cracks. It turned out to be easier than she thought: the tweezers in her bag were enough to crack the piece open. She passed it on to DCI Bland. This time it was not empty.

Bland's face lit up and, for the first time since Julia had met him, he smiled.

"Ah, a memory stick." This was his terrain; he felt in charge again. "I'll have it examined straightaway. You have been most helpful, Mrs Flowers. Thank you. I may have to contact you again."

"Of course, Mr Bland. Here is my card," Julia took out of a bag one of her business cards and added, "I'll write my mobile's number on the back. In case you want to contact me when I am not at work. I work part-time, you see."

While Julia was scribbling Bland realized she had kept calling him "Mr" Bland and that he had not insisted on being called by his job title. Was Detective Chief Inspector too long for Mrs Flowers or did she see him as a civilian?

"Very kind of you, Mrs Flowers. I'll leave you to finish your work here. I'll scoot to the station. This may be important," said Bland waving his precious piece of new evidence.

And he left as abruptly as he had arrived.

CHAPTER 4

MEMORY STICKS

Julia Flowers was proud of her new house in the East Neuk. Proud for what it meant more than for what it was. It was the first house she could call truly hers. She had not left home to go to college as the Edinburgh College of Art was where she wanted to study and her parents had turned the basement of the family home in Stockbridge into a separate flat just for her. Soon after graduation both her parents died in quick and terrible succession and she just moved upstairs. Marriage meant a move to Suffolk first and back to Edinburgh later, but neither the cottage in Haverhill nor the apartment in Heriot Row ever felt hers. They had been chosen by her ex and, nice as they both were in their different ways, they had been given to her, as if she were a welcome lodger.

No, the white house on the coast was most definitely hers and hers alone. She had decided to move away from Edinburgh. She had looked at dozens of properties. She had negotiated a good price for "Whitewalls" and sold her Edinburgh flat at a handsome profit. Even Maisie and Philip were told of the move after she had already exchanged contracts.

Julia loved everything about her new house. She loved that although it was only a stone's throw away from the harbour her house stood almost isolated on a limb of coast slightly protruding from the row of pretty terraced cottages. She loved the tiny white-walled garden, the welcome refuge of a few bushes too stubborn even for the bitter North wind. But most of all she loved that everything about the house was hers.

Saturday mornings were chillax time, as Philip would say. No alarms in the morning, a lazy late breakfast, Radio 4 in the background, googling a new recipe for the evening meal. What was definitely not part of her Saturday morning routine was the landline ringing furiously for attention. Her landline phone had come with her broadband package and she hardly ever used it and practically nobody knew the number anyway.

"Julia Flowers speaking. Who is calling?"

"I am very sorry to bother you at home and at the weekend, Mrs Flowers. This is Detective Chief Inspector Bland. I tried your mobile, but there was no reply."

"Not a problem, Mr Bland. How can I help you? It's the memory stick, isn't it?"

"Precisely, Mrs Flowers. I am afraid we may need your help again," said Bland, still apologetic.

"Sure. Why don't you email the file to me, Mr Bland and I will look at it."

"I am afraid it is not as simple as that. We may need a statement from you. I know this is really inconvenient for you, but could I see you sometime this afternoon, Mrs Flowers?"

"But I do not live in Edinburgh and ..." before Julia could continue, DCI interrupted her:

"I know where you live, Mrs Flowers, and I would not ask if it were not really urgent."

"I see. Fine. Can you come at three?" Julia relented.

"It is very kind of you, Mrs Flowers. I'll be there at three. Thank you again. Good bye".

Normally, at this time of day on a Saturday, Julia Flowers would be preparing a light lunch, a halloumi salad accompanied by a glass of Prosecco a distinct possibility, to be followed by a couple of hours lying on the George III chaise long that she had had re-upholstered, attending to her Facebook contacts, following up little queries that had been accumulating in her mind for the last few days, possibly Skypeing Maisie or Philip, if they were available, awake, and not too hung over.

Instead, she forgot completely about lunch and went straight to her old desktop in her study, determined to find out more about the late Dr Gordon. Once she started sifting through the many hits about his murder, she paused for a while and asked herself why she was doing this. It felt a bit like homework. Was she swotting so that she would not appear unprepared when Inspector Bland called? Or was this idle curiosity on an idle Saturday?

She decided that it was a bit of both and, discarding all the pages (and they were many) on the murder and on the investigation (much fewer), she tried to piece together who Dr Anthony Gordon was.

It did not take more than half an hour for Julia Flowers to realise that Dr Gordon had led a very strange life, a game of two halves, as the cliché goes. After graduating with a double First at Madgalen College Oxford, Gordon went straight to the Foreign Office, rising quickly through the Civil Service ranks. Barely in his thirties he left the FO to be appointed Director of Research at Chatham House where he was very active promoting research, seminars, and conferences on China. This was followed, not wholly unpredictably, by a return to the FO, but this time as Cultural Attaché at the British Embassy in Beijing. And then, Julia thought, something strange must have happened, because not only did he resign his Diplomatic Service job, but he took up a post as Visiting Professor of International Relations at the University of Abertay (the former Dundee Institute of Technology). Not exactly the crowning of a scintillating career – more a jumping into a big hole, in the hope no-one will see you. For the last 10 years or so, Dr Anthony Gordon had managed to hide in full view, giving the occasional lecture, editing the occasional book for minor academic publishers, that kind of thing.

"Definitely something must have happened in China," thought Julia, "something serious enough to change his whole life." And that was not all. Nothing in the fairly well documented life of Dr Anthony Gordon was there to suggest even the slightest interest in antiques, even though his collection was no random pile of disparate pieces, but instead the careful accumulation of very shrewd purchases, buying against fashion and with a remarkable nose for unappreciated little treasures.

Julia wished she could have found more about Dr Gordon's family because there was no way that even on a good Civil Service pension supplemented by his University salary could he have afforded to buy his Heriot Row apartment, not to mention some of his more expensive antiques.

Julia looked at the time on the bottom right corner of her computer screen and fretted – Detective Bland was due to arrive in less than 20 minutes and she was still wearing her tartan pyjamas.

She walked quickly to her bedroom and opened her wardrobe doors looking for inspiration: nothing suited the occasion. "Well," she thought, "it is not every day that I am visited at home by a senior detective on a murder case." She decided that a tweed skirt coupled with a short-sleeved cashmere jumper was the least inappropriate combination.

This time Detective Bland's ringing of the bell did not startle her. Julia opened the door without looking into the spy-hole (mainly because the door did not have one) and was surprised to see that Detective Brand had not come alone.

"Mrs Flowers, this is WPC Corby," said Bland, as if he had read Julia's thoughts, "may we come in?"

"Of course, please, come in. This way."

Julia let both visitors into the vestibule and shut the door behind them before showing them the way to the drawing room.

"Unfortunate name," Julia thought, feeling slightly bitchy, "her face looks as if had been pressed hard between two steel plates." Admittedly, WPC Corby did not possess much of a profile; her nose was not so much squashed as non-existent and her chin was certainly more protruding outwards than the tip of her nominal nose.

"We are really sorry to bother you at home like this, Mrs Flowers, but, you know, thanks to you we may have a breakthrough and there is no time to lose. WPC Corby will show you what we found on the memory stick retrieved at the scene." DCI Bland was on a mission and keen to get the job done.

WPC Corby opened her little bag and extracted her laptop. A couple of clicks and WPC Corby was up and running.

"The stick has 50 separate files on it and each file is the same. Photo of an individual, male, followed by the scanned copy of an invoice. We have not been able to identify any of the individuals – no criminal record, no Internet photos on the Web. Most unusual."

"I thought you could help us with the invoices," intervened Bland, "they are about antiques."

"Mr Bland," started Julia.

"Actually, it's Detective Chief Inspector." WPC Corby helpfully corrected her.

"I am sorry, Detective Chief Inspector," Julia rolled the final "r" long enough to show that she was not in the least sorry , "I do not mean to be unhelpful, but should you not consult someone more experienced than me. You know, a major auction house has an office in town."

"The thought of asking a major auction house – as you call it – had occurred, Mrs Flowers, and we have already interviewed their International Director, but no joy."

Bland was not liking the tone of the conversation and, somewhat incongruously, changed the subject completely:

"My uncle used to live just over there," he said pointing to the row of terraced houses framed by the large window in Julia's drawing room, "do you like it here, Mrs Flowers?"

"I *love* it here, Inspector, just love it," replied Julia, "and forgive me – I am not used to being questioned by the police – but would you like a cup of tea, or coffee?"

"A cup of tea would be great, Mrs Flowers," said Bland, happy that the tension had eased a bit.

WPC Corby was surprised by the sudden change of tone and by her boss accepting a drink while on duty, but thought best to follow suit and also settled for tea.

While Julia repaired to the kitchen, Bland took the opportunity to look around the room. It was sparsely furnished, but every piece of furniture had an inevitability about it, as if a confident hand had decided what its natural position was within the elegant design of the room. There was an oriental theme running through the room, but Bland could not put his finger on it, because none of the furniture was oriental. His attention was drawn to a strange object he had never seen before: on a simple three-legged stool there was what he could only describe as a perforated ball, indeed a series of perforated balls nestling inside each other. He was still looking at it when Julia returned with a tray and three mugs.

"One sugar for you," she said passing one mug to Bland, "No sugar, no milk for you." WPC Corby grabbed her mug. "Please do sit down."

Bland was still looking at the concentric ball carving.

"Amazing workmanship, isn't it? It would take a master carver over a year to produce it. You can hold it in your hands, Inspector. Just do not drop it."

Bland did not want to handle the thing, but now he could not chicken out. "Forgive my ignorance, Mrs Flowers, but what is it, exactly?"

"It's an ivory ball: thirteen concentric balls all carved out of a single piece of ivory, with astronomical designs, Flowers, animals, dragons …" explained Julia.

"Simply incredible. Incredible." Bland was truly stunned by the almost impossible artistry contained in those balls, the largest no greater than a tennis ball, the smallest the size of a pea.

Bland was not exactly disappointed that he had not found any evidence of a Mr Flowers.

"May I see some of the invoices? asked Julia, "I am a little curious, I must confess."

WPC Corby was only too happy to make herself useful and tapped the laptop back to life. Julia took possession of the laptop and started scrolling through the files.

After what seemed to DCI Bland a very long pause, Julia raised her eyes from the screen and asked:

"Are you sure there is nothing else on the stick?"

"Absolute positive," intervened WPC Corby, as if the question had been asked to her personally, "no deleted files, just what you see. I have checked and double-checked."

"Strange," said Julia, "and, for the record, these are not invoices."

"Yes, we know, because there are no prices on them. But if not some kind of invoices, what are they?" asked Bland.

"They are standard consignment notes. When we collect any item for sale at auction we issue the client with a short inventory of the consignment. But all of these are incomplete," Julia explained.

"In what way?" Bland was keen to know.

"Well, in two ways: there is no name or address of the vendor and there is no way of knowing who is issuing these notes. It does not make sense. That is why I asked if you had retrieved all the information on the memory stick," Julia continued, "and the descriptions are too detailed for a consignment note. They read like entries for a well- researched catalogue."

"Can you tell us anything about the items described in these files?" asked Bland.

"I doubt I can add anything to what your auction house has told you already." Julia's tone suggested that she would not mind too much having a go anyway.

DCI Bland got the message and insisted:

"Please. If you do not mind, Mrs Flowers."

Julia began examining the long list of consignment notes and, just to break the silence, thought best to provide a running commentary.

"As you can see, Inspector, all of these notes are single-item, which is unusual. Typically when clients decide to sell, they part with more than one piece. And another strange thing ..."

DCI Bland interjected: "Yes, Mrs Flowers?"

"... and another strange thing," Julia took a long breath here, as she did not particularly like being interrupted mid-flow "is that even pieces that are clearly part of the same set were sold by different clients and at different dates," concluded Julia.

"As if all the people on the memory stick were selling their share of a joint treasure," observed WPC Corby, who obviously was a lot smarter than she looked.

"Anything more on the actual items, Mrs Flowers?" insisted Bland.

"As they will have told you, the pieces are all Chinese, all top quality, I mean Imperial quality, and appear to come all from the same collection. In fact, it seems to me that someone had decided to clear a room in an Imperial residence of all its contents." said Julia, quite satisfied with her guess at possible provenance.

"They were very reticent. Very reticent." DCI Bland observed, more to himself than to anyone in particular.

"Sir," said WPC Corby addressing her boss, "but why would Dr Gordon go to the trouble of hiding what is, after all, just an inventory list of pieces some unknown stranger sold to some unknown people sometime in the past?"

"That, Corby, is a question I would love to know the answer to. Any suggestions, Mrs Flowers?"

"Well, I could check on the catalogues whether there were any single-venue sales of Chinese antiques sometime in the early 2000s," suggested Julia.

"Mrs Flowers, if I may," WPC Corby was clearly bursting to ask Julia, "how do you know that the items were sold at different dates and that the sale must have been 15 years ago or so?"

"I am sorry. I forgot that this is a police investigation. Of course, I do not *know*. But there are large gaps in the sequence of the vendor's numbers on the consignment notes, which suggests that they were not filled in at the same time. As to dating the sale, the pair of Doucai bowls belonging to Dr Gordon has a vendor's number somewhat in the middle of the sequence and I know as a fact that they were in Dr Gordon's possession back in 2005." If Julia had felt quite smug about her guess at provenance, now she was positively basking in her own cleverness.

"So, one of the notes refers to Dr Gordon's pieces, right? And how do you know that, if I may ask, Mrs Flowers." Julia liked the tone in Bland's voice, a tone that said "I really value your opinion."

"Again, I do not exactly *know* it, but why would Dr Gordon happen to keep a note describing in fine detail a pair of Doucai bowls matching exactly his own pair. In fact, I would bet a large amount that there is only one pair of Doucai bowls in the kind of mint condition of the pair I saw in his apartment." Julia knew what she was talking about.

"Mrs Flowers," intervened WPC Corby while opening her notebook and brandishing a pen, "it would be really helpful if you could try and

21

reconstruct the series of steps starting from the clearing of the palace to the writing of these consignment notes."

Julia did not like Corby's brusqueness and was surprised by the forwardness of a mere constable in the presence of a Detective Chief Inspector. Surely not a Bland-Corby liaison?

"Well, this is pure speculation, but it is my best guess. First, all pieces come from the same Imperial residence. Second, they are dispersed across these fifty individuals. Third, for some mysterious reason, these fifty people all approached the same intermediary or dealer, who duly issued a consignment note to each of them. Fourth, again for some unknown reason, the top part of all these notes is missing. Fifth, God knows why Dr Gordon kept a scanned image of the notes on a memory stick hidden in a puzzle box." Julia had finished.

"Mrs Flowers, this puts a completely different complexion on our enquiry. But before I ask you any more questions, I have to ask you something I forgot to ask when we first met in Dr Gordon's apartment. These Doucai bowls, how valuable are they in today's money?"

"I thought the auction house would have told you already," replied Julia, "but, sold as a pair, they would fetch in excess of seven hundred and fifty."

"That little!" intervened WPC Corby.

"Seven hundred and fifty thousand. Possibly a million, on a good day." Julia did enjoy the stunned expression on WPC Corby's squashed face.

CHAPTER 5

WILL SHE?

The weekend was over, but not for Julia. She did not work on Mondays. But she had a work-day routine: she would set the alarm for eight o' clock. Get up promptly. Wash and get dressed. Cup of tea. Radio 4.

But that particular Monday Julia Flowers did something that she had meant to do for some time, but had always managed to postpone for one reason or another.

She had decided that the time had arrived to think of herself and only of herself and that meant finding a companion, maybe a lover.

She had been celibate for nearly two years and even that had only been a one-night stand that had meant nothing at all.

She had not missed the lack of physical contact as much as she thought she would. She was happy with her life, with her job, with her new surroundings, with her independence, but would it not be even sweeter if shared with someone? She missed actual adult conversation, not the artificial exchange of words on Facebook or the progressively rarer Skype conversations with old friends.

She registered on a reputable online dating site and took the plunge. Before filling in her profile details, she started off by filtering for the kind of man she was interested in. The implied questions were surprisingly frank, brutal even. Did she want her man to be tall, medium, or short? Was being overweight a no-no? White, black, Asian, or "not relevant"? Divorced, separated, widower, or unattached? What average yearly income?

To be confronted with so many prejudices all at once was disconcerting for Julia, but not nearly as much as the next stage of her virtual quest for the ideal man. She had to admit to herself that she cared about looks much more than she feared: no matter how enticing the profile was, if the photo showed an accountant's face, she would swiftly move on.

And if the photo was enticing, but the profile showed a peppering of mis-spelled words, again she would pass.

Was she afraid? Was her pickiness just a defence mechanism? She was not sure, but she was not going to chicken out now. To the next stage: her own profile.

Julia felt on solid ground here. She regarded herself as a bloody good cataloguer: concise, precise, detailed, and with an occasional hint of irony.

However, when the object to be described for the highest price was herself, she found the right words a bit more difficult to come by.

The factual bits were easy. She was not going to lie about her age: she was 51 and proud of it. She was a graduate of the Edinburgh College of Art and she definitely had two children not living at home and at University. She was solvent and living in Edinburgh (a small white lie was allowed, surely). But the more ambiguous questions were less easy.

Was she "attractive"? Of course she was. But "very" attractive? On a good day, perhaps. After a long commute on Thursday night, less so. Perhaps she should have a quick look at the competition and then decide.

After ten minutes of browsing, Julia was no longer in the mood for self-advertising. Profile after profile, she could read between the lines and see genuine, disappointed and yet optimistic women with half their lives to forget and the rest to re-build.

Was she one of them? She was not re-building anything. She was very happy with what she had built. In fact, she was not aware of any building efforts on her part. Once she had picked up the courage to leave her sorry specimen and take two small children with her, everything just fell into place, with no need to arrange emotional bricks into neat rows of soldiers. She could be herself, independent, free, and, yes, very happy.

The moment had passed. She saved her half completed profile. She was not chickening out, just leaving the rest to another day.

CHAPTER 6

CHINESE FEATHERS

As soon as Julia arrived at her office on Tuesday morning she knew from Joan's expression that something was up. So she was not as surprised as she should have been when Joan told her that Alistair Reid was waiting for her in her office.

"Good morning, Alistair. I must say I am surprised to see you here. Has Joan offered you tea or coffee?"

"I am fine, Julia. Sorry for coming without an appointment. But I have to talk to you confidentially about the probate valuation for the late Dr Gordon."

"It will be ready later today and you can have it by tomorrow, but you had not mentioned it was urgent."

"Urgency is not the problem, Julia. Quite the opposite. We have been approached by the Foreign Office. This is strictly confidential, Julia. Very." Alistair Reid looked very uncomfortable.

"I do not understand. Is it anything to do with the missing Doucai bowls?"

"I do not think so. It's politics." This time Alistair Reid sounded mysterious.

Julia could not fail to notice that Alistair Reid did not seem at all surprised about the missing bowls, as if he knew already and was not bothered by a large part of Dr Gordon's inheritance having disappeared.

"You see, Dr Gordon left his entire estate to Rights for China, a charity that is banned in China. Too political. And it is a rather large estate and apparently Rights for China would not accept it quietly. It would be a propaganda coup for them, according to the Foreign Office, anyway."

Murder, missing bowls, now the Foreign Office. Sparring with DCI Bland had been almost fun, but this definitely was not. Julia took a step back away from Alistair Reid.

"The Foreign Office suggested a possible way out. But it would require your cooperation."

"I really do not see …"

"Let me explain." Alistair Reid knew he had to act quickly. "If a way could be found to delay the valuation, and therefore the execution of the will, it would buy time for the Foreign Office to smooth Chinese feathers, as it were."

"But the valuation is ready, Alistair. What you do with it is, well, not my concern." Julia wanted out of this unpleasant business.

"Not really, Julia. You said that some pieces are missing. Well, Reid and McHalm would like you to try and find them. You are one of Edinburgh's finest experts on Chinese ceramics, are you not?"

Julia was not flattered and decided to buy time herself:

"I have to think this over, Alistair, but I'll let you know as soon as I can."

"The firm would be most grateful if you could help, Julia. Most grateful." Alistair Reid was not going to let this go.

As soon as Alistair Reid left the office, Julia went to her computer and googled "Rights for China. Charity". Alistair was right: they were not pulling any punches. Julia was shocked by the number of death penalties in China – the exact number is unknown, of course, as it is a State secret, but running at 100-200 *a week*. She was even more appalled by the callousness of the system, which is slowly replacing death by firing squad with the less brutal method of lethal injections, not because of the complaints of the families about the disfiguration of the faces of their executed relatives (shot in the back of the head), but because they are cheaper and can be administered in mobile "death vans".

Julia shut her computer, upset and enraged. Then she started thinking: why would a Foreign Office official of Anthony Gordon's standing want to support such a radical charity? What this linked to his sudden resignations from his Beijing posting? Or, perhaps, to the missing bowls? And how on earth was she supposed to find them?

Julia had never liked Alistair Reid even though she had had very little to do with him personally. Mainly emails, the occasional telephone call. She found him insincere, even for a solicitor. And she had the distinct feeling that he did not want the missing bowls found. Worse, she thought he knew more about their disappearance than she did.

It was time to pay another visit to 55 Heriot Row.

CHAPTER 7

TREASURE HUNT

Even by Edinburgh's standards the weather on that Tuesday lunchtime was truly atrocious. The sky was a uniform dark grey blanket giving no intimation of the swirling gushes of horizontal rain that were buffeting everybody who dared walk the streets.

The cobbles that cover Heriot Row were shiny and busy reflecting the little sunlight that somehow managed to filter through the thick clouds. Having miraculously found a parking space not far from number 55, Julia Flowers hurried to her destination, made short shrift of the few slippery steps to the entrance of the apartment and quickly turned open both locks.

As soon as she was inside, she stopped dead. Her heart raced. She took a long deep breath. The lights were on and it was obvious that she was not alone in the apartment. She froze, unable either to rush back into the now welcoming embrace of the gushing rain or to venture past the vestibule.

Suddenly, a face peeked through the drawing room door:

"Ah, it's you, Mrs Flowers."

Never before had Julia been so glad to see the unremarkable features of DCI Bland.

"Inspector Bland. I was not expecting to find you here. Forgive me. I was scared for a moment."

"I was not expecting you either, Mrs Flowers. But I suppose we are both looking for the same thing."

"What are you looking for, Inspector?"

"The rest of the consignment notes, of course. And you?"

"I wish I knew. Inspiration, perhaps."

"Why would Dr Gordon keep separately the two halves of these wretched notes?" Bland answered his own question, "precaution. But for what purpose?"

"I do not mean to interfere, Inspector Bland, but could you show me the spot where you found the body of Dr Gordon?"

"I don't see why not. This way, Mrs Flowers." Bland led the way to a large public room, grandiose, in fact, and so spacious that the full length grand piano did not look at all out of place, but the natural complement to the very high ceilings and the floor-to-ceiling windows. "Right there." Bland pointed to the corner of the room furthest from the door and from the piano.

"I hope I won't make a total fool of myself, Inspector, but if Dr Gordon was so keen to keep the notes secret, it would make sense for him instinctively to move away from them when he was attacked."

"So you think he was murdered for these notes?" Bland had already entertained the possibility, but was curious to know how Mrs Flowers' brain worked.

"Unlike you, I do not have the full picture and so the hidden notes are my only clue."

"Carry on, Mrs Flowers. I did not mean to interrupt."

"Well, we found one half in the puzzle box in the next room. So, if the remaining half is in this room, and that is a big 'if', we could start looking away from this corner." Julia pointed to the spot on the floor where Dr Gordon's body had been found.

"Fine. I search the piano and you the big display cabinet. Presumably we are looking for another memory stick."

"Presumably." Julia was not so sure.

While she was handling the pieces in the cabinet, Julia thought that her job was not that different from Bland's. They were both looking for clues, she for age and provenance, he for guilt or motive. Most of the items in the cabinet were blue and white Chinese porcelain with some exquisite jades but none could be used as secret hiding places.

"Sorry, Inspector. Nothing here. Shall we swap, just in case I missed something?"

As he moved towards the cabinet Bland appreciated the delicate way in which Julia was suggesting that she'd better look at the piano herself.

"Dr Gordon was not into piano playing, was he?" Julia was rummaging in the large piano stool, "or he was so good that he had little use for sheet music." Before Bland could open his mouth, Julia continued, "a little Bach, a couple of Scarlatti sonatas, nothing too taxing."

Julia switched her attention from the piano stool to the piano itself, sat on the stool, lifted the heavy lid and stopped. "Inspector! This is strange."

Bland left the cabinet open and walked quickly to the piano:

"What is strange?"

"The candlesticks. The candlesticks, Inspector. They do not fit."

"What do you mean they do not fit?"

"The piano is clearly Austrian, early twentieth century. But the candlesticks are early Victorian and, anyway, this kind of piano would never have been fitted with candlesticks."

Bland started handling the candlesticks, without too much care, noted Julia, when suddenly one candlestick gave way to Bland's turning motion and got unscrewed from the piano.

Before Julia could complain about the damage, Bland kept disassembling the long thin candlestick and then, in a release of tension, he shouted, "Gotcha!"

Rolled inside the candlestick and, hidden by the floral patterned drip tray meant to collect the molten wax, there was a long scroll.

DCI Bland held his trophy very carefully in his large hands, but he knew that he had to pass it on to Julia Flowers, not only because the material was so thin as to be virtually transparent, but also because he could see that it was a Chinese script.

Julia understood immediately what was being asked of her and so she took out of her handbag a pair of cotton gloves that she kept in case she had to handle delicate or potentially hazardous items.

"Another similarity with police detective work," she thought as she wore the gloves.

"It is surprisingly tough, silk. It becomes brittle with age, but this roll is definitely modern, even contemporary." Julia unrolled the fabric slowly, but expertly. Fully extended the roll was about a foot long.

"It is incredible how so much fabric can be hidden inside a tiny candlestick." DCI Bland was not enjoying the definitely Oriental theme of this murder investigation.

"I need to search something online," said Julia after having scrutinized very intently the tightly packed Chinese characters on the roll. She took out her iPhone and started tapping on it.

"She types using her thumbs, like a teenager," thought Bland, rather envious of Julia Flowers' dexterity with her thin and elegant fingers.

She proceeded to stroke the screen in the unmistakable motion now necessary to enlarge an image, sliding index and thumb away from each other as if stretching an invisible rubber band, and showed Bland the result of her search:

羅伯特戈登

"What is this?" Bland was liking anything Chinese less and less.

"Probably nothing, but could I ask you to check with me if these characters appear anywhere in the roll, Inspector? I start from the top, you from the bottom."

Julia could not suppress a smile when she saw DCI Bland extract from his inside pockets, in rapid succession, first a pair of reading glasses and then a magnifying glass. Bland gave her the unmistakable stare of someone not in the mood for Sherlock Holmes jokes and said matter-of-factly: "Surprisingly useful."

After a couple of minutes of silent scrutiny, Julia and DCI Bland said almost in perfect unison, "Here!"

The characters were all there and in the right order on a line about three quarters down the length of the roll.

"Perhaps now Mrs Flowers you could share with me what is it that we have found?"

"Oh, it's very simple. I wanted to see if the name 'Anthony Gordon' was on this list and clearly it is," Julia was happy that her hunch had turned out to be right. "Perhaps you could have all the other names transcribed, Inspector."

Bland understood at once the importance of the list:

"So you think these are the missing names of the sellers on the memory stick?"

"It is a distinct possibility, but unfortunately I do not read Chinese. I know a few hundred characters, mainly names and surnames and things you find painted on ceramics." At this point Julia Flowers thought that the timing was right to ask DCI Bland a question she had no right to ask:

"May I ask you a question about this case, Inspector?"

"Of course, Mrs Flowers. And if I can, I will even try to give you an answer." Bland was glad to be back in charge.

"Did the late Dr Gordon move large amounts of cash in and out of his bank account?"

"Funny you should ask, Mrs Flowers, because this is one of the things that puzzled me from the start. Dr Gordon's monthly bank statements are all practically identical, month in month out, regular income in (pension and University salary), regular outlays out (utilities, Council tax, mobile phone), positive balances at the end of each month withdrawn in cash. And then nothing. No saving accounts, no investments, no cheques even."

"No trace of a three-quarter million cash injection, then? I was hoping …" Julia left the sentence unfinished.

DCI Bland stared into Julia's eyes without uttering a word and before Julia felt totally uncomfortable he asked her earnestly:

"Mrs Flowers, is there anything you are not telling me? I do not mean to sound official, but obstructing police enquiries and all that …"

Julia looked into DCI Bland's eyes at least as long and then she said: "I have been asked to retrieve or at least locate the missing Doucai bowls and following the money is the obvious route," she took a very long breath, "and apparently Dr Gordon left a very sizeable estate."

"Thank you, Mrs Flowers. I will make discreet enquiries with Reid & McHalm."

"Why don't you call me Julia, Inspector? It looks as if this is going to be a long investigation."

"Eric. Please call me Eric, Julia."

CHAPTER 8

AN UNEXPECTED VISIT

DCI Bland found his office profoundly depressing and, thanks to his understanding with WPC Corby, he was managing to navigate the turbid waters of police bureaucracy fairly successfully. But today was one of those occasions when WPC Corby had forewarned him that his physical presence was required.

Not ten minutes had passed since he had arrived in his office when WPC Corby was knocking on his door and announcing that his visitor had arrived.

After a minute or so the "visitor" appeared, framed by the open door, a very tall man, wearing an ill-fitting but expensive suit.

"DCI Grant, Special Branch, Metropolitan Police"

If the name was meant to carry weight with Bland, it failed to do so. Bland hardly lifted his ass from his office chair, waved his hands in a vaguely circular motion, sat back on his chair and mumbled:

"What can we do for you, DCI Grant?"

DCI Grant had done his homework and was expecting a less than wildly enthusiastic welcome, but nevertheless was taken aback by Bland's lack of curiosity, as if a visit from Special Branch was a matter of routine.

"It is the Gordon case." DCI Grant hardly fit into the visitor's chair and his long legs forced him into a very uncomfortable posture.

"I see. The Gordon case. And why the sudden interest, if I may ask? It's been over a year…"

DCI Grant pointedly ignored the question:

"I understand there have been some recent developments."

"And, if I may ask, how did you come to understand about these 'recent developments'?" Bland was not going to let Grant off the hook so easily.

"DCI Bland, we are on the same side here. We thought that you should be made aware of our interest in the case. A courtesy, if you like."

"DCI Grant, if Special Branch is interested in my case it means that you know something I don't and so I would really appreciate if you could tell me what the hell is going on. Please." Diplomacy wasn't Bland's strong point.

DCI Grant tried to cross his legs but only succeeded in sitting in an even more ungainly position. "There are international implications. China, specifically."

"I see. International implications. China. Ah, well, that explains it, doesn't it? And to think that I was afraid that you may want to keep me in the dark." Bland was running out of patience.

"DCI Bland, surely you, of all people, must understand my position. I am just relaying a message from London. Should your enquiries involve foreign nationals, we would like to be informed."

"My enquiries would move a lot smoother if you cared to elaborate. Which foreign nationals and why?"

"Chinese. Dr Gordon's dealings with Chinese nationals are of interest to us."

"Dr Gordon has been dead for over a year and, as far as I can recall, we never got any communication from your lot about Chinese 'dealings'. Let me repeat. Why now?"

"We understand you now have some new lines of enquiry. Which may involve Chinese nationals."

Bland realised that he was not going to get anything out of DCI Grant and decided to bring the discussion to a swift end. "Understood, DCI Grant. Should we discover any Chinese connections, you will be the first to know. Anything else we can help you with?"

"Here is my card and mobile number. We would really appreciate if this discussion remained confidential. No need to involve any of your colleagues. Or acquaintances." DCI Grant stood up, stretched his legs, shook Bland's hand and left.

Bland leaned back on his chair and then erupted: "Fuck. Fuck. Fucking fuck." He knew exactly what that little charade had been all about. This was London telling him that they had been watching him and Mrs Flowers and that if he tried to get smart and poke his nose outside Edinburgh, they would take over the case.

As if summoned by the triple fuck, WPC Corby appeared at his door with a cup of coffee.

"Bad news, Sir?"

"Since when is London good news? And Special Branch to boot. Any joy with Gordon's solicitors?"

"Spoke to Alistair Reid, but he would only confirm that they are the executors of Dr Gordon's estate. Perhaps he might be more forthcoming if you spoke to him, Sir."

"Perhaps," Bland was clearly not paying attention. The mug of coffee was getting cold. "Any news from the translators?"

"Sorry, Sir. I meant to tell you. We have just received the translation you asked for. Do you want it now?"

"No. Let us wait a couple of days. Of course I want it now." Bland stood up, practically pushed WPC Corby out of the door and walked swiftly to collect the piece of evidence he had absolutely no idea what to do with.

While walking out of the police station, DCI Bland had to fight his way through a gaggle of Fettes College students, all resplendent in their garish pink-blue striped blazers, probably on some community service mission. Bland glared at them with undisguised contempt. It was bad enough for the police station to be next to Waitrose and its snooty customers, but for some over-privileged tossers to walk into his police station and waste everyone's time was more than he could take after the visit by DCI Grant.

He walked slowly to the car park, opened the door of his police car, and slumped into the driver's seat. Over the years he had learned to cope with the intrusions from down South, but he could not stomach the thought that Special Branch had bugged Dr Gordon's apartment without informing him. This would have been the perfect time to light a cigarette but he was not going to break his 13-month smoke-free run just because DCI Grant got on his nerves. Still, Bland imagined taking out a pack of Marlboro from his pocket, selecting a cigarette, placing it languidly on his lower lip, and lighting it with his Zippo, inhaling slowly the first puff, the smoke travelling deep from his mouth, down his throat, and finally arriving into his lungs and lingering there till the next breath out. But there was no buzz in his brain, no hit at the back of his neck. He would have to think this case through unaided by nicotine.

Everything pointed to the list of names on the scroll as his main clue. Why was it written in Chinese characters? Anthony Gordon was not Chinese and yet his name was written down in Chinese characters. The obvious reason was that whoever wrote the list was Chinese. But then why was the list in Gordon's possession and why was he hiding it?

Before leaving the station he had asked WPC Corby to run the list of names through the police computer, just in case any of them was flagged up, but he was not optimistic. Bland thought that he would pay Mrs Flowers a visit. As he was in one of his navel-gazing spells, Bland had to admit that he could just as well give her a ring, but instead he wanted to see her. Nearly four years since Bianca had died, he still was not ready even to think about having a relationship, but he found Mrs Flowers's company very pleasant. Very pleasant indeed. He started the engine and drove off.

CHAPTER 9

TILTING AT WIND MILLS?

Julia Flowers should have been busy compiling condition reports on Oriental pieces in preparation for the big quarterly antique sale in two weeks' time and instead she was very distracted, unable to concentrate. She hated leaving tasks to the last minute, and had she been in her usual methodical frame of mind, she would have worked her way through her emails assessing the state of vases, the age of jades, the provenance of Satsumas with her characteristic precision. But not today. Something was bothering her and she did not know what it was. She decided that the saleroom was too chaotic for her and so she told Joan that she would take some pieces home and email the condition reports back to the office.

She had just finished loading her car with the carefully wrapped collection of vases, bowls, and jades when DCI Bland entered the large reception area at Hillman Roberts and nearly bumped into a very absent-minded Julia Flowers.

"Mrs Flowers. Eh, Julia. Sorry to barge in like this, but could we have a word, please?"

"Eric. I was not expecting you. Well, shall we go to my office?"

"If you do not mind, a more private place would be better."

Julia thought of her office as a private space, but perhaps DCI Bland meant a more neutral place.

"There is the Wind Mill not too far from here. Someone told me they do nice coffee there."

"Sounds ideal. You drive there and I'll follow."

The Wind Mill was a bistro-café-restaurant surprisingly elegant for its location. Some of the former mining villages peppered around Edinburgh are not known for their architectural elegance, but the Wind Mill had been converted with a lightness of touch that promised well for the quality of its fare.

Once they were shown to a quiet table, Julia and Bland sat down, each ready to unburden themselves of the questions and doubts that were bothering them.

"Julia, if I may," Bland still felt a bit awkward when addressing Julia by her first name, "there have been some developments."

"Same here," interrupted Julia.

"Well, this morning I was visited by Special Branch. Metropolitan Police," Bland added ominously.

"And I was told by Alistair Reid that the Foreign Office is involved, somehow." Julia thought best not to specify that she had known this for some time.

"Also, I have had the list of names transcribed and typed up." Bland took out of his pocket a rather crumpled up piece of paper. "It is for you. In case any of these names ring a bell." Bland was about to say that the list was confidential, but he knew in his heart that Julia was a naturally discreet woman.

"Thank you for the confidence, Eric. I will definitely look into it. But, I have been thinking …"

Bland came clean: "And you should know that Dr Gordon's apartment is bugged. And not by me."

"I see. Strange. Anyway, the more I think about Dr Gordon the more I am convinced that we should look back to his time in China. Why did he leave so suddenly? Was it political? If not, what drove him into obscurity?"

Bland was taken aback, as he certainly had not shared WPC Corby's background checks on Dr Gordon with Julia and yet she had worked out the crucial fact about Gordon in China.

Julia continued: "I have done a bit of digging online and two strange coincidences struck me."

Bland sat back on the comfy chair: "I am all ears."

"Well, the first coincidence is probably nothing, but Dr Gordon left the British Embassy in Beijing exactly at the time when Jiang Zemin unexpectedly stepped down as General Secretary of the Chinese Communist Party."

"Julia, that is not so unusual. A change in the regime is often followed by a change of diplomatic personnel."

"True. But Dr Gordon was not recalled or re-assigned. He resigned."

"And the second coincidence?"

"Promise not to laugh, because it is rather far-fetched."

"Of course. Carry on."

"Well, my brother had a liver transplant about twelve years ago and he was on immuno-suppressants until he died."

"I am sorry for you, Julia."

"This is why I know about cyclosporine. It's an immuno-suppressant. Well, guess what I found in Dr Gordon's medicine cabinet?"

"Very impressive, Julia. The post mortem report did say that Dr Gordon had had a liver transplant. But where is the link to China?"

"This is where you may laugh at me. Do you know the Falun Gong movement?"

"Falun Gong … Falun Gong. The name rings a bell, but I cannot place it."

"As far as I understand it is a version of Buddhism, but that is not the important bit. When Jiang Zemin was in power apparently he persecuted Falun Gong practitioners relentlessly, to the point that tens of thousands were killed and *their organs harvested,*" Julia carried on in the same breath, "and I am not a conspiracy theorist, please believe me."

"Really interesting, Julia," Bland was still processing Julia's theories, "this would explain something that has been bugging me since the beginning. Why did Gordon come to Edinburgh and not London after leaving China?"

Julia was on the same wavelength as Bland: "For its liver transplant unit."

Bland's brain was whizzing: "Falun Gong. Now I remember. There is a Falun Gong community in Edinburgh. They held some kind of parade some time ago and they informed us. Nice bunch of people. Totally harmless."

Julia noticed how tactfully Bland had ignored the more horrific and far-fetched side of her story, but in fact he was just getting there.

"So. Gordon somehow gets himself a new liver on the black market. Resigns. Comes to Edinburgh. Not altogether impossible. But how does the list fit in? Why the Foreign Office? And Special Branch. We are missing something."

Julia and Bland were so engrossed in their conversation that neither had noticed the polite waiter hovering round their table waiting for a break in their exchanges. "Would you like to order, madam, Sir?

"A decaf cappuccino, please," said Julia.

"Same for me." Bland was not this virtuous normally, but he thought he had enough adrenaline running through his veins to last him the day. At long last this investigation had somewhere to go.

Julia, too, was on a high. "Actually, Dr Gordon could have had a liver transplant here in Edinburgh. Which may explain why the Doucai bowls are missing."

"You think they may have been a payment in kind for his Chinese liver?"

"It is a possibility. Perhaps you can find out."

The cappuccinos arrived with the inevitable silhouette of a wind mill sprayed on the milk froth. Julia and Bland sipped them in silence, each following a different train of thought.

CHAPTER 10

RUTHIE AND RUPERT

On her way home, Julia thought she would call on Ruthie and Rupert. One of the great things about her old friends was that she knew she could drop on them unannounced and be met with a wide smile and a huge hug.

Ruthie especially had been a rock when Julia was in the throes of her terminally diseased marriage. She was older than Julia and had been divorced twice and so, in spite her apparently frivolous look and quirky spectacles, she had been a spring of wisdom and a warm blanket of comfort for Julia.

The reason why she wanted to call on her old neighbour in Heriot Row was that, if there had ever been any kind of gossip or rumour about Anthony Gordon, Ruthie was certain to have heard about it. Ruthie was not a gossip. Quite the opposite in fact. But precisely because people instinctively knew that she was discreet and without an ounce of malice in her, they would confide in her without even realizing it. And Ruthie would repay their trust by stripping down their secret revelations of any personal details and turn their experiences into miniature morality plays that she would perform at the appropriate time. The appropriate time being most probably at one of her famed gin benches. Ruthie and Rupert have had a remarkable gin cellar well before it became fashionable and throughout the late spring and summer on a sunny Friday evening the gated gardens of Heriot Row would be alive with exotic G&Ts and relaxed conversation. If the weather was particularly enticing a small gazebo would be erected and residents would drift in and out of Ruthie's gin bench throughout the lazy evening. Rupert would be sitting on a deck chair reading a book and doubling up as bartender when needed to cater for a sudden surge of thirsty patrons. He has long since retired from the University of Edinburgh and was enjoying every single day of his life away from research assessments, teaching quality assurances, and the demeaning subservience to third-rate administrators that these days passes for University life. Rupert was the perfect foil to

41

Ruthie's exuberance and vivacity – softly spoken, ironic without being acerbic, understated to the point of self-effacement and always reliable if an obscure fact or episode needed instant retrieval.

Of course, Ruthie and Rupert's code of confidentiality only applied to current residents at Heriot Row: as soon as someone moved away, the implicit covenant was broken and former residents became fair game. Julia knew this did not apply to her, because she and Ruthie were not just neighbours but best friends.

Julia rang the little brass bell that served as doorbell at Ruthie and Rupert's and, as expected, immediately she found herself hugged tightly to Ruthie's ample bosom.

After the usual exchange of family news, children at University, grand-children misbehaving, and Edinburgh City Council being obtuse, Julia asked Ruthie about the recently departed Dr Gordon.

"Funny you should ask me about him. Just the other day Clara Bellingham, you know, lives above Gordon's apartment, was complaining about the comings and goings from his place. The apartment had been vacant for over a year and quiet as a cemetery and then, boom, lots of strange people turning up."

"Yes, funny that. But did you meet Gordon when he was living at 55? What kind of person was he?"

Ruthie knew that Julia would not ask without having a good reason and so she spoke without inhibitions:

"Very strange character he was. Came a couple of times to my gin bench, but did not touch the stuff. Teetotaller, I fear. He had virtually no visitors. Bit of a recluse. But he would talk to Rupert endlessly about international affairs, which, of course, was right up Rupert's street. I asked Bruce whether he thought Gordon was gay, but he was adamant he wasn't."

Bruce was a friend both to Julia and to Ruthie, a shy gay guy with an infallible gaydar.

"But unless he had a lady friend somewhere else, nobody had ever seen him with a woman."

Julia had been hoping for more informative details and Dr Gordon being an abstemious celibate bachelor was not much of a revelation.

"More boring than mysterious," continued Ruthie, "except for the fracas with the Chinese couple."

Julia's ears pricked up: "What Chinese couple? What fracas?"

"It was well after you left. Clara told me all about it at the time. She and Jack heard very loud voices and a bit of a commotion coming from Gordon's apartment and so they went downstairs to see what was happening. Well, Theresa and John, who live on the ground floor, they are new, you do not know them, were also outside their front door and so the four of them walked into Gordon's apartment, as the front door was open and they thought they should do something. Gordon's apartment being usually so very quiet, you see."

"And?" Julia was anxious to know the rest of the story.

"Well, they found Dr Gordon in a terrible state, shaking and everything, and this Chinese couple shouting at him. In Chinese. Well, Clara thought it was Chinese as the couple were definitely Chinese."

"And then?"

"Well, John asked Dr Gordon if he was alright and if they should call the police, but Gordon said that it was just a misunderstanding and apologized for the noise. Clara told me that the apartment was a mess, as if it had been burgled."

Julia was trying to process all the information Ruthie had been pouring out and after a while she asked:

"Do you remember when this was?"

"Of course I don't, but I know a man who does. Rupert!" Ruthie shouted so that her husband could hear her.

"Yes, darling. Hi, Julia. I did not know you were here." Rupert had brought with him the book he had been reading.

"Do you remember when I told you about the kerfuffle in Dr Gordon's apartment? When would you say that was? About a year ago?

"It was the 7th of February last year. My mother's birthday. Bye, Julia. Nice to see you again." Rupert was keen to repair to his study and finish his book.

"May I ask you why the interest in the late Dr Gordon, Julia?" Ruthie could not keep her curiosity in check any longer.

"It's a long story. I am doing a valuation in his apartment and I am curious to know who he was. That's all."

"Nothing to do with your rendezvous with a mystery man at number 55, then?"

Julia should have known better than trying to pull the wool over Ruthie's big blue eyes.

"Ah, that. There is no mystery, unfortunately. He is a policeman investigating the case."

Julia turned down Ruthie's invitation to stay for dinner, shouted a good-bye to Rupert and left.

CHAPTER 11

MR PATTERSON

Julia had been thinking for a while about Patterson, whether contacting him would be worth the risk. But her quest for the missing Doucai bowls was going nowhere. If there was anything not quite above board involving Chinese antiques, Patterson was the man. He had carved out a niche in the Edinburgh antiques market by establishing himself as the intermediary of choice for wealthy Chinese dealers and businessmen wishing to buy back some of the more valuable Chinese antiques held in Scotland. Conveniently he had married a well-connected Chinese woman and between the two of them they had an impressive network of buyers, dealers, and auction houses. Patterson had had a major slip-up a couple of years ago: he had bought nearly £80,000 worth of Chinese porcelain for a client of his who then decided that he did not like the merchandise, landing Patterson with a large unpaid bill and with the auction house threatening legal action. Everybody in the business knew that Patterson was just an intermediary, but when you bid at an auction you enter into a binding contract. It took over a year to negotiate a compromise, but Patterson's reputation as a reliable bidder had been seriously tarnished and some auction houses had discreetly blackballed him.

Julia Flowers has been advised not to have any dealings with him, a piece of advice that she had been more than happy to take, as she found Patterson to be sleazy, untrustworthy and, not to put too fine a point, physically repulsive.

It would not be an easy call to make.

"Mr Patterson, Julia Flowers of Hillman Roberts. I hope I am not disturbing you."

"Mrs Flowers, must have been more than year. Always nice to speak to you, but I should tell you that at the moment I am not buying."

"Actually, for a change I am the buyer, or rather a client of mine."

"I am all ears, Mrs Flowers."

"Well, to be honest, this is well out of my league, but my client is interested in some specific and very expensive Chinese antiques and so I thought that you, with all your contacts, could point me in the right direction."

"Flattery always works with me, Julia." Patterson knew how to extract maximum advantage in his dealings with people hence the sudden change to first names. "What are you looking for?"

"Doucai Lingzhi bowls with a neat Yongzheng signature."

"And what is your client's budget?"

"You have been long enough in the business to know that I cannot tell you that, but I can assure you that my client is prepared to pay a fair price for the right bowls."

"If I may ask, where are you calling me from? This is not your mobile number and the connection is terrible."

"My mobile is broken and BT has not connected my new landline. That is why I am calling from a telephone box." Julia certainly did not want to reveal her landline number to people like Patterson.

"I see. Well, your client is out of luck. A very nice pair was sold some years ago, but nothing since."

"If you could find the buyer and convince him to sell to my client, my client would pay you a very generous commission, I am sure."

"Even I could not convince the buyer to part with his precious bowls."

"You are too modest, Mr Patterson. If you really try …"

Patterson changed tone abruptly. "The buyer is dead. Murdered, to be precise. And I would advise your client to develop an interest in anything but Doucai bowls."

Julia Flowers was not expecting this turn of events and could not find anything to say.

"Well, I shall see you at the next antique sale, Julia. No hard feelings, then? Bye."

Before Julia could utter a word, the long-forgotten continuous sound at the end of the line reminded her that her telephone box conversation had ended.

She always enjoyed the short walk from the harbour to her cottage, the surrounding terraced houses pretty enough to remind her of their glory days but not picturesque enough to feature in a tourist brochure, the cobbled streets that not long ago must have been alive with the sounds of fish being unloaded, the faint smell of rotting seaweed in the air.

Should she believe Patterson? She could not think of a good reason why he would lie, but Dr Gordon buying back his own bowls did not make any sense.

She turned away from the main street to walk the short distance to her front door when she saw the undistinctive features of DCI Bland waiting for her.

CHAPTER 12

VALENTINE'S DAY

"Sorry, I did try to call, but there was no reply."

"I went for a walk and left my mobile at home. Have you been waiting long?"

"Not really," Bland lied, "but there is something I had to tell you in person."

"Do come in," Julia unlocked the door and led the way to the sitting room, "fancy a cup of tea?"

"Not now." Bland obviously had some bad news.

"For a change London was actually helpful, but this complicates things considerably."

"What is 'this'?" Now it was Julia's turn to sound worried.

"Well, an antique dealer was murdered in Soho and, for reasons not entirely clear, Special Branch thinks that this may be relevant to our investigations."

Julia liked the sense of joint ownership of the investigation, or was Bland referring to Police Scotland?

"Clearly you think that it is relevant. Perhaps there is something you cannot share?"

"The reason why I am here is that he was not just murdered. His tongue and ears had been cut out while he was still alive. It is a clear message. And Special Branch recommended to alert people connected with the case to be vigilant."

"Am I connected with the case? Should I be concerned?"

"There no harm in being prudent, Julia. I just wonder whether your own search for the missing bowls may have attracted the interest of we know not who."

Julia's brain was buzzing. She needed space. "I do need a cuppa. Sure you do not want one?"

"Not now, thank you."

Julia repaired to the kitchen, put the kettle on and sat down. She could not deny being excited, but the vague nature of the menace was upsetting, too. Perhaps she should come clean with DCI Bland.

When she returned to the drawing room with a steaming mug in her hand, she found Bland looking at some photos.

"Maisie and Philip. She has just started at Aberdeen and Philip is finishing his degree at Exeter." She knew what Bland was thinking. "Happily divorced."

"I did not mean to pry. But Philip looks very much like you. Handsome fellow."

Was Bland paying her a compliment? Or were his just two statements of fact?

"Eric, it may be nothing, but perhaps I should tell you all the same."

Bland sat on the armchair. He was in listening mode.

"I asked around about Dr Gordon and two facts struck me. Do you know of the brawl with Gordon and the Chinese couple?"

Bland ran quickly in his head through the list of door-to-door reports on the case and could not recall any brawl. "No, I don't."

"Well, on the 7th of February last year Dr Gordon had a row with a Chinese couple loud enough for his neighbours to call in to his apartment as this was very much out of character. And the apartment looked as if it had been burgled."

"Gordon was murdered on the 14th. Some Valentine's day," Bland said aloud to himself, "and the other thing?"

"Well, this may or may not be true, but apparently a couple of years ago Dr Gordon bought back his own Doucai bowls – which makes no sense."

Now it was Bland' turn to need some time to process all this new information. "If you do not mind, Julia, I'll have that cup of tea, please?"

"I need a top up, too." Julia disappeared to the kitchen. While the tea was brewing she could just hear Bland talking on his mobile. She waited until the conversation was over before returning to the sitting room.

"I was on to Special Branch," Bland was explaining his telephone call, "and there is something else you should know. The wife of the murdered Chinese dealer is missing." Julia's next question left Bland speechless.

"Do you think they are the couple that had quarrelled with Dr Gordon?"

Bland had just had the thought himself and to see Julia getting there as fast as him confirmed his hunch that Julia Flowers was no ordinary woman.

"They may be."

"Easy enough to find out. You could ask Clara and Jack Bellingham. If you have a photo."

"Are these the neighbours who witnessed the row?"

"Yes, but there may be a slight problem," warned Julia, "Clara is, how can I put it? She is a very highly-strung person and may not react well to a police interview."

"Can you explain?"

"Clara has had mental health issues," Julia hated the expression, but could not find an alternative, "and if she has a panic attack you would not be able to get anything out of her."

"What about her husband?"

"Jack is, ehm, lackadaisical, shall we say. Not an ideal witness."

"It may not be protocol, but I wonder whether you would mind coming with me to see the Bellinghams, just to keep things informal and cool."

"I don't mind at all."

Bland remembered the mug of tea getting cold in his hand and started sipping it. A pleasant silence ensued.

"Let me get my diary." Julia returned with her black leather diary bulging with loose sheets of paper, business cards, and assorted stationery. "I am free tomorrow at 10."

"Great. I'll see you at 55 Heriot Row tomorrow at 10, then."

DCI Bland went all reflective on his drive back to Edinburgh, helped in no small measure by the perennial traffic jam to and from the Forth Road Bridge. Luckily his excursions to the Kingdom of Fife were infrequent, but every time he could not help thinking how patient Scottish drivers are. Once he did some back of envelope calculations and found the results astonishing.

More than 50,000 vehicles use the bridge each day. Suppose the queues waste 30 minute per vehicle. Considering an average value of time of £25 per hour and adding the cost of extra petrol and pollution, the cash wasted by the traffic jams amount to more than half a billion pounds a year. Enough to start a revolution in most countries.

But Bland was not thinking about economics. He was not even thinking about the investigation and the new leads. Rather he was admitting to himself that he could not remember when he had felt so excited by his job. Bland would be the first to confess that he had lost his enthusiasm for policing a long time ago and was counting the days to drawing his pension. The only reason he wanted to close the Gordon case was his promotion to Superintendent and the extra £12,000 salary. But not now. He was genuinely looking forward to following up the lead on the Chinese couple. And tonight he was not going to eat a take-out. Instead he was would stop at that restaurant just off London Road next to the gay public toilets as he had meant to do for months. And about time, Bland thought.

CHAPTER 13

THE BELLINGHAMS

It was a glorious Edinburgh morning. The high winds of the night before had swept away all traces of dust and pollution from the air and the April sunshine was of a brightness unknown south of the border. One could almost smell the sea air as far as Heriot Row, or so thought Julia as she was waiting in her car in front of number 55, with her window rolled down.

As she saw Bland's car approaching, she got out of the car, and smoothed down her skirt so as not to reveal too much of her gorgeous long legs.

"The gods are conspiring against me, again," apologized Bland, "a last-minute emergency in the office. I hope I am not too late."

"I do not mind waiting when the weather is this lovely." Julia's smile managed to brighten an already bright day.

Bland pressed the bronze bell and waited for the intercom to crackle into life.

"Yes. Who is it?" croaked a metallic voice of indistinct gender.

"Detective Chief Inspector Bland."

"About time somebody showed up. Come up," was the unexpected welcome.

Bland and Julia walked up the stairs to find a bellicose Clara Bellingham standing on her threshold ready for them. On seeing Julia, Clara Bellingham was visibly mollified:

"Julia, how nice to see you. But I do not understand. What are you doing here with the police?"

"Hi Clara. It's a long story, but nothing to worry about. How's Jack?"

"Come in, come in. We are still upset by the incident. Sorry, what did you say your name was"?

"DCI Bland of Police Scotland. Before talking about the incident, would you mind if we ask you a few questions about an unrelated enquiry?"

"You mean you are not here to investigate the incident?" Clara Bellingham was on a war path now.

"If I may, Clara. It would be really helpful if you could assist the inspector with some antiques that went missing. A client of mine, you understand."

"Missing antiques. How exciting! Of course, I'll help. But first you have to try some amazing jasmine tea Jack found in that new shop in Stockbridge. And you, too, Inspector." Without waiting for a reply, she disappeared out of the drawing room's door.

"What did you call her? 'Highly strung'. That covers it." Brand smiled at Julia.

Even before Clara Bellingham returned to the room one could smell an intense jasmine perfume pervading the apartment. Not really Bland's cup of tea, but he had had worse. She put a tray down on the coffee table and starting pouring a very pale green liquid in rather exquisite bone China mugs.

"What antiques are we talking about, Julia?"

"I'd better let the Inspector ask the questions."

"Mrs Bellingham, I know it's a lot to ask, but you would not remember an incident involving Dr Gordon and a Chinese couple in February last year, would you?

"Of course I do. It was so extraordinary. Normally Dr Gordon would be quieter than a mouse. The ideal neighbour, really. But that night there was a huge row coming from downstairs: shouts, furniture being shunted about, even broken glass, I think. So Jack and I went downstairs, to check that Dr Gordon was alright. Such a gentleman, you know."

"Did you see who Dr Gordon was quarrelling with?"

"Well, Jack and I went in – the front door was open, you see – and we saw Dr Gordon, very distressed he was and this Chinese couple shouting at him. In Chinese!"

Bland took a couple of large photographs out of a folder he was holding under his arm.

"Do you know these people, Mrs Bellingham?"

"It's them. It's them. Who are they? Very rude they were."

"Are you positive that these are the people you saw arguing with Dr Gordon?"

"Of course I am. Totally positive. You can ask Jack, too." Clara Bellingham moved swiftly to the door and shouted: "Jack, Jack! Come down, please. Quickly."

After a brief moment, Jack Bellingham arrived, wearing a rather fetching velvet dressing gown with beige and green piping. A silk cravat would not have been out of place or out of character.

"Yes, dear. Oh, my word. Julia? How nice to see you. Such a long time." Then Jack noticed an unfamiliar presence in the room: "I am afraid I do not think I know you".

"DCI Bland, Police Scotland. Nice to meet you."

Clara interrupted the formalities: "Jack, Jack. Do you remember the awful mess with Dr Gordon last year. The unspeakable Chinese couple. The Inspector knows who they are!"

This is not exactly how DCI Bland would have asked a witness to identify someone, but there was no way of stopping Clara Bellingham mid-flow.

"Show him the photos, Inspector."

Bland obliged. "Oh yes. It's them. Have you apprehended them, Inspector? They terrified poor Dr Gordon. I always thought they were up to no good."

"Why do you say that, Mr Bellingham?"

"Well, you see, the next morning I paid a visit to Dr Gordon …"

"You never told me that! Why did you never mention it, Jack? Why did you?" Clara Bellingham's voice was now a full octave higher.

"It was nothing, dear. Just a courtesy visit, to check that everything was okay. You were still asleep and later I just forgot."

"You were saying, Mr Bellingham? You saw Dr Gordon the next day, and?"

"He asked me not to mention the incident to anyone, as a personal favour. And he said something to the effect that it would never happen again. When I asked him who those frightful people were, he said that they had been sent to frighten someone, but obviously they had the wrong person and the wrong address."

"And you never saw them again?"

"Certainly not! Frightful people," intervened Clara Bellingham, "and now Inspector can you please do something about the intruder?"

"I must come clean with you, Mrs Bellingham. I confess I have taken the wrong file with me this morning. Could you remind me of your complaint, please?" Julia admired the way Bland was able to think on his feet and get on the right side of Clara at the same time.

"Well. First we reported strange noises coming from downstairs and even stranger people coming and going in and out Dr Gordon's apartment. And these were not estate agent types, I can assure you."

Bland had a pretty clear idea of who these strange types were. Typical London. "And then?"

"Two days ago, it must have been well past midnight, Jack and I heard noises coming from the back garden and what was worse was that the security lights did not work. So we got a torch and we saw the intruder."

"What intruder?" Now Bland was interested. Very.

"Middle of the night. Not the ideal time for gardening, is it? There was a man, digging up soil in Dr Gordon's garden. When we shone the torch on him he looked up, stopped digging, and walked slowly into Dr Gordon's apartment as if *we* had disturbed *him*!"

"Did you see his face? Could you recognize him?"

"Recognize him? You must be joking! He was wearing a woolly hat and dark sunglasses. At midnight, for goodness sake!" Clara Bellingham suddenly seemed to switch gear, her excitement fading, as she appeared to resume an earlier inner conversation. "But what about your missing antiques, Julia? What is your story?"

Bland was keen to bring proceedings to a swift conclusion:

"I am really sorry Mrs Bellingham, but Mrs Flowers and I must be going now. You and your husband have been very helpful. Thank you again."

Julia understood the situation: "Clara, I'll see you at Ruthie's soon and then I'll tell you all about it. Bye."

Bland and Julia walked quickly down the stairs and into the bright April morning, both knowing that they, just like the Chinese couple, had been to the right address and had talked about the right man.

CHAPTER 14

TEA FOR TWO

Bland accompanied Julia to her car and, as she was about to unlock the door, he erupted:

"Do you fancy a cup of tea before going back to work? Your friends are quite something."

Julia let a gentle breeze flow through her hair and squeezed her eyelids to avoid being dazzled by the rays of sunshine that seemed to be emanating from Bland's balding head.

"Yes, why not? In fact, I have a question I have always wanted to ask you."

Bland nodded and opened up his arms waiting for the question to be revealed. "But tea first." – continued Julia.

As they walked across Queen Street Julia suggested a self-styled exotic tea room for no other reason than it had a good selection of gluten-free cakes.

"It must be so annoying this gluten allergy. I would not survive without toast." Bland was trying to sound sympathetic, but in his heart of hearts he thought that the gluten thing was a bit of a middle-class indulgence.

"It's not just bread. Gluten is used everywhere and if I am not careful I feel really sick."

Bland did feel a pang of remorse for his secret lack of sympathy for gluten-phobes.

The décor of the tea-room was post-modern kitsch and Bland hated it.

"Different." Bland murmured. He did not wish to offend Julia.

"Do not worry. The teas and cakes are much better than the interior decoration." Julia reassured him.

After ordering, chai tea and carrot cake for Julia and black breakfast tea for Bland, Bland returned to the unasked question:

"You wanted to ask me something?"

"Oh yes, I forgot. I am a bit of a sucker for crime dramas and I have always wondered how you identify people by their dental records? I do not think my dentist keeps a record of my teeth, or does he?"

Bland took a while before answering, as he was doubly disappointed: somehow he was expecting a personal question and also he was hoping Julia would not refer to him as "you, the police".

"It's mainly x-rays. Not very exciting, I am afraid."

"Is that how you identified Dr Gordon, then?"

"Not really. He was not registered with a dentist. Strangely enough. So we struggled a bit, as he has no family to speak of."

Julia kept silent as she wanted to know more.

"Eventually it was the head of department at his University who had to formally identify him."

Julia was allergic to split infinitives as much as to gluten, but tried not to show it.

"Why do you ask?"

"It's nothing. Watched too many crime movies, I suppose. I just thought, what if the body with the smashed-up face wasn't Dr Gordon's."

"His University colleague seemed pretty certain it was Gordon's." But now Bland was not so certain himself. After all, he had been put in charge of the case after the body had been identified as Gordon's. He did not see it himself.

"As I was saying, it's nothing. You do not mind if I ask you about the case. Probably I shouldn't, but in a strange way, I feel involved somehow."

"You have been very helpful, indeed. But, yes, you are right, in theory I should not be discussing the case with you. But I am not so keen on protocol …"

"So, the murdered Soho dealer and Dr Gordon not only knew each other, but quarrelled about something just before Gordon was killed. Possibly the Doucai bowls? Was the dealer trying to swindle Dr Gordon or the other way round?"

"His name was Guangyao Liang and he had no criminal record, but the way he was tortured suggests no ordinary murder. It's a warning. But for whom? For what?" Bland was following his own train of thought and had not been paying much attention to Julia's ramblings.

Julia did not desist: "Do you not think that the bowls are the key? Mr Liang was either selling to, or buying from, Dr Gordon. You did not find the bowls in his shop, by the way?"

"I shall make enquiries, but London seems to be more interested in the missing Mrs Liang at the moment."

"How does the intruder fit it, do you think?"

"It doesn't. But that was the point, wasn't it? Now I am supposed to order a search of the garden, even if I bet you one million pounds that we won't find anything. Which, again, has the hallmarks of a professional job. Nobody is hiding or searching for anything in the garden, or anywhere else. Not when the place has been empty for over a year. It's all window dressing."

Unlike Bland, Julia was listening to her companion and was uneasy about the mere suggestion of shadowy people working in the background, murdering and mutilating with impunity. Perhaps she should report back to Reid & McHalm and stop her pointless quest for two lousy bowls.

Bland must have noticed the cloud that had descended on Julia's bright eyes:

"I do not mean to alarm you, Julia, but you should have my mobile number, just in case you notice anything out of the ordinary."

"Thank you, Eric. Knowing that if something out of the ordinary should happen to me I can always ring a number miles away in Edinburgh does not alarm me in the least." She sounded more sarcastic than she meant to be.

Bland insisted on paying and they walked back to their cars in Heriot Row in complete silence.

CHAPTER 15

HOUSEKEEPING

For the whole of that day DCI Bland sat in his office, prompting speculation that he must be preparing for the Superintendent's interview. He was not the desk type.

In fact, Bland had been clearing his mind and the Superintendent's job could not have been farther from his thoughts. He had had a hunch and was looking for the evidence to support it. It was not even a hunch, more of a malaise, a discomfort, a vague sensation that wool was being pulled over his eyes. Mrs Flowers had been a great help, he could not deny it, without her and her missing bowls the case would have been shelved by now. But she had also been a distraction, he could see it now. Bland did not want to admit it to himself, but somehow he had fallen under her spell, the more powerful for not being intended. And because of his carelessness, now she could be embroiled in a mess she was not even aware of. He would go back to basics, do some proper boring policing, and try to get to the bottom of the case and he knew exactly who would help him.

WPC Corby was the person you want on your team but would never invite for a coffee afterwards. It was not so much her looks, which initially would put anyone off, so asymmetric, so quirky, but rather her complete coolness. What made her the perfect colleague also made her the most imperfect person to spend time with. Although she had joined the police only very recently on a fast track stream – in the office nobody knew why a graduate in medieval history would want to be a copper – it was obvious to everybody that she was a rising star and nobody resented it. She was good. Very good. The person you do want on your team.

Later that afternoon Bland decided to have some Corby time.

"WPC Corby, take a seat, please. I could ask you to do some background work on the Gordon case, but, knowing you, I think you have done that already. And more beside."

"Well, Sir, I followed up on your query about Dr Gordon's identification and you were right, it is not as watertight as we thought."

"What have you found?"

"I interviewed Professor Stolper, Dr Gordon's boss at Abertay. He had moved from Napier only two years ago and had met Dr Gordon only a couple of times. I showed him a photograph I had prepared and he identified it as Dr Gordon without batting an eyelid."

"What do you mean 'a photo you had prepared'?"

"I went through a few mug shots and chose one that looked like Dr Gordon. A retired accountant charged with fraud – pretty close resemblance, but not perfect by any means."

"Very clever," thought Bland. Corby's fast track was now even faster.

"I am trying to find a reliable DNA sample, but after all this time …"

"Good work, Corby. And the solicitors?"

"No joy, Sir. They would not release the terms of the will. Not without a court order. I have spoken with Corporate Fraud just in case there was scope for some leverage, but, no, not even a hint of shady accounting."

"There may be a way round," suggested Bland.

"Linking the Gordon case with an ongoing investigation, Sir?"

Of course, Bland was not supposed to have shared the Special Branch report with a mere WPC, but Corby was far from mere, and, true enough, she had made the connection.

"I'll prepare the paperwork, Sir."

"Anything else, Corby?"

"Well, I spoke to DS Peng."

"Vice Squad? Really, WPC Corby?"

"It is not what you think, Sir. DS Peng is a Mandarin speaker and pretty good on Weibo."

"Weibo?"

"It's a mix of Twitter and Facebook used in China, Sir. Well, he is working on the list of names we got from Dr Gordon's memory stick. I mixed in a few other names. Need to know and all that."

"I cannot believe that on the web there is no trace of any of fifty people, whoever they may be. Perhaps these are nicknames, aliases, not real names, something."

"That's why I thought DS Peng may help. I have also done a background check on Mrs Flowers. I hope that's okay."

"I was about to ask you to do just that," Bland hoped that his lie was convincing, "to be on the safe side."

"Nothing to report. A single speeding ticket. Ex-husband a bit of a sleaze bag, but aren't they all?"

Bland's curiosity wasn't altogether professional. "In what way, sleazy?"

"Bank accounts in Switzerland, undeclared income, does not believe in paying support to his children, that kind of thing, nothing too illegal."

Bland was relieved that there was an ex, and not an exemplar husband either.

"Sir, may I make a suggestion?"

Now it was Bland's turn to be one step ahead: "I know, I should really get in bed with Special Branch."

"Only a suggestion, Sir."

Bland had one more job for WPC Corby, one he was not sure should be done at all.

After Corby left, Bland felt that for the first time since he had taken the case on, he was finally going somewhere, even though he would be damned if he knew where he was going.

He just had to call Murphy, whether he liked it or not. And he most definitely was not liking it.

Bland looked at his mobile on the desk beckoning him and realized he had ran out of excuses to delay the inevitable.

"DCI Murphy? This is DCI Bland of Police Scotland. Perhaps you do not remember me." As if, thought Bland.

The voice at the other end was surprisingly friendly:

"Eric Bland. How can I possibly forget? All well North of the border? I suspect not, otherwise you would not have called, right?"

Bland was not fooled by the friendly tone. If there was a pound of flesh to be taken, Murphy would take it. And to hell with the pint of blood.

"Yes, Murphy, you are right. We need some help."

"And who is "we"? Because if memory serves the last time "we" turned out to be just you, Bland. Last time "we" did not include any other fucking Scottish officer, did it? So pardon my insistence, but is this just you, again, or is this a proper request, DCI Bland?"

Bland had already decided that if he was going to make the call he would restrain himself and not be dragged into going over the Wilmot case.

"I assure you this is all kosher, DCI Murphy, I am just following up a report you kindly shared with us. All proper and above board."

"This would not be about the Gordon case, would it?"

Bland was surprised that Murphy knew about an obscure and nearly dormant local Edinburgh case.

"As a matter of fact, it is. It looks as if we may have to liaise on this one. Joint investigation, even."

"Not too fast, Bland. We already know about Gordon and Liang. That's why we thought we should pay you the courtesy of letting you know about the Liang murder. We are the sharing type, you know."

Bland had no choice and so he gambled: "So you know about the list, right?"

The silence from Murphy sounded beautiful to Bland's ears. He had landed a big one.

"Is this one of your jokes, Bland? This is a fucking serious case and we are not going to let some fucking Scottish clowns mess it up. Is that clear?"

Murphy was on the defensive. Bland gloated: "So you do not know about the list, then?"

"No, we do not. Should we?"

"Well, we Scottish clowns have found a list of fifty names that Gordon took great pains to kept secret and most probably is the reason why he was killed and his skull smashed in. My officers are looking into it, big red noses and all."

"We need your list, Bland."

"Who is moving too fast now, Murphy? Sharing is caring. You share your files with us and we do not care a fuck about what you do with our files. Seems fair to me."

"Listen, Bland. If I wanted to, I could have your fucking list on my desk by tomorrow morning, do you understand?"

"I am sure you could, DCI Murphy. But would it be the right list, I wonder."

"Bland, stop fucking about. This is a very serious case."

"So you keep saying, Murphy, but all I know is that a little Chinese dealer in Soho got done in and his wife is missing. Does not sound that serious, with all due respect, unless you guys have so little to do that you keep busy with dinky toy investigations." Bland was enjoying every word he was uttering.

"Listen, Bland. We set off on the wrong foot here. Let us keep things fluffy and informal. What do you say I come up north, you feed me deep fried Mars bars, and we have a friendly chat?" Murphy was sounding the retreat and Bland knew it.

"I can't wait, DCI Murphy. Let me know when you arrive so I can book the limo."

CHAPTER 16

ANTIQUITEAS

In spite of the silly name, Julia liked the antiques-shop-tearoom combo. After all, if bookshops and petrol stations can be partners with coffee shop chains, why not antiques and teas? The atmosphere at Antiquiteas was relaxed, the service unrushed, the teas properly brewed. Julia was sitting at a table waiting for Rosita – although born in India, Rosita had lived in Spain as a teenager, had married an Argentinian, and was imbued with a thoroughly Hispanic sense of time-keeping. Julia was effectively Rosita's replacement mother: she had been Maisie's and Philip's *au pair* and after the divorce Julia, no longer able to employ her, became Rosita's confidante and moral support, providing the warmth and love that Rosita's own mother was so singularly unable to dispense.

The owner of Antiquiteas recognized Julia and approached her table: "Julia. I thought you had deserted us for good. How are you?" William McLeod was the most unlikely businessman in Edinburgh, who had opened his small antiques shop as a form of bereavement therapy after his wife's sudden death in a hit-and-run accident.

"Not at all, William. I have been very busy. How's Daphne?"

"She had to take leave of absence from Uni to concentrate on her sailing. Rio, you know. She has a real chance of making the team." Daphne had been a sailing fanatic since primary school and after her mother's death she had spent more time on the water than on dry land.

"I am sure she'll make it. She is a star. William, I wonder whether I can talk shop for a moment." William McLeod did not know the meaning of talking shop, but he was the most affable person to engage in any conversation about antiques. "Business gossip, really," continued Julia, "do you know of anyone buying for or selling to Dr Gordon?"

"You mean Anthony Gordon, the diplomat?"

"The very same."

"Well, my little curiosity shop is small beer for the likes of Dr Gordon, although he did visit me a couple of times. Very knowledgeable on Chinese porcelain, I do not have to tell you. And on Chinese teas, too. His views on the merits of Da Hong Pao were a bit too controversial, but I did not want to antagonize him. Difficult man to read, I thought. I would not have guessed he was into baby grands, but there you are."

McLeod's stream-of-consciousness conversation was not easy either to follow or to interrupt and so Julia had to take advantage of his brief pause for breath to jump in.

"Baby grand? What baby grand?"

"I do not remember the details. It must have been more than a couple of years ago, but someone told me that he had paid a small fortune for a Steinway baby grand."

"Are you positive it was a baby grand?"

"Absolutely. Bill Devonshire. That's who told me. I remember now. We argued for half an hour, my point being that even if their model S is not really a baby grand, it has none of the musicality of their full size beauties."

"Very interesting, William. Thank you for the information."

McLeod was obviously keen to continue the conversation, by Julia was saved by Rosita's arrival.

"So sorry, Hoolia. I missed the bus." Julia had given up years ago on having her name pronounced in a non-Hispanic fashion, and now she would have been disappointed if Rosita had called her anything other than Hoolia. Only after she had hugged and kissed Julia did Rosita realize that perhaps she was interrupting something. Julia, as usual, deftly defused the awkwardness by introducing William to Rosita: "Rosita, this is William, who owns this lovely place. William, my friend Rosita." Pleasantries over, Julia and Rosita ordered, quite appositely, some oolong tea.

During the exchange of news about children, jobs, and husband, Julia was somewhat distracted by what William had just told her. She had been trying to get news about the elusive Dr Gordon from all her contacts in the antiques business, but with no success. Was Gordon doing business with London dealers? Or possibly with China directly? After all he could access the network of contacts that allowed him to acquire those beautiful Doucai bowls.

Rosita was full of the enthusiasm of a mother whose children are finally both in school, combining the joy for their daily achievements and the relief for a life rescued from incessant involvement with toilet training, ingesting comestibles and not chemicals, building with Duplo, and other drudgeries.

Julia was reminded of that very same time in her life, and saw in Rosita the same unacknowledged anxiety, the same vague feeling of a new chapter being written without any idea of the plot, just a jumbling of characters moving in and out of the pages, pages that were inexorably being turned.

Rosita, intuitive and bright, must have sensed that something was preoccupying Julia: "Hoolia, is there anything wrong? I know that expression."

"It's work. Something I have not done before. Looking for some missing antiques."

"Sounds exciting."

"No, it isn't," Julia thought best not to involve Rosita, "I have just realized that you have not been to my new house. Francisco and the children will like it: it's right on the seashore." Julia knew of Rosita's strange dislike for anything aquatic. "You must come soon."

They agreed that it was a good idea, but no firm date was fixed.

CHAPTER 17

PIANOS

One of the sadder aspects of Julia's job was to do with pianos. Even the plainest of pianos has a nobility, an emotional resonance, an accumulation of labour and workmanship that are missing in modern furniture. And yet most pianos have a negative market value, in so far as even if they are sold at all, the realized price is invariably less than the cost of moving the piano. But in the perverse economics of second-hand pianos there are winners, actually a single winner, the removal firm that has carved a niche for itself specializing in the removal of pianos. Four men would appear on your door step, wrap the piano in a strange harness – upright, baby grand, full concert size, whatever – lift it and weave it down the most intricate of Edinburgh stairs, load it on a truck and disappear. All done in virtual silence, with the same rehearsed efficiency of first-class funeral directors, no questions asked, the necessity of disposal taken for granted.

Every time a piano was dispatched to the Council's skip yard, Julia's heart sank and the rest of the day would be darkened by a suffused sadness, a sense of loss for the senseless disposal of a potential dispenser of harmony and culture.

And so it was that for the first time ever Julia rang the telephone number of the piano undertakers without a heavy heart. Quite the opposite, in fact, as she hoped that it would lead to an interesting discovery.

"This is Julia Flowers of Hillman Roberts. I wonder whether you can help."

"Always happy to oblige, Mrs Flowers, but I should tell you straightaway that we are fully booked for the next two weeks."

A piano massacre, thought Julia. "That's quite alright, Mr Moody, as I am trying to locate a piano, not to dispose of it."

"And how can we help?"

"I have been asked to help with a probate valuation for the late Dr Gordon, but I seem to be unable to locate a baby grand he acquired some time ago. This is a valuable piece and so I thought he could have used a reputable firm like yourselves."

"If you give me a minute, Mrs Flowers, I'll check our records. Hold the line, please."

After a couple of long minutes, Mr Moody was back: "Here it is. Dr Gordon. 13, Dean Park Mews, EH4 1ED. Steinway baby grand."

"Thank you very much Mr Moody. You have been a life saver."

Julia knew the place quite well. Upper class lock-up garages, really. Little cobbled streets, wooden double doors, painted green or pink, stone-walled one-storey terraced cottages. She had not thought her next move through. Was she going to break an entry? It would not be too difficult. A pair of bolt cutters and the muscle power of Colin, the head porter at Hillman Roberts, would be enough to break the genteel locks that adorn Dean Park Mews. But almost certainly there would be a burglar alarm. Julia sweated at the thought, as if she had already committed the hypothetical crime, and was hearing the whining sound of the burglar's alarm in her ears. Probably there was no power in the premises. Julia relaxed slightly. Unless Dr Gordon had set up a standing order in which case the garage would be alarmed. Even a few seconds of merely imagining her break-in were enough to convince her that well-intentioned burglary was not on the cards.

She would have to think laterally. And she did.

Parking at Edinburgh Airport was one of the few perks enjoyed by DCI Bland: instead of submitting to the fantastically exorbitant parking fees charged by the daylight robbers known as Edinburgh Airport ("Where Scotland meets the world" and robs it blind), he could park just in front of the main entrance and ask the PC on duty to keep an eye on the vehicle.

Waiting for DCI Murphy in domestic arrivals, surrounded by the traffic of generally bored or pissed off passengers, Bland was wondering whether he would recognize his Special Branch visitor after so many years since they had met in London. That was a disaster that Bland was only too happy to have forgotten almost completely, except Murphy's stereotypical Irish features, his curly ginger hair, the freckles, the long pointed nose, the gangly demeanour.

Bland need not have worried. He recognized Murphy immediately, in spite of the now absent curly hair, and the freckles replaced by liver stains.

"Welcome to Scotland, Murphy."

Murphy shook Bland's hand with exaggerated vigour, as if to reassure him that the loss of hair did not mean a loss of purpose: "Thank you for meeting me here, Bland. Very kind of you."

"I know you haven't much time, and so I thought we could start talking on the way back to town." What Bland really meant was that the sooner Murphy buggered off back to London the happier he would be.

Murphy, who was carrying a small cabin-sized holdall, obviously was not planning on a long stay, either.

Throughout the usual snarling drive from the airport to Edinburgh city centre Murphy steadfastly refused to engage in any meaningful conversation with Bland, concentrating instead on how much more easily car traffic was flowing in London since the introduction of the congestion charge, on the pointlessness of automatic cars, especially sports cars, anything under the sun in fact, except the reason why he had travelled all the way to Edinburgh.

As they approached the even more badly congested city centre, Murphy suggested they stopped at the George Hotel, much to Bland's surprise.

"Have you not heard of austerity, police manpower cuts? You know, deficit reduction, Tory drivel, down in London?"

"You forget you are talking to Special Branch. The clue is in the name, Bland. Special, that's what we are." Murphy smiled broadly revealing his working class origins and his badly aligned teeth. "Let's us say that the George owes me a favour. And, of course, there are operative reasons, too."

"What? They procure the best hookers in Mid Lothian, do they?"

"Ouch, Bland. No, the bar at the George is one of the few places in town where there is live piano music almost non-stop." Murphy was setting a trap and Bland fell right into it.

"And without live piano music Special Branch cannot operate, is that it?"

"Not exactly," Murphy took a small object from his pocket, "combined with this little gizmo, a scrambler to you Bland, piano music makes interception practically impossible." One nil to me, said Murphy to himself.

Bland acknowledged the uppercut by raising his eyebrows in a resigned fashion and regrouped quickly.

"Instead of these stupid spy movie shenanigans, if you had come clean on this case from the beginning, perhaps we would not need your gizmo, would we, Murphy?"

"Better safe than sorry. Cannot be too cautious." said Murphy as he and Bland stepped into the piano bar at the George. Bland pretended not to be impressed by the impressive glass cupola and attached giant cut-glass chandelier. Predictably, Murphy sat at the table nearest to the piano, which at the moment was silent, as the pianist was sipping a well-deserved freshly squeezed orange juice.

Bland and Murphy took advantage of the momentary silence to order soft drinks as, after all and in spite of the unusual surroundings, they were two coppers on duty.

As soon as the inevitable Gymnopedie started filling the vast empty space of the George piano bar, Murphy filled Bland in on the details of the Gordon case.

"Dr Gordon was an awkward sod. Too clever by half, you might say. Left a very good posting in Beijing for reasons unknown. For reasons even more unknown he settled in Edinburgh to lead a near-monastic life. Then he managed to get himself killed in the most horrible fashion. So far so nothing to do with us, but then his will is brought to our attention, as the mysterious Dr Gordon not only leaves a very substantial estate – five million pounds min. – but leaves it to the worst possible charity in the world. Rights for China, for goodness' sake, the most radical human-rights organization you can find. And that's where the Chinese come in. All guns fucking blazing. We are talking major diplomatic incident. We-stop-investing-in-your-nuclear-power kind of incident."

Bland lost his patience. "Are you fucking kidding me, Murphy? Did you come all the way from London with your fucking scrambler to feed me this plateful of bullshit? When are going to start telling me something worth listening to? I have better things to do than hanging from your very special branch. And, as to my list, you can fucking forget it, Murphy."

"Take it easy, Bland. I was setting the scene."

Bland was not in the mood for contextual conversation. "What is the link with the murdered Chinese dealer? Was Gordon involved in illegal antiques dealing? Why were you bugging his apartment? What the fuck was the digging up of his garden all about?"

Murphy was taken aback by the ferocity of Bland's outburst. Some retrenchment was called for.

"Calm down, Bland. I came all the way from London to bring an olive branch and to start some serious joint work with you. So let us forget the past. Let's start afresh and let's nail this case together. What do you say?"

Bland was not convinced, but did not show it. "Fine by me, Murphy. But if you want my list, you have to put something substantial on the table."

"The charade in the garden and the bugging had nothing to do with Special Branch. It was an MI6 show for the benefit of the Chinese, just to show that they were taking the case seriously. River House are pissed off because Gordon was totally off their radar and when he managed to get himself killed they realized that they had virtually nothing on him. We ourselves are being leaned on very heavily from all sides. Foreign Office, MI6, even the Home Office. You name it. They all want to make sure that the Chinese do not get tarnished in any way. I am asking you to trust me. Believe me when I tell you that if you or I come across some Chinese involvement with the case that would spell the end of the case. Period."

"So why are you here? What is there to investigate if as soon as we find out anything the case is taken away from us?" Bland was not sure about Murphy's angle in the case.

"I am investigating Liang's murder personally. Truly horrific, but it can give us the key to crack this case. In my humble. The wife is missing, but I am not holding my breath. I do not think we will ever find the body." Murphy was scrutinizing Bland's face looking for any signs of rapprochement, but Bland's was not a face easy to read.

"Okay, Murphy. If you tell me about your Chinese dealer's details, I'll tell you what I know about him and Gordon."

"In my opinion, and it's only a hunch, the murder was staged to look like a revenge killing in Chinatown, but I do not think that Liang had any connection whatever with organized crime."

"So you think he was killed by the Chinese?"

"Not directly. It was a professional hit and anyone could be behind it. Including the Chinese. I have tried to keep the investigation low profile and so far at least MI6 have not made the connection with the Gordon case."

"I can tell you precisely when and how Gordon and the Liangs were 'connected'". Bland waited for a moment to see the reaction on Murphy's face and then continued. "They met for sure on the 7th of April two years ago at Gordon's apartment and it was not a cordial exchange."

"That's great. Now we know for sure that there was a connection. Which leaves the small matter of finding it. Has your antiques consultant got any ideas?"

Bland was taken aback by Murphy's knowing about Julia. "My consultant, as you call her, only consults about antiques. She is a specialist in Oriental porcelain, not in murders."

"Sorry for touching a raw nerve, Bland. Let's carry on. Liang's shop was thoroughly searched by the killer or killers and my guess is that they were looking for your list."

"Ah, the blessed list. You have to give more before I share it with you."

"Bland, I have come clean with you. Everybody here has an agenda. You want superintendent, I want to poke MI6 in the eye, and MI6 have a lot to be forgiven for. The little River House has shared with me I have shared with you. The truth is that none of us has much to go on."

"Fine, Murphy. I take your word for it, but if I find you are playing games with me, I swear I'll make you pay. Now, Gordon kept a secret list of names, all of Chinese people presumably, and all untraced. Are they aliases? I don't know. But he took a lot of care to hide this list and from what you say Liang got gutted for it, too. And before you ask, yes, I have made a copy for you to take back to London."

"That's grand, but are you sure you don't have more on the case?"

Bland was not in a hurry to reply. He was not going to bring Julia into this business with Special Branch and, anyway, he did not have anything concrete to share with Murphy. "I'll play fair. When I have solid news, I'll let you know. I have a question for you: have you spoken to Gordon's solicitors? My impression is that they are keeping their cards a bit too close to their striped chests but for the life of me I cannot work out what they are so secretive about."

"Shall we say that a chat with Reid & McHalm may be in order now, partner?"

Bland was not so sure about the "partner" bit, but bringing Murphy along was likely to make Reid & McHalm a little less reticent.

CHAPTER 18

GOLF CLUBS

Julia's gamble had paid off: she guessed that the unseasonal warm weather and a slow Friday would be sufficient to drag Alistair Reid away from his office and to the Gravelstone Golf Club. So when she turned up at 4.45pm at the offices of Reid & McHalm asking for the keys of 13, Dean Park Mews, Sue, the meticulous legal secretary, could not reach Alistair Reid to check whether the keys could be released. Julia's reputation and her winning smile were sufficient for Sue Mollison to deposit the heavy old-fashioned brass key to Dr Gordon's lock-up in Julia's hands.

Julia's heart was pounding, in spite of her repeated self-assurance that she was not doing anything illegal. After all she had been instructed by Alistair Reid to leave no stone unturned to find the Doucai bowls and 13, Dean Park Mews was as good a stone as any to look under. Key firmly clenched in her hand she left the HQs of Reid & McHalm and headed straight to her destination.

In Edinburgh's needlessly chaotic Friday rush hour – the result of the breath-taking incompetence of the most inept collection of traffic managers in the whole of Europe – it took nearly half hour for Julia to cover the short distance between the solicitors' and Dean Park. But for once Julia did not mind, as she was not at all clear how best to proceed.

Ten minutes later, having finally found a parking space and having paid the extortionate ransom that Edinburgh Council euphemistically calls a parking fee, Julia arrived at 13 Dean Park Mews. Her heart was beating furiously as if it wanted to jump out of the rib cage and bounce along the cobbled street. Her mouth suddenly went completely dry, her tongue unsuccessfully trying to find a drop of moisture on the inside of her cheeks. Trembling, she inserted the heavy brass key into the keyhole and turned it purposefully. The key took only a half turn and then stopped. Julia's long experience with keys and locks told her instantly that this was not the right key. She took it out as if to interrogate it and then looked at the key label, with its spiky but clearly handwritten sign: 15 Dean Park Mews. The secretary had given her the *wrong* key. On the bright side, Julia's heart resumed its normal beat and her mouth regained its moisture, as if a secret tap had been turn on. The sense of anti-climax was palpable. Her shoulders unclenched and a long sigh came out, unprompted but welcome.

"Why would Reid and McHalm have the keys of the lock-ups at *both* 13 *and* 15?" Julia suddenly thought, her heart speeding up again. She had been given permission by the solicitors to enter the property to which the key belonged, hadn't she? And she had paid the exorbitant parking fee for the full 60 minutes. She took the few steps to the door at 15, Dean Park Mews, put the key in the lock, turned it without hesitation and opened the door. Or tried to open the door, because the travel of the door was impeded by something offering gentle but obstinate resistance. She pushed the door a bit further and found the source of resistance: strips of heavy thick black rubber were hanging just past the door, the sort you find in industrial freezers, but in white, not pitch black. She forced the door past this plastic protection and fumbled for the light switch, as the space she had entered into was totally dark. Before finding the switch, her skin first and her brain later alerted her to the strange feel of the room: it was as if she had stepped out of a chalet in the Swiss mountains and into the fresh air of a late spring morning. The lock-up at 15, Dean Park Mews was temperature and humidity controlled. The light switch was refusing to cooperate and was nowhere to be found. Julia fumbled into her handbag, grabbed her iPhone and switched on the torch, as on automatic pilot.

When she shone the surprisingly intense light beam round the room, her heart stopped for a beat or two, and then restarted at much faster speed. She was not aware of it at the time, but her beautifully designed jaw literally dropped an inch or so. It was as if she had walked into one of her recurring dreams: the room was full of the most exquisite Chinese ceramics you can imagine. In fact, to Julia's trained eye it was as if she had walked into one of the emperor's display halls. When she finally located the light switch, the full glory of the treasure trove was revealed. A shiver ran down her spine: she was not supposed to have seen this abundance of beauty, not to mention the twenty million pounds worth or so carefully shelved in the lock-up. Whose was it? Dr Gordon's? Had she been given the wrong address? Most probably not, as there was no trace of the Steinway baby grand piano and Mr Moody was nothing if not meticulous.

It was not the chilled air in the temperature-controlled space that was giving Julia a cold sweat. This was not the accumulated collection of a passionate buyer, it was not the obsessive life work of a completist, it was not the academic precision cataloguing of a museum curator. It was cold, detached, clinical, shorn of any passion. Julia had an image that she could not shake from her mind: the place looked like the evidence depository of a surreal police station. The reference to police reminded Julia of DCI Bland. Should she mention her fortuitous find to him? Or was she breaking and entering, in spite of her possession of a legally acquired key? Too many thoughts were swirling in her head. She needed time to process all the fears and plan ahead. A quick stopover at Waitrose and a nice long recipe to follow to the letter. Supper for one need not be bleak. She carefully locked 15, Dean Park Mews and its Ali Baba trove and gingerly made it back to the car, strangely triumphant.

≈≈≈≈≈

On the way to Reid and McHalm, while Bland was raging about something or another, Murphy suddenly asked him to stop the car in a way that Bland instantly regarded as over-dramatic.

"Listen, Bland. Perhaps I am going to regret this, but I am going to share with you something I have never shared with anyone else."

"You are not going to tell me you are gay, Murphy, are you?" said Bland in a flat attempt to defuse the situation.

"I am serious, Bland. This is a fucking serious business, much more serious than you can imagine. I am going to introduce you to a source no-one knows about. Not Special Branch, not MI6. N-o-o-n-e, do you understand? "

"Keep your pants on, Murphy. I did not like you either, but I think you are alright, actually. You can trust me. Really."

"Let's go to the Gravelstone Golf Club then."

Bland and Murphy were silent for the rest of the car journey. Gravelstone Golf Club is an urban oddity. Located between Murrayfield and Corstorphine, surrounded by very expensive real estate is an oasis of snobbery and greens, and its car park, on that busy Friday afternoon, was stereotypical. Porsche Cayennes and Audi A8s disgorging golf club bags and people in ridiculous outfits.

Murphy seemed strangely at home in surroundings that were totally alien to Bland, who meekly followed his new partner into the foyer and the reception hall.

"Mr Murphy. I am expected by a member who, I believe, has already signed me in. I have a friend with me. I trust this is okay with you."

The receptionist smiled without uttering a word and accompanied both policemen to the members' bar, opened the door for them and withdrew, silently and discreetly.

Murphy moved swiftly towards a table where a small man with greasy hair and what Bland anticipated correctly as very sweaty hands was sitting, sipping what looked like whisky and water. The small man was expecting Murphy to be unaccompanied and imperceptibly raised an eyebrow when Murphy introduced him to Bland. "This is my friend Eric Bland. Eric, meet Alan Patterson."

After shaking Bland's hand and transferring a fair amount of moisture unto it, Patterson turned to Murphy and in his unctuous voice said:

"I do not mean to be rude to your friend, but you told me this would be a, ehm, confidential meeting".

"I know, Alan, but Eric can be totally relied on and he has some very, very useful intelligence."

"If you say so, Patrick, if you say so."

"Of course, Murphy would be a Patrick." Bland said to himself.

Murphy summoned the waitress with a backward tilt of his head and ordered a tomato juice for himself, followed by fizzy water for Bland. Patterson had already drunk enough – for the time being.

"Alan had been following Dr Gordon for years," Murphy started, when Bland interjected: "What do you mean 'following'?"

"We had intelligence that Gordon may not be the innocuous former diplomat he appeared to be and Alan discreetly followed his career, especially as far as trading in antiques was concerned."

It was Patterson's turn to take over the account:

"He was a very crafty trader: selling high-value items at the right time and buying undervalued quality antiques. He definitely knew his onions, but it was never clear to me how a part-time University professor on a Foreign Office part-pension could be in possession of really big-ticket porcelain – Imperial quality I mean, top-drawer stuff."

"I confess I know nothing about this antiques business, but if Gordon was such a smart dealer, treating antiques as commodities to be disposed at the highest price and bought cheaply, why make copies of his precious Doucai bowls and where are they, anyway?"

Patterson's sweaty face did not betray any change, but he had just realized that behind Bland's anodyne face there was a pretty smart brain.

"He made a killing on the Doucai, but God knows why he made a copy. And he did not sell the bowls through the usual channels."

"Forgive my ignorance, but what are the usual channels?"

"When you know the quality of what you are selling you do not sell at auction. Why pay 20 percent commission or more to sell to people you can sell to directly? So you contact the right dealers whose client list include people with taste and deep pockets, have a couple of nice lunches and seal the deal. But for the Doucai bowls Gordon dealt directly with a buyer, cashed a very, very big cheque and, for reasons best known to him, had fairly good copies made."

"Why was Patterson keeping the final card close to his no doubt sweaty chest? I'll just ask him," thought Bland, "and who was this buyer, who obviously trusted Gordon on provenance?"

"I'll be buggered if I know."

The image of Patterson being buggered made Bland queasy for a moment, but he was not going to let this slippery customer get away with bullshitting him.

"Given that you were so intimate with Gordon's dealings, perhaps you can tell me where exactly the proceeds of his clever deals have ended up?

According to my source the collection in his apartment had hardly changed in the last ten years or so."

"Let me tell you two things, Bland," Patterson's tone changed from matter-of-fact to menacing, "first, your source, Mrs Flowers, is not what she seems and you should not be taken in by her charm. And second, Gordon had a secret life and a large amount of cash to go with it."

Murphy thought that he'd better step in before the meeting turned sour. "Alan, I am sure Eric knows how to deal with his sources and, anyway, Mrs Flowers has given him some very important leads." This was Murphy's clue to Bland to start talking about his damned list.

But Bland was not going to play his trump card before he had managed to extract more information from Murphy and his informant.

"Just one more thing," as soon as Bland pronounced these words he regretted sounding like a bad impression of Inspector Columbo, "what do you know about Gordon's liver?"

Bland scrutinized intently both Murphy's and Patterson's reaction: Patterson appeared to be genuinely surprised by the question, Murphy less so.

"Liver? What liver? Gordon wasn't a heavy drinker, if that's what you are asking." Patterson's expression was one of true puzzlement.

"I think Eric is referring to Gordon's health issues with his liver."

"So Murphy knew about the transplant, but had kept quiet about it." Thought Bland who made a mental note of asking Murphy directly as soon as they were alone.

"What I do not understand is why Special Branch, or the Counter-terrorism Command, to give it its proper name, is interested in antiques dealings, to the point of having Gordon "followed" for years. Where is the threat to national security coming from? A flood of ceramic fakes? A dotcom porcelain bubble?"

Murphy and Patterson looked at each other for a split second, each wondering whether to answer Bland's question. Murphy moved first. "Eric, I will not sell you any BS about 'National Security', but let's just say that Gordon left his Beijing post under a bit of a cloud and we were asked to keep a discreet eye on him."

"You have to do better than that, Patrick," Bland spelling out each letter of Murphy's newly revealed first name, "with terrorists rampaging all over Europe you are telling me that Special Branch has so much spare time and cash to 'keep an eye' on a minor former diplomat with a side line in antiques?"

"China is the second largest economy on the planet," intervened Patterson, "it trades on world markets, but it is not a market economy. It is capricious, with its own rules. You irritate the wrong Party official and thousands of people thousands of miles away lose their jobs."

Bland was taken aback by Patterson's interjection, spoken with unexpected authority and he wondered who was employed by whom. "All very true, but if you are not more specific, if you do not tell me the connection between little Dr Gordon, China, and the next Great Depression I cannot see how I can help you."

Murphy realized that Bland was not going to give up the list without getting substantial intelligence in exchange.

"Eric, I really should not be telling you this, but we think that Gordon was a small cog in a much bigger clockwork movement the Chinese do not want anybody to see, let alone interfere with. All we know is that he was involved, but how and to what extent, we have no idea."

"When you say "the Chinese", do you mean the Chinese government?" asked Bland with pretend naïveté.

"The Chinese concept of 'government' is different from ours," Patterson was in lecture mode, again, "without support from the Party you cannot build a multi-billion dollar business and without multi-billion businesses you cannot keep a surveillance state functioning. We think Gordon stumbled upon a Party-Business liaison he was not supposed to be a part of."

Bland was now clear who wore the trousers in the Murphy-Patterson household. The time had arrived to give Patterson something of what he was after.

"Well, Gordon went to great lengths to keep a list of fifty names well away from prying eyes. The thing is that the names, as far as we can make out, are just that, we cannot attach them to any real persons."

"Who is 'we'?" asked Patterson anxiously.

"Do not worry. I kept my search very low key. Only a couple of officers know of the list, and neither are aware of its significance or origin."

"What about Mrs Flowers?" Patterson insisted.

"She found it." Bland was not going to involve Julia any more than he had to.

"Anything else on the list?" asked Murphy.

Bland put a memory stick on the table. "You can check for yourself. Only names and antiques."

Patterson grabbed the memory stick and pocketed it slowly.

"You will let me know if you find something out, won't you, Mr Patterson?"

"Of course, Patrick will keep you abreast of developments." And with that he got up, tilted his head upwards imperceptibly as if to mean a silent farewell, and left.

"And who exactly is Mr Alan Patterson?" asked Bland as soon as the departing grease-ball was out of ear-shot.

"It is well above my pay grade to know for sure who he is. He was assigned to me years ago as an 'external consultant', but now it very much looks like I am working for him. He is a slippery bugger, I do not trust him a bit, but he knows stuff that no-one else does and he gets things done."

"Like bugging Gordon's apartment?"

"Quite possibly." replied Murphy, but Bland was not paying attention. In fact, he got up hurriedly and almost ran to the door linking the Members' Bar to the veranda. Murphy had to follow suit, just not to look like a complete idiot.

"Mr Reid, a word, if you do not mind" shouted Bland at a foursome of garishly attired golfers who had just finished their Friday afternoon round. The four, and everybody else in a twenty metre radius turned to Bland, but he was impervious to the dozens of daggers being darted at him in typical Edinburgh middle-class fashion. Alistair Reid stopped while the rest of the group proceeded in their slow march to the changing rooms. He tried to distance himself from the faux pas: "Do I know you, Sir?" and in the same breath, "yes, I do know you from somewhere …"

"DCI Bland and this is a colleague of mine, Mr Murphy."

"Pleased to meet you, Mr Reid," said Murphy in a rare display of social nicety.

"Has anything happened? Is my wife alright?" Alistair Reid was still playing to the stalls and Bland went along, whispering in his ear: "Absolutely nothing to worry about, Mr Reid, more of a social call. If we could talk somewhere quiet …"

Social propriety restored, the three men walked to an empty outdoor table and when all three were sitting down, Bland went right down to business.

"Mr Reid, this is about Dr Gordon's investigation. We now believe that in your previous statements about Dr Gordon you were – what is the phrase? – oh, yes, 'economical with the truth'".

Alistair Reid was not as impressed with Bland's gambit as Bland was hoping.

"DCI Bland, I have been as forthcoming as my fiduciary position allows me to be, but if you have any more questions that I am permitted to answer, I shall be only too happy to assist you." Reid was as cool as a cucumber dressed up as a golfer can be.

Murphy thought best to pile up the pressure: "DCI Bland was himself economical with the truth when he introduced me as a colleague. I am from Special Branch, Metropolitan Police …"

"I thought you were now called Counter Terrorism Command," interjected Reid, not all impressed.

"… we prefer the old name. Anyway, the very fact that I am here should tell you that this is not a run-of-the-mill case and that we expect all citizens to help us in whichever way they can."

"This is interesting, Mr Murphy, because my contact at the Foreign Office told me exactly the opposite. To treat this investigation as closed and to be as discreet as it is legally possible."

Murphy and Bland could not help looking at each other for a split second and to admit to themselves that Alistair Reid had wrong-footed them. If the tables had not been turned, they certainly had been comprehensively re-arranged and it was Reid who was sitting pretty, golf garb and all.

Murphy was the quicker to re-group:

"Of course we are aware of the Foreign Office's interest in the case, but, as you know, all investigative powers rest with us, not them."

Bland weighed in. "And if it turned out that you failed to disclose material evidence or even that you were an accessory, it would not look good on your c.v., would it?"

"Our involvement with the late Dr Gordon was merely as executors of his estate, nothing more."

"Yes, but if you aided and abetted Dr Gordon to hide part of his estate, then that would not make you mere executors, or would you call it 'estate forward planning'?" Bland had decided to take off the gloves he never intended to wear in the first place.

"If I were you I would be more careful and would not make ludicrous accusations against a respected solicitor."

"What DCI Bland is suggesting is that it would be better all round if we cleared the air and clarified a few points." It was unusual for Murphy to play Good Cop, but he did not dislike the experience.

"As I said before, I am always happy to cooperate with Police Scotland and even with Special Branch."

"To put it simply, there is a large discrepancy between the activity on Dr Gordon's bank account and his activities as antiques collector and dealer. Any light you wish to shed on this, Mr Reid?" Bland did not like the guy, but was trying very hard not to show it.

"We acted as executors, not as financial advisers. We drew a will according to the instructions of our client and, upon his death, we were the appointed executors." Reid was on the defensive and stating the bleeding obvious did not help his position.

"Talking of wills, did Dr Gordon change any of his dispositions?" asked Bland.

"I suppose this could be regarded as privileged information, but, on the other hand, in view of Dr Gordon's passing, it could also be regarded as non-material and therefore open to disclosure. Yes, he changed his will on the 10th of February, four days before his untimely death."

"In what way?" interrupted Bland, tired of legal niceties.

"That, I cannot disclose. Or rather," Reid paused for dramatic effect, "I can disclose only in part. The new beneficiary is a matter of public record. Or rather it will be once the will is officially open. It is the Rights for China charity."

"But you won't tell us who the previous beneficiary was." stated Murphy.

"I can tell you only that it was not an organization, but an individual."

"This is very helpful, Mr Reid," said Murphy, now totally immersed in his Good Cop character, "but it leaves the matter of the missing assets still unresolved."

"I am afraid that here I cannot be of any help. You will have to talk to Dr Gordon's financial adviser."

"And who is he?" asked Bland brusquely.

"Or she," corrected Reid, "I wish I knew."

"But perhaps you may have an idea, an inkling, a hunch, something." Murphy was clutching at straws.

"Well, if I were involved in aggressive estate planning, which I am not," stressed Reid, "there is an obvious firm I would want on my side, if you know what I mean."

"I do not know what you mean." Murphy was getting tired of playing in character.

"I think I do," intervened Bland," perhaps Dr Gordon had an interest in water springs."

"A distinct possibility, I would say," concluded Reid standing up. "If there is to be another meeting, and I hope there is not, it will be in my office and arranged in the proper manner. And perhaps I could ask you another favour. Let Mrs Flowers do her job without hindrance. She has a delicate task to accomplish. Have a good rest of the day." Bland and Murphy were left at the table like two discarded fag ends in an ashtray.

Murphy turned to Bland with the look of someone who is owed an explanation: "Water springs?"

"Strathmore & Strathmore are the financial advisers Gordon may have used. And also a Scottish mineral water, as you ask. I will follow this up and let you know."

Murphy knew that nothing more would come from chatting to Bland: "I hope this meeting has been useful Bland and, more important, that we can start trusting each other."

"Of course, Patrick. Sharing is caring. I am sure you can survive the evening on your own. I have quite a lot to attend to before the weekend."

"No worries, Eric. I'll manage."

Bland could not wait to leave the Gravelstone Golf Club and its fake Edwardian atmosphere behind him.

CHAPTER 19

AN UNEASY WEEKEND

On Saturday morning Julia woke up annoyingly early and even more frustratingly she could not go back to sleep. Waking up late was one of Julia's Saturday little pleasures and so this was not a good start to the weekend.

She walked unsteadily to the kitchen, put the kettle on while still on automatic pilot and sat next to the pine table that had accompanied her ever since her college days. She knew why she was upset, but did not want to admit it to herself. She should not have set foot in 15 Dean Park Mews and she knew it. But she could shake off neither the sense of excitement of seeing some many wonderful works of exquisite beauty all in one place, nor the thrill of being on the brink of making a breakthrough in the case of Dr Gordon's murder. She was sure that the contents of 15 Dean Park Mews matched item for item the list hidden by Gordon in the Chinese puzzle box. Did Gordon own or rent both 13 and 15? If not, what were all those treasures doing in somebody else's lock up? And whose were they? She could not wait for Monday to arrive, but nothing is longer than an unwanted weekend.

She needed something to take her mind off the case and suddenly she realized that she had not spoken for a long time to Mizuki, her best friend. Mizuki, too, had married the wrong man, someone genetically unable to appreciate her kindness, charm, and intelligence. Luckily she had happily divorced him and, like Julia, was enjoying a life of fulfilled independence. And she was a terrific cook, patient and precise in imparting her sophisticated knowledge of Japanese cuisine to Julia.

Julia rang Mizuki's mobile but the only reply was from a recorded message. Julia left a message, but was not hopeful of a quick response, as probably Mizuki was on one of her frequent trips back to Japan. Julia had no time to be disappointed because her iPad sounded off beckoning her to answer a Skype call. Even before opening the iPad she knew it was the customary weekend call from Maisie. So she was very surprised when the caller turned out to be Philip.

"Hello Mother, how are you?" Philip being awake early on a Saturday morning sent alarm bells ringing in Julia's head.

"I am fine, Philip. What has happened? Are you all right?"

"I am very well. Do not worry. I called to ask you if it is okay if I come home next weekend."

"Of course, it would be great to see you again, but aren't you busy revising for your finals?"

"Lectures will be over and I think I would work better at home, if that is okay."

Julia knew Philip too well not to realize that there was more to Philip's call. "And would you be coming alone?"

"The thing is that Melissa is also going home next week and so I thought that we could stay over for a while."

"And who is Melissa?"

"Oh, didn't you know? She is my girlfriend."

"No, I did not know, but she is very welcome. Of course. Where does she live?"

"Her mum lives near Aberdeen and her dad works in Hong Kong, I think."

"How is the studying coming along?" Julia was not over-keen on romances blossoming during revision time.

"Lots of work, but Melissa is helping me with the ECHR paper."

"What's ECHR?"

"European Court of Human Rights. The place the Tories want us to get out of."

Philip had never been particularly political. Maybe this Melissa was not such a bad influence after all.

"Send me a draft. I like reading your work. And correcting your grammar." Philip had a habit of dispensing the right number of capital letters but in a random fashion so that rome would be found next to the Traffic warden Directing the chaotic roman rush Hour.

"You couldn't pick us up from Waverley on Saturday, Mum, could you?"

Since Maisie and Philip had left home for university, Julia enjoyed the sharp reduction in the complimentary taxi service that she had provided throughout their school years and now it was almost a pleasure to know that Philip still depended on her for basic transportation needs.

"Remember to text me your arrival time." Julia said more in hope than expectation as Philip was not exactly a planner-ahead type. So she was dumbfounded when he replied instantly that he and Melissa would arrive on the 6.34 from King's Cross.

"What have you done with my son, stranger? Philip would never plan this far ahead."

"It is a lot cheaper if you book in advance, Mother." And now she was getting a lecture on personal finance, too.

The unexpected call from Philip and the news of his homecoming – and with a girlfriend – cheered Julia up. She walked to what was supposed to be Philip's room but was effectively an additional wardrobe space. She walked round the room, looked at the walls, the smallish but pretty window and its sea view, and decided that a signature wall would add style. She had a strange fascination with decorating walls with Farrow & Ball paint, its luscious viscosity, its docile yielding under the brush, the glorious finish. When she opened the front door to reach the shed where paint cans and other DIY material were stored she was so engrossed in her new task that she nearly bumped into the postman.

"Morning, Mrs Flowers. Lovely day, wouldn't you say?"

"Most definitively, let us hope it stays." Julia was embarrassed not to know the postman's name and made a mental note of asking him at the next opportunity. She took the bundle of letters and junk mail held precariously together by a beige rubber band and entered the shed full of purpose. She put the mail bundle on a shelf, but before she could start her quest for the right paint pot, the rubber band snapped and the assorted correspondence spread all over the wooden floor. Julia's attention was immediately drawn to an A5 Manilla envelope: her name and address were rubber stamped on it. Julia thought it curious and proceeded swiftly to open it. As soon as she took out the single sheet of paper inside it, a shiver ran down her spine.

"S T O P   M E D D L I N G   O R   E L S E " was rubber stamped across the white sheet, this time in much bigger letters. She let both envelope and sheet fall off her hands, transfixed for a very long couple of seconds, frozen to the spot. A knock on the shed's door shook her from her stupor, but not in a good way. She did not have the time to panic, as the reassuring voice of the nameless postman was proffering some kind of apology: "Sorry, Mrs Flowers. Forgot this little packet for you. Are you alright?" Julia's delicate face had been drained of all its usual hint of pinkness and the light had gone out of her eyes.

"Thank you for asking. I am fine, really; Mister ... ehm, I am afraid I don't know your name."

"William Bland, but everyone calls me Billy."

Julia burst out in a loud laugh and immediately apologized to Billy. "Forgive me, Mr Bland, but I had a friend in primary school with the same name," she lied through her teeth, "and it brought back funny memories."

From his frowned expression it was clear that William Bland had not bought the explanation. He politely greeted Julia a whispered "Goodbye" and left.

Julia looked at the small brown packet tied neatly with a thin string with the attention, no, with the apprehension that normally would be reserved for receiving a ticking bomb. It had a green customs sticker on it which revealed its origin as China. Julia left it where Mr Bland had put it, on the window sill and walked quickly back to the house. She locked the door behind her, collected her thoughts, went to her handbag and picked up her mobile.

"Eric. Julia. So sorry to bother you. I know I am over-reacting, but could you possibly come to my cottage. Something very strange. I am sorry. It does not make any sense."

"Julia. Stop. Big breath and tell me what happened. Slowly."

"I think I just received an anonymous letter. It said 'stop meddling or else'. I am being silly. I should not have called you."

"Not at all. Do not touch the letter. Anything else?"

"Probably it's nothing, but I also got a small packet in the post. From China."

"What's in it?"

"I have not opened it."

"Excellent. Leave it. I'll come as soon as I can. You are right: probably it is nothing to worry about, but it is my job to check these things. Make yourself a nice cup of tea and wait for me."

Instead, Julia sat on her chaise long and stared out of her favourite window looking at the gentle ripples on each wave that eventually would die on the sandy shore yards away from her.

Driving towards the East Neuk, DCI Bland could not disguise to himself that he was worried. Even before receiving Julia's telephone call, he had been recapping the events of the previous day and if there was one thing that had preoccupied him was the unexpected role that Julia had played in his conversations with Murphy, Patterson, and Reid. All three had mentioned Julia: Murphy knew of her, even if he had never mentioned her name or existence to him; Patterson effectively had told him not to trust her, and Reid had warned him to leave her alone. He had a hunch that sweaty Patterson was the key to solving this riddle. How could he know of Julia Flowers? His sleazy world was miles apart from Julia's genteel habitat and yet apparently he knew her well enough to doubt her motives. Bland felt he was missing something vital, but he could be damned if he knew what it was. He put his foot down and sped his way along the A92.

Julia was strangely calm. Bland's professional tone and soothing voice had turned something that for Julia was extraordinary and frightening into a routine matter to be dealt by DCI Bland. She put the kettle on and put five tiny balls of jasmine tea in a white China mug. While pouring the near-boiling water on to them she lingered on their slow unfolding into five Flowers jostling for space on the surface of the water which started to turn pale yellow. The intense jasmine perfume hit her smell receptors and she felt secure. She was about to switch the kitchen radio on Radio 4 when she remembered that the Saturday morning programme was presented by a vapid celebrity reverend she could not stand and so she tuned into Radio 3 instead. The opening bars of Mozart's *Requiem* stopped her in her tracks: as she looked at the jasmine Flowers in her mug a solitary tear dropped right into it. It was physically impossible for her to have heard the almost imperceptible sound of the teardrop splashing on her tea, but it did resonate in her head adding a thumping note to the already booming echo of the bassoons in the *Introitus*. Was this the effect of Mozart's sublime music or was she not as tranquil as she thought she was. "OR ELSE …" or else what? She was a specialist in Oriental antiques. She could not be the target of some obscure plot. Anonymous death threats just did not happen to people like Julia.

The doorbell rang. Julia rushed to the door and opened it. "He must have driven like a maniac to arrive so quickly." Julia thought as soon as she saw Bland standing there.

"Eric. Thank you for coming so quickly. I am a bit shaken, I must admit. I do not know what to think."

"Your reaction is perfectly normal. Let me do my job now. Where are the letter and the packet?"

"In the garden shed. Follow me." Julia walked swiftly to the shed, but when she was about to enter she found she could not move her legs and all she could say was "In there," pointing to the inside of the shed.

As Bland stepped past Julia he put on the regulation latex gloves. Inside the shed he saw immediately the Manilla envelope and the white sheet. He examined them both for what seemed to be an eternity to Julia, who had regained movement in her legs and had followed Bland inside the shed.

"I'll have these examined by forensics, but I can tell you right now that this is a professional job. Pretty untraceable. The ink is from a biro and the characters are etched from linoleum to form a home-made rubber stamp." Bland's voice was shorn of any emotion and delivered in the tone expected of a police witness on the stand in a court of law.

"Also, the people behind this seem to know you well. No need to spell out gruesome threats. Just a hint of menace."

"Nothing to worry about, then." Julia chuckled nervously.

91

"Quite the opposite. You will need police protection without the shadow of a doubt."

Julia herself was surprised by her own determination: "I do not need any protection when I am in Edinburgh, but if someone could keep an eye on the house when I am home, that would be great."

"Where's the pa …" Before he could finish the question, Bland saw the small packet on the shelf. He held it with two fingers in a pincer motion.

"We should take it to forensics, really. But if you are okay with it, I could try and unwrap it."

"I do not want you to take any risks."

"To be on safe side, I'd better unwrap in the open air. In case there's a powder inside. Totally different ballgame, this. Handwritten address." Bland crouched on the grass and very slowly untied the string round the cubical package. The brown wrapping paper, released from its constraining string, unwrapped itself like a blooming and wilting tulip on a time-lapse video-clip, to reveal a small white paper box. Bland hesitated for a moment, looked at Julia, and slowly lifted the paper lid. Then he raised an eyebrow and purposefully showed the content to Julia. She leaned forward slightly, took a quick peek and burst out in a loud laugh. "Bamboo buttons. I totally forgot. I bought them on eBay a long time ago. I feel such an idiot. I am so, so sorry."

"Let us concentrate on the letter. I never thought the parcel was any danger whatsoever, by the way, otherwise I would not have touched it with a barge pole. I am not the hero type, in case you haven't noticed."

"You seem pretty brave to me. Let us go inside. Tea or coffee?" Julia felt a cold shiver run down her back followed by a sudden burst of sweat on her forehead.

"Coffee would be perfect."

Bland sat himself in the kitchen while Julia busied herself with kettle, cups and saucers. Suddenly he realized how long it had been since he had been in a kitchen with someone making coffee for him, on a sunny Saturday morning with the rest of the day unplanned and all the better for it.

"Sorry. I have forgotten whether you take it black."

"A spot of milk and one sugar, even though I shouldn't, please."

A gorgeous smell of coffee hit his nostrils and he wished he could smoke. "Your coffee smells delicious."

"Thank you. It is a coffee blend I got in Indonesia. It is almost chocolatey, isn't it?"

Bland saw the steaming cup in front of him and inhaled over-dramatically. "Ahhh, you do not need to drink the stuff. The aroma alone is enough to make you feel alive." He measured a level teaspoonful from the sugar pot and stirred it methodically, first clockwise then counter and finally he took a sip. It was the best coffee he had ever tasted. And probably the strongest, as the caffeine rush blasted straight into his brain.

"Julia, you realize you have a choice to make. Either you leave the investigation to us or you carry on with your amateur sleuthing running the risk of upsetting some very unsavoury characters." Had Bland known Julia a little less superficially, he would never have posed such a stark alternative to her.

"I am very grateful for your concern and even more for your protection, but I intend to carry on with my life as normal." Julia was surprised by her own words, as if they had been spoken by someone else, an alter ego who was far more determined and independent than she herself ever thought she could be. If before she was unsure whether to tell Bland about her little expedition into Dean Park Mews, now she was certain she should keep it to herself for a couple of days or so.

In spite of his lack of psychological perspicacity Bland felt that he had put his foot in it, although he was not sure what 'it' was. He thought best to carry on regardless, no point in dwelling on his faux pas. "Do you know Alan Patterson?"

"Of course I do. Anyone working in antiques in Edinburgh knows Patterson."

"I should have asked – how well do you think he knows you?"

"Well, as it happens I spoke to him recently. I asked him about Gordon's Doucai bowls and he warned me off. Rather rudely, actually. But I would not say we are other than distant business acquaintances. Patterson is a bit of a pariah. Unpaid auction bids on behalf of some of his mysterious Chinese clients, that sort of thing."

"I see. Well, according to him he knows you so well that he warned me about you. 'She is not what she seems' were his exact words."

Julia was lost for words for a long while. She tried to recall any of her meetings with Patterson, but all she could remember were business discussions, nothing personal. And if Julia had a fault it was her total inability to dissemble, which was one of the reasons why people generally warmed to her instinctively.

"Really? Did he really say that of me? I think he is a bit of a fantasist, believes himself to be a world-class wheeler-dealer, when in fact he is just a rather unscrupulous mediocre middleman."

"Patterson was certainly skilful at hiding his second job for Queen and Country," thought Bland.

"Well, I'd better go back to base and let forensics check the letter, even though I am sure they cannot tell us anything useful. But you never know … And thank you for the great coffee."

"I am truly, really, sorry for having troubled you for nothing, but I am grateful that you came. I was in such a state …" Julia was not the blushing type, otherwise she would have turned bright pink at this point, such was her embarrassment.

"You have done absolutely the right thing. And I beg you to treat your safety seriously. I cannot force you to stay at home for the next week or so, but remember that every time you go out, you are at risk. How high the risk is I cannot say with any certainty, but if I were you I would take time off work and enjoy a rest."

"I'll be careful. I promise."

CHAPTER 20

MONDAY, BLOODY MONDAY

Julia had set the alarm even earlier than usual, but she needn't have bothered as she was wide awake well before six. She had forgotten to draw the curtains in her bedroom, which now was bathed in the wonderful suffused light of East Fife in April.

She got up, walked slowly, pulled up the sash window, and inhaled the sea air, still cold, but with a promise of warmth. Spring had been late and the garden seemed reluctant to show any sign of blossoming, apart from the primroses which had already produced a chromatic explosion of violet, red, yellow, white, and purple. Instinctively, she leaned out the window to see the shed, only to find that the door was wide open and swinging gently in the breeze. Suddenly she felt cold, as she was sure that she had shut the shed door the night before. She put on her dressing gown and fluffy slippers and went to the front door, unlocked it and walked to the shed. Perhaps the drop lock was a bit loose and had come undone.

As soon as she arrived at the shed she had a very vivid memory of the instant when the previous night she had locked the shed door *and* had checked that it stayed locked. Julia had to think on her feet, literally. She could not possibly call Bland – she could not risk another embarrassing moment like the bamboo buttons incident. Should she check the shed out? Or was the open door enough of a warning?

The decision was taken for her by her legs, moving as if pulled by invisible strings. She went over the threshold, automatically switched on the light as the half-opened door allowed only some of the pale morning light through. The shed had been systematically emptied. Even the wooden shelves had been carefully removed; only the carcass of the shed was left. Somewhat incongruously, Julia appreciated how much bigger the shed was once its entire content had been cleared. Obviously this was neither a garden burglary nor a prank. This was as clear a warning as the anonymous letter of the day before. In fact, it felt much closer and more direct: actual people had worked during the night blind to the danger of being spotted by a passer-by or a neighbour, and all to scare her.

She jumped out her skin when she heard, or thought she heard, branches rustling loudly near the bottom of the garden. She did not want to be trapped inside the empty shed and so she ran outside, her heart pounding, her feet hardly touching the ground. A muffled screech came out of her mouth when she bumped into a dark figure wearing a cap.

"Mrs Flowers. It is the police, PC Gavin Dale. DCI Bland told me to clear the shed and turn it into our stakeout pad. He sent you a text, I believe."

"You have to excuse me, PC Dale, I am rather tense. You understand."

"Not a problem at all, Mrs Flowers. You just carry on as normal. I'll try to be invisible. DCI Bland had clear instructions: keep watch on the house and do not trouble you for any reason whatsoever."

"Fine, PC Dale, fine."

Julia was mightily relieved and the thought of the 6'2" young policeman guarding her house discreetly reassured her perhaps more than it should have.

She took a quick shower – today she could not afford to be late. She left her morning cup of Earl Grey half drunk, got into her car and enjoyed the light traffic on the A92 to Edinburgh. She had an appointment and a script to follow.

≈≈≈≈≈

Bland was already sitting at his desk when WPC Corby arrived, punctual as usual, passing by Bland's open door.

"Corby! Good morning. When you have a minute, please."

"I'll get my notes, Sir. Back in a jiffy."

Corby was indeed back in a minute with a very voluminous set of notes.

"Thank you, Corby. It's the Gordon case. There have been developments."

"You could say that, Sir. All very interesting."

Bland was taken aback as his was not a question, but a statement and he was not expecting Corby to add to his already full plate. After a while he regained his inner composure and asked Corby: "So you have news on the DNA front, do you?"

"Oh, yes, Sir, and more."

Bland raised an eyebrow and Corby quickly realised that she was not going to be allowed to milk the situation any further.

"As you had suggested, Sir, the idea of checking on upper class gay bars has paid off – big way. Forensics are still working on it, but I am 100% certain that the corpse is in fact Dr Gordon's. What is very interesting was how I got to get Dr Gordon's DNA. I have never come across a dominator before."

"Do you mean a male dominatrix?"

"Precisely, Sir."

"Dr Gordon a dominator? Surely not."

"No, no, Sir. Dr Gordon was a client of the dominator. Goes by the name of Mister Meaner. Very strange character, but exceedingly useful. Forensically, I mean."

"Please explain, Corby."

"Well, to be a client of Mr Meaner, you have to play by his rules. No exceptions. And one of his rules is that he keeps specimens of all his clients' semen. Sir."

Bland had a rather tenuous grasp of Edinburgh's gay scene, but was not wholly surprised.

"I see. So Gordon is indeed Gordon and he is, was, gay."

"Not quite, Sir. According to Mr Meaner, Dr Gordon never engaged in homosexual sex. He was into masochism, but not into anyone, if you see what I mean."

Bland tried not to imagine the series of steps required to get from Dr Gordon's penchant for flagellation to his semen being stored by Mr Meaner. "Anything else, Corby?"

"Well, yes, Sir. Mr Meaner's real name is Steve Min and he, like most of his clientele, is Chinese. A niche market. Anyway, apparently Dr Gordon was a regular until about three months before his death, when he had a quarrel with Mr Min and stopped seeing him altogether."

"And do we know the reason for the row?"

"No, Sir. But I guess that you and DS Peng may have better luck than me. How can I put this? Mr Min does not appear to warm to the gentler sex."

Bland had never associated Corby with anything gentle, but he got the message. "Very good work, Corby. Very good indeed."

"Sir," it was obvious that Corby wished to carry on, "I hope you do not mind, but there is something that has been bothering me for some time, but I am afraid you may not like it."

"You know I trust your instinct, Corby. Out with it."

"Well, you may say that I am going far too much by the book, but at training college we were told that there are two main reasons why new key evidence should be reviewed afresh."

"One. When the new evidence seems to invalidate all previous evidence …" – interrupted Bland, who, in spite the intervening years, had not forgotten training college.

"… and two," carried on Corby, "when the direction of the investigation is driven by a single source."

Bland looked at Corby intently for a second or so and she saw in his eyes that, deep down, he had admitted that hers was not a baseless concern.

"I have dug a little bit deeper and, it may be just a coincidence, but it would appear that Mrs Flowers' uncle was an MI5 agent. Fairly high up, it's my guess. I can show you the file, Sir."

"Carry on, Corby. Carry on." Bland was deep in thought.

"If I am allowed to play devil's advocate, Sir. Mrs Flowers is the single source of the investigation, but there may be more to her than meets the eye. If you see what I mean."

"I do not think I do see, Corby. Do not be coy with me. If you have doubts, now is the time to tell me."

"It is just a hypothesis, Sir, but what if all the evidence that Mrs Flowers has unearthed had been put in by her in the first place?"

Bland was following his own train of thought, but was willing to stop at Corby Central to take more passengers in: "Carry on, Corby."

"Well, there is no way of knowing when the data was transferred to the memory stick found inside the puzzle box. Which is unusual to say the least. Again, the list found in the piano, b-y M-r-s F-l-o-w-e-r-s," Corby lingered on each letter, somewhat unnecessarily according to Bland, "it could have been written by anybody at any time."

Bland immediately reached the next step in the logical progression: "And the same applies to the anonymous letter." he muttered.

"Sorry, Sir. What letter?"

Bland pointed to the evidence bag on his desk: "Mrs Flowers received a threatening anonymous letter on Saturday."

"All I am saying, Sir, is that perhaps we should also consider another angle. Mrs Flowers could be more than an innocent by-stander. Could."

"You are right, Corby. Of course you are. Can you please try and get DS Peng for me. Let's meet here in one hour. I have to do some checking of my own first. And leave the file on the MI5 link on my desk, please."

As soon as WPC Corby shut the door behind her, Bland sank into his office chair with a loud sigh. He had been in the same situation a few times before in his career. The fork in the road. And a few times he had taken the wrong turn. Was Julia literally too good to be true or were Corby's concerns a little too well aligned with the hints that Murphy, Patterson, and Reid had been so careful to drop for his benefit?

Bland was too long in the tooth to know that he could not rely on his hunches. He needed some solid evidence.

≈≈≈≈≈

Julia arrived at her destination with time to spare. She fed the no-arm bandit known as the Edinburgh Council parking meter with a cascade of pound coins and walked resolutely to the little pastry shop where she was hoping to bump accidentally into her target. She did not have to wait too long as Sue Mollison was extremely punctual and, luckily for Julia, very methodical. She would always stop at the pastry shop for a croissant followed by her morning cigarette, just in time to arrive at Reid & McHalm at 9am precisely.

"Good morning, Sue," said Julia brightly.

"Oh, it's Julia. Sorry. I was miles away. Monday morning, eh. Have you come to see Alistair?"

"Oh, no," nothing was farther from Julia's intention than meeting Alistair Reid, "I have come to swap keys. I am afraid you gave me the wrong key for Dr Gordon's place at 13 Dean Park Mews. These are the keys for number 15, I think." Julia produced the keys from her handbag.

"I am sorry, Mrs Flowers," Sue always switched to a more formal address when under stress, "how silly of me. I gave you Mr Patterson's lock-up keys instead. What was I thinking?"

Julia surprised herself with the speed of her response. "I knew Alan had a lock-up in Dean Park Mews, but I thought it was farther along."

"No, no. He rented it about a year ago. I remember because I drew up the rental agreement." She realized that now she would not have the time for her morning fix of nicotine and so she invited Julia to the office to pick up the right keys. Julia was only too happy to oblige.

When she returned to her car with the keys to 13 Dean Park Mews firmly clutched in her hand, Julia sat in the driver seat and tried to recollect her thoughts. She knew she had no time to lose and yet she was not quite sure what to do next. Throughout her drive to Edinburgh she had been agonizing whether to call Bland or not. Calling him was the safe option, but how could she justify it? He had been quite clear: she was supposed to stay indoors and any escapade would be at her own risk. She would have to be extra careful – that was all. Checking on Dr Gordon's estate was part of her job, it could not be regarded as "meddling", or could it? And if so, by whom?

A thousand half-formed thoughts were swirling in her head and she felt almost dizzy. The scariest thing about the anonymous letter was that she had no idea whatsoever who could have sent it. In what way was she "meddling"? She was well used to squabbling heirs making her job difficult when it came to valuations for probate, but Gordon had no heirs. The whole affair made no sense. Perhaps she wasn't the intended target of the letter. The people who sent it must have known that she would show it to Bland, so perhaps it was a message to him. That did not make much sense either. She would go to Gordon's lock-up and that would be the end of her search. End of.

When she raised her eyes from the steering wheel, which she must have been staring at while she was trying to sort out her next move, she gasped as an ugly acned face was looking at her on the other side of her car window. After a couple of seconds, she returned to her Edinburgh city centre universe: the ugly face belonged to a traffic warden who was not looking at her but at the time printed on the parking sticker stuck on the inside of the car window. She looked at him with all the contempt that loathsome creatures deserve and drove away.

≈≈≈≈≈

Bland was looking at the Julia Flowers' uncle's file with a fixed stare. Corby was right. Mr Durward Flowers had all the features of a typical counter-intelligence officer. Background as a journalist, postings to many hot spots in post-colonial British Empire – Aden, Jakarta, Nairobi, Cyprus – and a non-descript job description: "Trade Attaché". But something else was bothering Bland. Not so much what was in the dossier, but the very fact that there was a dossier at all.

Putting together a fairly detailed account of the "diplomatic" career of a deceased employee of the Foreign and Colonial Office was pretty far from what was expected from a WPC in charge of carrying out some routine checks for the investigation of Dr Gordon's murder. And all because this guy happened to be Julia's uncle. Some connection. Corby was undoubtedly thorough and conscientious, but why would she think of running a check on a relative of an antique specialist who merely happened to have valued Gordon's collection? *Quis custodiet ipsos custodies?* Bland's feeling of being played by someone unknown for some unknown purpose was growing uncomfortable. He decided that for the next couple of days he would run his own investigations without involving anybody else, because he knew that at this stage there was nobody he could trust. Nobody.

≈ ≈ ≈ ≈ ≈

Julia Flowers found easily her way back to 13 Dean Park Mews. As soon as she arrived she switched to professional mode, put on her latex gloves, checked her handbag, and proceeded to her destination. She inserted the heavy key in the lock, turned it and opened the door. There was a shaft of light coming from the tiny window at the back of the room, but Julia was not at all interested in locating antiques or even the Steinway baby grand piano, as she was hit by a nauseous smell that permeated the whole place and seemed to be sticking to her body, too. She looked for and found the light switch, but no light was forthcoming – a familiar experience for someone like her who visits houses that have not seen a living soul for months, even years. She flicked the torch on her iPhone and as she did so she had a strong feeling of déjà vu. And not surprisingly because these were almost exactly the same actions that she had made in Patterson's lock-up just a few days earlier. She immediately saw the source of the smell and for a very long couple of seconds she felt as if she was going to faint. Instinctively she recoiled, took two steps backwards, and averted the torch beam away from the corpse. The naked body was tightly bound in layer upon layer of cling film, only the head, or rather the partly skin-clad skull, was exposed to the air. Julia realized she had been holding her breath and was in urgent need of fresh air. She gently closed the lock-up door behind her and leaned against the wall, still unsteady on her legs. For a moment she thought that she could pretend that the previous couple of minutes had never happened. She could forget the whole Gordon affair, and return to her normal, happy, life. Thanks to the latex gloves there would be no prints of hers in Gordon's lock-up. But that was not the point. She would never be able to live with herself and she knew it. She just had to do the right thing, no matter what. She removed the latex gloves and with some difficulty as her hands, like the rest of her skin, were perspiring profusely, picked up her mobile and rang Bland.

Bland was irritated by the whirring noise of his mobile – he was deep in thought and did not welcome the distraction – and when he saw that Julia was the caller he was tempted to ignore it, but for some reason, sense of duty perhaps, decided against it.

"Hi Julia. Everything okay?"

"No, not really. I think I have found a dead body."

CHAPTER 22

SHORROCK AND HORROR

Driving through Stockbridge in his police car, Bland knew he would get to Julia before uniforms and forensics. He needed to see her face fresh from the experience of discovering a dead body. A murdered dead body. His years on the force had taught him that one can learn an awful lot from someone's reactions to such an extreme and rare event. Misled by all the crime drama on TV (not to mention the awful Midsomer Murders), people do not realize how few murders are committed in the UK every year. Fewer than 700 is the surprising answer and for most of them the victim knew the murderer, typically a husband or boyfriend. It was one of Bland's gripes – how the media manage both to trivialize and to glorify violent death, which, when it happens in real life, is so shocking and unexpected.

As soon as he arrived at Dean Park Mews, Bland muttered a silent "Fuck!" to himself, as uniforms were already on the scene, busy with crime scene bunting and keeping away the morbidly curious. A couple of panda cars must have happened to be very close to the place, Bland thought. Shame.

He got out of the car in a hurry and looked for Julia. The young PC taking down her statement must have been a very recent recruit, as he had taken Julia back into the lock-up and the two of them were incongruously close to the cling-filmed naked body of the poor murdered woman.

"DCI Bland," stated Bland unceremoniously, "I'll take over from here," and proceeded swiftly to take Julia by the arm and out into the cobbled street.

"You seem to be a magnet for trouble, Julia. Perhaps you should have listened to me." Bland seemed to have forgotten his previous desire to observe at close quarters Julia's reactions and now, deep down, he was more concerned about her safety.

"I was here for my job, Eric. This is Dr Gordon's lock-up and I was looking for antiques to value – which is my job, if you remember." She was being economical with the truth, but truthful nonetheless.

"So it is just a happy coincidence that instead of finding antiques you have bumped into a corpse, right?"

"I would have settled for antiques, believe me." At this point the built-up tension was too much for Julia. She turned her back to Bland, rummaged in her handbag for a tissue, and pretended to blow her nose while wiping away tears from her eyes.

Bland stood there feeling like a total prick and all he could manage was "Please stay here, I have to talk to the constable."

"What's your name, young man?"

"PC Wilson, Sir."

"Well, PC Wilson, for future reference when you are interviewing a member of the public perhaps you could avoid doing so right next to the naked body of a dead woman stinking of death. Two good reasons, really: one, it may contaminate the scene and two, the sight of a corpse and the smell of rotting blood may not put the witness in a state of complete ease, would they, PC Wilson?"

"I am sorry, Sir. I was not thinking. Not my area. I am in Traffic."

"Make yourself useful and get me a torch. Please."

Bland returned to Julia who was standing a few meters away, leaning on the door of number 15, as it happens.

"Would you mind terribly waiting in my car? There are a couple of things I have to do now, but we need to talk." It was clear from his tone of voice that there was only one possible answer to his question and so Julia meekly followed him to the car and sat on the passenger seat. Bland took a plastic bag from the gloves compartment and promised "I won't be long. Thank you."

The rest of the uniformed policemen had done a better job than PC Wilson, cordoning off the area and standing guard at the entrance of 13 Dean Park Mews. In the meantime forensics had arrived and Bland was pleased to see the familiar face of Dr Shorrock, his favourite pathologist.

"I would not have expected you so soon, David. Very timely of you."

"Just a coincidence, Eric. I was talking to your bright new thing, what's her name, Corby, when the call arrived."

"Coincidence indeed," thought Bland.

For the next minute or so the two men were busy wearing the regulation plastic gear and then entered the lock-up which in the meantime had been lit extremely brightly by the traffic police emergency lighting that PC Wilson had brought in from his car.

"I hope the lighting is acceptable, Sir." PC Wilson was visibly pleased with himself and his resourcefulness, but his barely hidden smirk of satisfaction was instantly wiped off his face when the 10,000-lumen emergency light suddenly changed from steady beam to intermittent red flashing, giving the inside of the lock-up the look of a clandestine stage set for snuff movies.

Sitting in Bland's car, Julia could not help noticing the intermittent bright red lights pulsating from Dr Gordon's lock-up and thought that it must have been some special infrared photography or some such high-tech forensics. Although she had had a glimpse of the dead woman's face for a split second, the image was etched in her eyes, especially the sunken cheeks and the badly bruised lips, not to mention the grotesque wrapping of her naked body, a sort of sub-Damien Hirst attempt to depict the futility of the human condition. Julia was surprised by how little the experience had touched her. In spite of her furtive tears, probably the after effect of days of repressed tension, Julia could not honestly say that being feet away from a murder victim had shocked her. She felt ashamed because all she could think of was whether her discovery was just a coincidence, being in the wrong place at the wrong time, or, more sinisterly, another coded message directed at her personally.

She could not recognize the distorted face of the poor woman and she had always had the knack of remembering faces. Even a fleeting glimpse was enough for her to recall a face years later. Although she was sure that she had never seen the woman before, she had the uncomfortable feeling that somehow she should know who the woman was.

Dr Shorrock started his preliminary examination from the woman's face, delicately opening her bruised mouth. "Just as I thought," he said to Bland in a matter-of-fact tone, "the tongue has been torn off. And I have a pretty good idea where we can find it. Very similar to the Fang case in 2001, methinks."

Bland remembered the Fang case only too well. Probably the goriest murder in his career. Internecine warfare between Chinese gangs involved in the hugely lucrative heroin business in Edinburgh. Most likely that the tongue had been torn off either with industrial-strength tongs or with the old-fashioned chain-operated clasp used to castrate cattle. Either way, the pain is beyond comprehension. She was not well liked.

"Judging from the smell and the decomposition inside her mouth, I guess she must have been dead for at least a week, possibly more. I'll tell for sure after the post mortem."

"As soon as you unwrap her, could you send me her fingerprints, please?"

"Of course, Eric. If there are any, that is. Dental imprints would be a safer bet. They may have done the fully Monty on her."

To an external observer, the crude and callous way in which Shorrock and Bland had been referring to a fellow human being could seem inexcusable, but in fact there was no lack of respect in their harsh words. Quite the opposite. Only by distancing themselves from the humanity of the victim could they keep their emotions in check and achieve the degree of rational thought required to carry out a proper investigation, the kind of investigation most likely to produce the desired result – the apprehension of the truly callous and despicable people who had inflicted such pain on the poor woman.

In no time the corpse was encased in a body bag, placed on a stretcher and taken away.

"Bye, Eric. Will be in touch asap, don't worry."

"Thank you, David. Give my regards to Erica."

"Will do. Will do." Shorrock felt sorry for Bland, as he could not reciprocate. Bianca had been dead for nearly four years, but he knew that Bland still missed his wife. They had been such a close couple, managing somehow to keep their jobs (surgeon one, police detective the other) well separate from their personal life together. And Bianca's death had been so sudden – three months from diagnosis to funeral.

Bland walked slowly round the lock-up. A fair proportion of the space was taken up by the baby grand. Automatically, he raised the keyboard lid and tapped on a couple of keys. All he got was a muffled thud so I raised the heavy piano lid and peeped inside: no sign of the heavy brass frame with its metal strings. The piano was an empty carcass. Why would Gordon keep a useless piano in a lock-up? All the shelves on the walls were empty, too. Empty, but almost dust free, he noticed. Someone must have kept the place tidy after Gordon's death, as he could not imagine the people who had placed the wrapped corpse in the lock-up also doing a spot of dusting on the side. The place had not been cleansed. They must have deposited the cling-filmed body against the wall and left. Job done.

When Julia saw Bland walking back to the car, deep in thought, she knew she had to make up her mind quickly. It was a no brainer, really: she could not possibly keep certain facts to herself. Not now that there was another murder in the picture.

As soon as Bland slumped in the driver's seat, Julia told him. "Eric, there is something I have to tell you."

"I should well bloody think so. What were you doing in Gordon's secret hideout just after you had received a death threat? Do you really think this is some kind of *Corpse in the Attic* game show?"

"Most, if not all, of Gordon's antiques are kept next door. In Alan Patterson's lock-up. I thought you should know."

Bland's shoulders sank deeper into the car seat. He sat there, speechless, for a very long minute.

"How long have you known this little detail of no importance, Julia?"

"Since last Friday. I am sorry. I have been … economical with the truth."

"Economical? Economical? Is that the best you can come up with? Try devious, irresponsible, deceitful."

"I was going to tell you. I just did not expect to find a dead woman in there. How could I?"

"You realize that now you are a witness in a murder investigation, don't you? I'd better call you Mrs Flowers, if that's okay with you."

"Fine with me, Bland."

CHAPTER 23

MIZUKI

Just as Julia was getting out of the car, Bland told her:

"I am afraid we will need a statement from you. Anytime tomorrow. But it may be a good idea to meet beforehand on neutral ground. I'll explain. Give me a ring when you can. Please. One more thing: any idea why Gordon would keep a piano with no frame and strings in a lock-up?"

Julia was still adjusting to being a witness to a murder investigation and hardly took on board Bland's question. "I am afraid not. No idea. I'll ring you as soon as I have sorted myself out," Julia was tempted to parrot Bland and say 'one more thing' but did not, "you may want to get a warrant to search Patterson's lock-up."

She did not wait for a reply, gently shut the car door and walked to her car. Subconsciously an idea must have formed in her head during the short walk because when she got to her car she knew exactly where she wanted to go. She would call on Mizuki on the off chance she was at home. While driving towards Ravelstone Dykes she tried not to think of any of the extraordinary events of the last few days, but found it impossible: a fast sequence of images, a crazy version of a PowerPoint slideshow, would run in her head: the anonymous letter, bamboo buttons, PC Dale, the acned traffic warden, cling-film and bruised lips, flashing red lights …

Finally she reached Mizuki's house. It was impossible to miss the beautifully and precisely trimmed privet arch that leads to a Japanese-style front garden where the perfume of lavender complements perfectly the soothing noise of footsteps on Cotswold Buff pebbles. She rang the bell expecting no reply and was about to return to her car when she heard the unmistakeable yapping of Fusty, Mizuki's irrepressible white Cairn terrier.

"Julia. How nice to see you. I have just arrived from Japan. Come in." After sniffing the well-known smell of Julia's clothes, Fusty lost interest and returned to his favourite armchair, leaving Julia to hug Mizuki.

"I am really sorry to barge in like this Mizuki, but the last few days have been truly unbelievable. I just had to talk to you. But you must be jet-lagged and tired, I'll come another day."

"Nonsense. I am fine and I, too, have something exciting to tell you."

Mizuki and Julia repaired to Mizuki's immaculate kitchen and to the inevitable cup of green tea. Julia briefly gave Mizuki the edited highlights of her extraordinary week (leaving out some of the more upsetting details) and Mizuki's exciting news turned out to be her imminent trip to China to meet her daughter's fiancé's parents.

"I had not realized that Anzu was so serious about Jon. Anzu engaged! I can still picture her playing in a sandpit with Maisie and Philip …" Julia welcomed her involvement with normal, family business, young people falling in love, mothers being apprehensive, impetuous Anzu perhaps making a rash decision.

"I know. I cannot see her as Mrs Hon Chi Lin. Everything is happening so fast." Mizuki mimicked something that looked like a very fast rollercoaster.

For a while everything stopped for Julia: she could no longer hear the muffled sound of traffic coming through the open kitchen window, or Fusty's furious scratching of his collar, or whatever words were coming out of Mizuki's mouth. Hon Chi Lin was one of the names on Dr Gordon's list. She was certain of it.

"Are you alright, Julia?" Mizuki seemed worried by Julia's temporary absence from planet Earth.

"Oh, nothing. Forgive me. Did you say Hon Chi Lin?"

"Yes, I know, it is strange, isn't it? Anzu has known Jon since high school but I never knew his surname. Apparently his father used to be a high-up party official, but now is a businessman, exporting solar panels. Very wealthy, but does not speak a word of English."

"You would not know his first name, would you?" asked Julia.

Mizuki was taken aback by the very strange question, but tried not to show it. "As a matter of fact, I do. He and his wife sent me a very kind invitation only last week." A few expert keystrokes on her iPhone quickly yielded the required name: "Shuin. Shuin Hon Chi Lin. Bit of a mouthful. Why? Do you know him?"

"No, no," Julia was quick to put some distance between herself and the mysterious name, "someone mentioned a very similar name at the office the other day, and I just wondered whether it may be the same person."

Julia was very happy to accept a refill of green tea, as this would give her a bit of time to process the news. She had come to talk to Mizuki to restore some semblance of normality to her life and instead she found herself back into the darkest bowels of the Gordon affair.

"How exciting to be involved in a real crime investigation! I do not follow this kind of things, but I do remember the British diplomat killed in his own house by burglars. In fact, it was what made me install a burglar alarm."

Mizuki was an avid reader of crime novels and would have gladly swapped places with Julia, who had refrained from telling her the scarier facts of her involvement – no anonymous letter was mentioned, nor the cling-film wrapped body.

"Why do you not invite your Bland for dinner?" exclaimed Mizuki.

Julia was speechless for a while because that was the last thing she would expected someone as reserved as Mizuki to have said. Perhaps it was the delayed effect of jet-lag.

"First, he is not 'my Bland', second, I am a witness. A proper one. Bland cannot possibly have dinner with me."

"Why not? Dinner in a public place surely is allowed. He seems a nice guy."

Julia was again astounded by Mizuki's forwardness. And how could she have formed the impression that Eric was a 'nice guy'? She herself must have subconsciously given Mizuki that idea. Well, she did think that Bland was a decent person, but not someone she would ever consider in a romantic way.

"Do not be ridiculous, Mizuki! At the very most, I'll invite him for breakfast."

"Whatever," Mizuki's half smile seemed very suggestive to Julia, even though there was nothing to be suggestive about. Nothing.

Julia's chat with Mizuki had the desired effect, because Julia was a lot more relaxed when she drove back to the East Neuk. Once at home she would text Bland, suggesting a working breakfast and then she would tell him all she knew about the Gordon case and that would be the end of it.

CHAPTER 24

BREAKFAST PREPARATIONS

Julia woke up in a good mood. She had gone to sleep really early the previous night and had had nearly twelve hours of uninterrupted slumber. She went for a quick shower like every other morning. If someone had stood outside her glass cubicle and had seen her naked, lathering her thighs and massaging gently her beautifully rounded buttocks, this someone could not have helped being impressed by her delicately alluring body (if the someone was not interested in women) or being sexually aroused (if he or she was), but Julia was blissfully unaware of how attractive she was and all her shower moves were for the purpose of hygiene, and not some form of self-congratulatory appreciation.

When she came back to her bedroom and opened the large wardrobe, it dawned on her that she only once before had been a witness in a court case. She remembered it well, as it was rather surreal. It was a divorce case between a very rich Malawian businessman and his very Scottish wife, a former Miss Scotland – no less, on whose side she was appearing as an expert witness. The husband's wealth was somewhat elusive and so one of the few assets the wife had managed to secure was the palatial matrimonial home, but the husband, driven by resentment and revenge, was questioning the valuation of every single item in the house. Julia remembered distinctly the suppressed guffaws that greeted her expert valuation of the family portrait that the husband had commissioned – a tasteful depiction of the man standing in full tribal attire while the wife was sitting, sporting a Burberry coat and a large Prada handbag. Considering that the businessman had paid £100,000 for the masterpiece, the wife's barrister had assumed rightly that Julia would have to appear in person to justify the resale value she had put on the oil painting, a whopping £750.

Still with a smile on her face, Julia was contemplating which outfit would be serious enough for a formal interview in a police station but cheerful enough for breakfast at Harvey Nicks. The previous night she had been slightly surprised when her suggestion to meet for breakfast there had been swiftly accepted by Bland. She could not picture Bland as an H&N habitué, but perhaps he did not wish to appear unfamiliar with its rather posh clientele.

She settled on a two-piece suit, turquoise skirt and turquoise and pink check jacket with a green velvet collar. Initially she had discarded the idea of a pink shirt, but later she warmed to it and wore it without regrets.

≈≈≈≈≈

Bland had an early appointment and had set his radio alarm accordingly. He was a deep sleeper, but had found a fool-proof method for getting out of bed at 7.45 sharp. He would place his alarm radio out of reach of the bed, tune it to Radio 4, and wait for Thought of the Day. He could not stand the cascade of platitudes, pieties, and sloppy thinking that would pour out of the radio and so he would jump out of bed and switch the damned radio off. If it were up to him he would set the *Thought of the Day* studio ablaze – the Bonfire of the Banalities.

DS Peng was due to pick him up at 8.30 and so, at 8.25 Bland, washed, dressed, and breakfasted, had a few minutes to spare. He looked round his house: it was as if Bianca was still there, but it really was not. Although he had not changed anything since her death, had she been alive, the house would now look quite different. Bianca would have potted the money plant in a bigger pot, would have had the curtains in the living room steam cleaned, probably would have repainted the hall. Bland was totally blind to all these little details, but nevertheless he sensed Bianca's absence in every room in the house and had long since stopped expecting her to emerge from the shower or coming out of the kitchen. He was alone and lonely, in a house that made no sense to him. Probably he should move and move on – he thought. Luckily the doorbell rang and he returned to the immediate concern of the day: trying to interview the Dominator.

DS Peng was not your average second-generation Scottish Chinese. He was 6'2" tall, not at all reverential, had a sarcastic smile, and an Edinburgh accent that did not happen by accident. Bland liked him.

"DS Peng. Thank you for coming. I hope Bateman did not mind if I pinched you for an hour or so."

"DCI Bateman was only too pleased Vice could be of assistance, Sir."

"Excellent. Let's walk and talk," said Bland shutting the front door behind him and walking to the police car, "has Corby filled you in on the Dominator?"

"Yes, Sir. I understand why you may need a Mandarin speaker."

"Well, actually, it is more your Vice background that may be useful, Peng. We shall see."

Peng drove expertly through the early morning traffic and arrived at the Dominator's address in Stockbridge well before 9. Bland rang the bell at the entrance of the rather expensive block of flats and waited patiently. After a minute or so, he rang again. Eventually, a deep voice crackled over the intercom: "Who is it? At this time of day!"

"It's the police, Mr Min. Can you please open the door?"

"Carl, if this is one of your stupid pranks, I will make you pay for waking me so early, you naughty boy."

"No, Mr Min, this is DCI Bland. I will show my ID if you let me in. Please."

"I am sorry, officer. You sound just like Carl. Do come up and see me. Third floor."

Panting up the stairs, Bland thought it strange how people living in apartments worth at least £750,000 could not find a way of fitting a lift. Planning regulations, probably. When he and DS Peng finally arrived at Min's door, they paused before hitting the heavy dragon-shaped knocker, so as to catch their breath.

Mr Min opened the door and was not at all what Bland was expecting. He was ready for someone in a kimono wearing patchouli essence and a demonic goatee and instead he was confronted by a middle-aged mortgage advisor wearing a Marks & Spencer plain shirt, non-descript dark trousers and the kind of slippers that would not look out of place in a Saga magazine advertisement.

"Mr Min, I am DCI Bland and this is DS Peng," Bland and Peng showed their ID to a rather puzzled Mr Min, "and we hope we could have a quick chat with you."

"Of course, gentlemen. Please do come in. I do remember Mr Peng. Difficult not to. Such a handsome young man, don't you agree, Mr Bland?"

Bland was not quite sure how to reply but he need not have worried as Mr Min carried on regardless.

"It's about Anthony, isn't it? I thought the case was closed."

"We have not apprehended the murderer, Mr Min, and we hope you can help us," said Bland in a pleading tone of voice.

"Always happy to give a hand to our brave boys in uniform, me. Green tea alright with you?"

"No thanks, Mr Min. Very kind of you, but we are pressed for time. How long have you known Dr Gordon, if I may ask?"

"You go straight to the point, don't you Mr Bland? No foreplay for you. What about you, Mr Peng?"

"I never knew Dr Gordon, Mr Min."

"Handsome and smart, isn't he, Mr Bland? So. How long have I known Anthony? I would say ever since I moved to Edinburgh. Before I plied my trade in Soho, you see."

"And when would that be, Mr Min?"

"About eight years ago. Doesn't time fly? Yes, eight years."

"And was this a professional relationship?" asked Bland.

"Strictly. I can be very strict, Inspector, if you catch my drift."

Bland could not reconcile the stereotypical patter heavy with double entendres with the Dominator's extraordinarily ordinary appearance. It sounded like a dated radio comedy with all the innuendos in the script being spoken by a mediocre actor.

"The Detective Chief Inspector would really like to know the precise nature of your relationship with Dr Gordon, Mr Min."

"Well, Detective Chief Inspector, all my clients want the same thing from me. Attention. Sometimes in the form of a whipping across the arse, sometimes sexual humiliation, sometimes just silence."

"We are aware of the range of your services, Mr Min, but we are rather more interested in what Dr Gordon's specific needs were."

"Well, normally I would not breach my clients' privacy, you understand, but, given poor Anthony's, ehm, end, I suppose I could enlarge."

"Enlarge away, Mr Min." Bland decided to play Min's game.

"Well, Anthony was a very reserved man, Inspector, but I could see that he was carrying a heavy burden and needed relief occasionally. And he must have found my rules reassuring and satisfying. Before you ask: One: Total confidentiality. Two: Total obedience. Three: Total submission. Four: Payment in advance. But please keep rule four to yourself and do not tell the Inland Revenue."

"I understand that your relationship with Dr Gordon came to an abrupt end. Could you expand, please?"

"Of course, Inspector. Well, Anthony wanted me to go away with him for a while. He was very worried and anxious and told me he could not stay in Edinburgh for much longer."

"Did he tell you why he was worried?" Bland pressed on.

"Not in so many words, but I could see he was not himself. Something or someone really scared him. Of course, I told him I could not leave all my other clients just for him. They need me, you know, Inspector. He became furious, left, and never came back."

"He did not leave anything behind, did he?" intervened Peng.

"No, not really. Apart from his set of tools, that is."

"What set of tools?" asked Bland.

DS Peng helpfully explained: "Each of Mr Min's clients has his own set of tools, Sir."

"Handsome, smart, and well informed. Aren't you lucky to share a car with this young man, Inspector? Well, yes. I still have Anthony's stuff. I was expecting him back and after his … end I thought best to keep quiet."

"Do you think we could see it, Mr Min."

"Of course. Let me fetch it for you."

While Min was gone, Bland tried to imagine the alcove the Dominator had disappeared into. Velvet drapes, gold ribbons, leather columns? Probably it was four-drawer office cabinets, a dentist chair, and a Dell computer.

Min came back with a large cardboard box, placed it on the coffee table, and started to extract one item at the time from this little cabinet of curiosities. "One cock ring. Medium. One gagging ball and strap. One glass dildo. Small. One riding crop. Two nipple clamps. One packet of condoms. Still wrapped. One notebook."

At the mention of the last item, both Peng's and Bland's ears pricked up. Bland was first off the blocks. "May I see the notebook, please?"

"Of course, but I doubt it will be any use to you. It's just doodles."

Bland thought for a split second whether to wear his latex gloves, but he agreed with himself that there would be no point, as Min's fingerprints would be all over it. Still, he handled it as if he were wearing gloves, trying to minimize contact with the expensive moleskin cover of the small notebook. He fanned the pages quickly enough to see that they were indeed covered in strange doodles.

"May we keep this, Mr Min?"

Mr Min was smart enough to know that Bland's was a question with a single possible answer and duly obliged.

"One final question, Mr Min. Has anyone approached you since Dr Gordon's death?"

Both Bland and Peng noticed how Min physically winced at the mention of the word "death", as if an invisible elf had squirted lemon juice in his eyes.

"Let me think. Certainly none of my clients. Chinese walls, you might say," Min looked pleased with his little pun, "oh yes, I do remember, I do not see many women within these walls," Min threw a very suggestive look in Peng's direction, "she said she was looking after Anthony's estate, or something like that. I do not recall exactly."

"Could you describe her, Mr Min?" asked Bland somewhat anxiously.

"Not really, Inspector. I do not have much of an eye for the ladies, you know. Stylish. Forties, maybe. Nice shoes. Italian, I am sure."

"And what did you tell her, Mr Min?" Bland was not liking where this interview was going.

"Nothing. I told her that Anthony was an acquaintance of mine, which she knew already. I certainly did not mention Anthony's private box. It was private, wasn't it?"

"Mr Min, you have been very helpful. And what goes on between consenting adults is of no interest to Police Scotland. Should you think of anything else or be approached by anyone about Dr Gordon, please do get in touch with me." Bland produced his card and left it on the coffee table.

"It was a pleasure to assist you. And you Mr Peng can get in touch with me anytime you want."

If DS Peng had been the blushing type at this point he would have blushed, but instead he replied "Should I bring my truncheon, Mr Min?"

"Handsome, smart, and funny, too. You are one lucky Inspector." And with that, Mr Min led the police duo to the front door and gave them a pretty wave of the hand.

Walking down the stairs, DS Peng took a long breath and then he spoke: "Min is not what he seems, Sir. I know as a fact that he is a vicious man who exploits the sexual needs of gay men for financial and personal gain. And he is straight, by the way."

"Thank you, Peng. For asking if Gordon had left anything behind. It would not have occurred to me. Getting rusty, I suppose."

"It's second nature when you work in Vice, Sir. We see it all the time. Mementoes, sex souvenirs, strange gizmos. I am pretty sure that Min took some stuff out of Dr Gordon's box of tricks. Far too lame."

Bland felt glad that he was not involved with Vice. The sex scene wasn't what it used to be. Much nastier and weirder. If Peng did not move soon, he would be marked for life, thought Bland.

When they returned to the car, Bland asked Peng to stop by Silverknowes before dropping him at Harvey Nicks. "We have to see Mrs Carter-Reid, don't we, Peng?"

"Didn't she use to work at HQ, Sir?" asked Peng, puzzled by Bland's sudden desire to see a long-retired secretary.

"Yes, Peng. And she is probably one of the very few people alive in Edinburgh who can decipher Gordon's shorthand. A dying art."

Peng was far too young to have ever encountered Pitman's in his life and was mightily impressed by Bland's knowledge.

Peng took Bland's request for an intermediate stop as a good excuse to put on the wah-wah and whizz through the traffic. Bland was too deep in thought to notice or care. In a few minutes Peng reached Silverknowes and had to ask Bland for more precise directions.

"I do not know the exact address, but I will recognize her block of flats when I see it. It is somewhere off Pennywell Road."

Peng switched off the siren and switched to a walking pace speed, as if he were following an invisible suspect. I was surprised at Bland's ability to distinguish between the near-identical blocks of flats that were slowly passing by, in a panning shot of the unbelievable aesthetic incompetence of Edinburgh's town planners.

Finally Bland exclaimed: "Next block on the right!"

Peng parked the car in front of a block of flats so anonymous, so shorn of any architectural appeal, so banal and brutal, that he felt a surge of pride for his Victorian terraced house in Musselburgh. Bland got out of the car quickly. It was clear that he did not need company. He returned after five minutes or so, wearing a self-satisfied smile: "Mrs Carter-Reid is a treasure. She will give us a transcription by the end of the day."

CHAPTER 25

BREAKFAST AT NICKS

On the lift going up to the cafeteria on the top floor of Harvey Nicks, Bland was repeating to himself what Min had said about the strange female visitor enquiring about Dr Gordon's estate.

During the short drive from Silverknowes to St Andrews Square he had googled images of Julia Flowers and had finally found one that bore a vague resemblance to Julia. None of the photos managed to capture her subtle beauty that perhaps resided in imperceptible movements of her mouth and eyes and thus was transparent to any camera. He had instructed Peng to go back to the Dominator and show him Julia's photo, just in case he recognized her. Peng was not particularly thrilled at the assignment, but did not show it, beaming a sardonic smile instead.

As soon as he reached the cafeteria, or rather the *Brasserie*, as HN would have it, Bland immediately spotted Julia. The stark difference between the dull photos and the radiant beauty of the real thing hit him hard. He slowed down and had to admit that perhaps he was, what was the right word, yes, perhaps he was smitten with Mrs Flowers. But she was a key witness in a murder enquiry and he was determined to remain professional and unbiased.

Julia, too, spotted Bland quickly, but that was not a difficult task, as he stood out as a sore thumb with his unfashionable wool jacket and non-matching trousers, surrounded as he was by people who would be prepared to pay £899.99 for a 'reduced' leather bag.

"Mrs Flowers, I hope I am not late."

"Not at all, I arrived earlier just to enjoy the view." Julia turned round as if to introduce Bland to the magnificent views of the New Town afforded by the enormously large windows that adorn HN's fourth floor. True enough, Bland, blinded by Julia's appearance, had not noticed them. "Not bad. And included in the bill, I am sure." He regretted his words as soon as they came out of his mouth as they made him sound like a tight-fisted stereotypical Scot. But when later he perused the menu and saw the £9 price for a French Toast he felt that his concerns were not completely misplaced.

The waitress took their order efficiently and friendly and disappeared as quickly as she had materialized earlier.

"Mr Bland, I have been worrying all day yesterday, as you must think that I am incredibly stupid, but the truth is that I am completely out of my depth here. My only contact with the police before this case, was for a speeding ticket."

"I understand, I understand, Mrs Flowers. No need to apologize. But before we take your statement, you have to come clean with me. Me, personally, do you understand?"

"Not really, Mr Bland. What do you mean?"

"Well, this is a very delicate case and there may be some aspects of your statement that I may want to keep confidential at this stage."

"You mean you do not want your colleagues to know?"

"Somewhat untactfully put, but yes. Exactly."

Julia proceeded to unburden herself, starting from her fortuitous piece of intelligence about Dr Gordon's baby grand, followed by her tracing it to Dean Park Mews, the incident with the swapped keys, the visit to Patterson's Ali Baba cave, the lot.

Bland could not help being impressed with Julia's enterprise and cunning, but quickly switched back to copper mode: "Is that all? There is absolutely nothing else related to Dr Gordon that you are keeping from me?"

"I give you my word." Julia was about to add "on my children's lives", but thought it over-dramatic.

"So you have never met an acquaintance of Dr Gordon's, a Mr Min who lives in Stockbridge?"

"Why would I meet anyone acquainted with Dr Gordon? I never met him, let alone his friends. I only valued his collection, years ago." Julia was genuinely puzzled by Bland's most unexpected question.

"You are absolutely certain? Mr Min's alias is The Dominator."

Julia burst out laughing, but quickly regained some degree of composure:

"I can categorically assure you that I have no interest whatsoever in dominators, whatever they might be."

"Fine. As far as your statement is concerned, just repeat what you have told me, but do not mention Mr Patterson's name, if you do not mind."

"As you wish, Inspector."

Bland asked for the bill and begrudgingly admitted to himself that, given the ambience, six pounds for one Americano and one Decaf Macchiato, was not as overpriced as he had feared.

The drive from Harvey Nicks to the police station in Fettes Avenue was a silent affair, even though Peng, who had picked up Bland and Mrs Flowers on his return from Mr Min, was bursting to talk to Bland about the news.

Julia had never sat in the back of a police car. It was like the back of any other car, except for the extra instrumentation on the dashboard, but, perhaps because of the influence of a thousand police films and TV dramas, there was a certain tension in the air, an unspoken understanding that this was not a normal ride. Julia tried not to be affected by all this and rehearsed in her mind the statement she was going to give. She certainly was familiar with the surroundings of the police station, ensconced between Waitrose and Fettes College, one her favourite shopping place and the other the destination of ten years' of school trips taking Philip first and Maisie later to the architectural Gothic overstatement that is Fettes College.

When they arrived at the station, Bland proceeded to escort Julia to his office, but eventually DS Peng managed to get his attention: "Sir, if I could have a word. It's about Mr Min." Bland asked Julia to take a seat in his office and reassured her that he would be back very shortly. He shut the office door, took a few steps away and then turned to Peng: "Well?"

"I showed the photo to Mr Min and he said that he was not sure, but it could be her."

"Did you press him? Would he testify?" Bland had no time to waste.

"I did, Sir, but he would not commit. 'It could be her, but also it could not' these were his words. I wrote them down."

"Well done, Peng. Come and see me after the interview."

As he was about to enter his office, Bland saw the large figure of Chief Superintendent Corstorphine, escorted by the less large figure of WPC Corby. Bland thought that he could do without a chat with Phil Corstorphine, but it was obvious that the feeling was not mutual.

"Good morning, Bland. A quiet word, if I may."

Given Corstorphine's booming voice, this was a physical impossibility, thought Bland, who knew instantly that something was afoot.

"Of course, Sir. Is it about your trustee thing?"

"No, no, Bland. That can wait. It's the Gordon case. I'd like to sit in on the interview with your witness, while WPC Corby takes notes, if you are happy with that."

"Well, Sir," Bland looked at Corby with some intensity, "perhaps you have been mis-informed. The witness is just giving a statement, there is no interview as such."

"Just do not mind me, Bland. You carry on as if I were not there. Not my idea, you see. I have been asked to keep things on the level."

Bland was not surprised that this was not Corstorphine's idea, as that would involve breaking a habit of a lifetime, but he was not sure what to make of Corstorphine's cryptic "on the level" remark. The Chief Superintendent always spoke in clichés, carefully avoiding any sentence that would actually say anything of any interest. Probably this was the reason why Corstorphine, only two years older and about 50 IQ points shorter than Bland, had made Superintendent and then Chief.

Bland decided that he would worry later about what was behind Corstorphine's unusual request and let him and Corby into his office.

"Mrs Flowers, this is Chief Superintendent Corstorphine and WPC Corby you know already."

Julia hesitantly shook Corstorphine's large hand: "Pleased to meet you. Should I be worried that a Chief Superintendent is here?"

Before Bland could attempt a reply, the Chief answered Julia's question: "It's these new guidelines, you see. The Chief Constable has this idea that senior officers should take a more hands-on stance. And so I thought, this morning I'll drop in on DCI Bland, if you are agreeable, of course."

"Well, why not? I myself am not sure what is involved, actually."

"This is standard procedure, Mrs Flowers," interjected Bland before Corstorphine got ideas above his police station, "when someone finds the body of anyone who has died under suspicious circumstances, we are required to take a statement."

"I see." Julia felt reassured by Bland's taking charge of proceedings.

"Perhaps you can start by telling us how and why you happened to find yourself at 13 Dean Park Mews yesterday morning." Bland was following his script and would not let anyone interfere with it.

The statement-taking followed the agreed steps exactly and at the end Chief Superintendent Corstorphine felt obliged to thank Mrs Flowers for her 'superb' help with the enquiry and Bland for his 'exemplary' handling of a witness. He shook everybody's hand vigorously and disappeared.

Bland apologized to Julia for the additional attendee and he, too, thanked for her time and asked her if she needed a police car to return to her car. Julia had had enough of police cars for one day and declined the offer.

As soon as she left, Bland turned to Corby: "Well?"

"WPC Ferguson and I went to 15 Dean Park Mews this morning, having received permission from the owner and the key from his solicitor, Sir."

"And?" sometimes Bland could not stand Corby speaking as if she were reading an official statement.

"We found the premises completely empty, Sir."

"What do you mean, 'empty'? Did you search the place?"

"Of course, Sir. It is a single-room lock-up. The only items on the premises were several shelves and they were all empty, Sir."

"Thank you, Corby. Have you returned the key?"

"No, Sir. I thought you may want to take a look yourself."

"Yes. Maybe be later. Leave it on my desk, will you? I have to catch up with Corstorphine." Bland left the office in a hurry and reached the Chief Superintendent's office one minute later.

"Come in. Ah, it's you Bland. I was expecting you."

"Sir, I'll come straight to the point. I think I am owed an explanation. There are no hands-on guidelines, are there? So why, if I may ask, the charade with Mrs Flowers?"

"Take a seat, Bland. Nothing to worry about. It was the Chief Constable, no less, who asked me personally to witness the witness, if you see what I mean."

"No, Sir. I do not. Why would you want to witness a routine statement?"

"Ah, Bland. This is where you are wrong. Apparently there is nothing routine about the Gordon case. The Chief Constable was adamant. By the book. Down the line. Cross all Ts and dot all Is."

Bland knew he would get no joy from Corstorphine for the simple reason that the idiot was just playing a part written for him by someone else and was not even aware of it.

CHAPTER 26

A TANGLED WEB SHE WEAVES

When Bland returned to his office and saw the key that Corby had left on his desk, the myriad of thoughts that were swirling in his brain were about to get out of control. He slumped on the desk chair and tried to get his head sorted out. He needed a plan, but first he had to contact Murphy. Corstorphine was just a pawn, and he had nearly messed up the simple move that he had been told to make.

"Hi Eric. You never call. You never write. I feel spurned." Murphy sounded annoyingly chirpy.

"Patrick, I am not in the mood. Things are happening here. Things I do not like. The corpse of Mrs Liang has turned up in Gordon's secret lock-up and it was not a pretty sight. Tongue torn off. The works."

"It's nothing to do with us, Eric. But good for you to have found her. I'll tell MI5 to stop looking. Send us a file, when you can, will you?"

"That is not the worst of it. I have been leaned on by the Chief Super to take it easy in my investigation. You would not know anything about that, would you, Eric?"

"You are a miserable sodding Scot, Bland. When I promised that I would keep things on the level with you, I meant it. Why would I want you to slow down, especially now that you are going somewhere?"

Bland had had the answer he was looking for, but pretended to be still interested in the conversation.

"Any idea why they would want to wrap Mrs Liang in cling film, Eric?"

"I am reliably informed that the aim is to let the face rot away while preserving the body. It intensifies the smell and makes it last longer. Apparently."

If Bland had been interested in what Murphy had to say, at this point he would have asked why Chinese gangsters would bother to transport the wrapped body of a woman all the way from Soho to Edinburgh, but he wasn't and so he didn't.

"Thank you, Patrick. Let's keep in touch."

"Same here, Eric. Bye."

Deep down, Bland had never trusted Murphy and so he felt a pang of satisfaction at having had tangible proof. What were the chances of Murphy and Corstorphine both using "on the level"?

Bland had gambled when he identified the corpse as Mrs Liang's, but Murphy had not appeared to be particularly surprised.

Bland decided that, instead of getting obsessed why London should suddenly get interested in the Gordon case and not in a good way, he would get stuck in and carry on regardless. He now had a plan and was going through with it.

Dr Shorrock's telephone manners were not indicative of the nature of the man. On the phone he was brusque to the point of rude and succinct to the point of monosyllabic, whereas in person he was affable and chatty.

"Bland. I haven't finished yet. I do teach at the Royal Infirmary, too, you know. But I have already sent the only things you are interested in to your sidekick. Fingerprints, dental, time of death. Etcetera. Something does not quite fit, but I'll tell you when I am done. Which is not going to be today. Bye."

Bland liked Shorrock. Had he continued with medicine, he would have ended up as someone quite like Shorrock. He never regretted his sudden change of career, but he was sorry for the disappointment that he had caused his parents, especially his old man. Things were never quite the same with his father; the police uniform was a barrier that he could not or would not overcome.

Why did Corby not mention to him Shorrock's interim report? Bland had some difficulty in imagining WPC Corby as his sidekick, but perhaps he could not see himself as the main protagonist in the first place. Shorrock was right, as always. Something most definitely did not quite fit.

On his way to the car park Bland thought that checking Patterson's empty lock-up was going to be a waste of time. Corby was nothing if not thorough and anyway even a blind idiot could not have missed the abundance of riches that Julia had described so precisely to him. Still a little recce may provide some inspiration.

Before entering 15 Dean Park Mews, Bland ran simultaneously in his head the account of the place that Julia had given him and Corby's statement of her inspection. Apart from the minor detail of the presence or absence of precious Chinese antiques, there were other discrepancies that Bland was keen to explore.

The first difference was obvious as soon as he opened the door: Julia had mentioned heavy plastic sheeting to keep the room temperature-controlled, but there was nothing to impede the smooth inward movement of the door. After locating the light switch Bland shone his torch at the top section of the door frame and instantly noticed that someone had very recently applied instant plaster on two spots that looked very much like the previous homes of two very large raw plugs, probably holding some hooks. The place was cold, but not particularly so: again it was clear that the temperature- and humidity-controls that Julia had mentioned had also been taken away, if they had been there in the first place, that is. The room was spotless, as if waiting for a Trading Standards inspection in a food-preparation laboratory. Bland made a mental note and proceeded to go round the room tapping on the walls. They were solid. Very. There was only one cupboard, with neatly stored brooms, mop and bucket, and various cloths. The rest were rows of empty shelves. Bland, uncharacteristically, sat on the floor cross-legged. His visit had not advanced his enquiry by one inch: yes, there were the new plaster marks above the door, but, if Julia Flowers was not the person he assumed and was a devious bitch instead, she could have patched up the plug holes herself. After all her shed was full of DIY materials. Something was niggling him, though.

He decided to return the key himself to Reid & McHalm and soon thereafter he introduced himself to Alistair Reid's secretary. "DCI Bland. I believe you gave this key to my colleague WPC Corby".

"Sue Mollison, Mr Reid's assistant. Pleased to meet you".

"Interesting name for a legal clerk." Bland chuckled to himself.

"Oh yes, quite a popular key, 15 Dean Park Mews. First Mrs Flowers, then WPC Corby and now returned in person by a Chief Inspector." Sue Mollison's attempt at humour was not wholly successful.

Bland was not distracted and ask for a clarification: "You gave the key to number 15 to Mrs Flowers in error, did you not?"

"Oh no, Chief Inspector. Last Friday she asked me for the key to number 15. No mistake about it."

"And why did you give it to her? What was her business with number 15?"

"What do you mean, Chief Inspector? I presume she wanted to see the place before renting it. I believe it is standard practice. I asked her if she wanted me to accompany her, but she said she could manage on her own. She is well known in the office, and so I had no problems with giving her the key. Should I not have?"

"And when did she return the key?"

"First thing on Monday morning. I remember it very well as she bumped into me at the pastry shop opposite the office. I always stop there for a quick break before coming to work."

"And when did she get the key for number 13, Dr Gordon's lock-up, Mrs Mollison?"

"Ms Mollison, actually. How would I know? Probably she has her own key."

"So you did not give Mrs Flowers the key to number 13."

"Certainly not. Not even if I wanted to. Mr Reid keeps it in the safe in his office, together with the other bits and pieces to do with Dr Gordon's estate."

Bland was trying to process this flow of information and nearly forgot to ask the very question that had made him stop at Reid & McHalm.

"Ms Mollison, could you give me the name and address of the person or company that does the cleaning for the lock-up at number 15, please?"

"Of course. That is easy. Polish Polish do the cleaning for all our clients." When Sue Mollison saw Bland's raised eyebrow she continued in the same breath: "Polish Polish is a bit of a joke name, but they are very thorough

131

and efficient. They are Poles, you know. I can dig up their address, but they are on the internet."

"Do not trouble yourself, Ms Mollison. I am sure I can find them. Many thanks for your help."

For the first time since he had met Julia Flowers, Bland doubted not so much her integrity but rather his own instinct. Why would she lie to him? What was her angle? Better: why did she have an angle at all?

He needed time to think and as soon as he left the rather over-decorated offices of Reid & McHalm he somehow decided to make a stop at the Meadows. He drove without hurry, almost without purpose, as a tourist with time to spare before catching a plane home. As he approached the large splash of green just off Lothian Road he suddenly realized why he wanted to sit on a bench surrounded by undulating lawns and passing cars. The Meadows was the place where he had proposed to Bianca. He could remember with perfect recall the shocked expression on her face, followed by the loudest burst of laughter that ever passed through her throat and lips. He remembered with a shiver down his spine the fork in his life then: would he beat a strategic retreat and pretend that the whole proposal thing was just a silly joke or would he turn serious and tell her that he knew she was the woman who had defined happiness for him in ways that he had never imagined could exist. And how could he forget Bianca's response to his stuttering attempt to convince her that he loved everything about her, even the things he did not know yet? The best kiss in the world, the perfect way of showing him that he, too, was what Bianca had been looking for all her life.

But these were memories without emotions, scenes from a well-directed movie, seen from a comfortable seat in the cinema of his mind, illustrations in the book of his life, but there were, there had to be, new pages to be written.

Bland had just parked his car when his reverie was interrupted by the whirring of his mobile. It was Shorrock.

"Hi David, I was just thinking about you." Bland was lying to himself as well as to Dr Shorrock without any discernible reason, "have you good news for me?"

"It depends what you mean by good. Erica wants to see you tonight for dinner. I did try to dissuade her. Told her what a miserable sod you are these days, but to no avail. So 7.30 it is, I am afraid."

"And the good news?" Bland was not sure if his attempted joke was too close to the bone, but he liked Erica a lot and Shorrock knew it.

"I rest my case. Anyway, I do have news. Not sure on the "good" part, but we'll have to meet before 7.30. House rules. Shall we say Ryries, at seven?"

"Thank you, David. See you at seven."

Erica Shorrock's house rules were unbreachable, written in permanent ink and etched on granite tablets: David's job was not part of family life and no mention, however indirect, to forensic pathology would be tolerated at 45 Eglinton Crescent. Bland admired Erica's unbending stubbornness as it made for far more interesting social interactions and had prevented David from becoming the coarse human being that many forensic pathologists slowly turn into.

Shorrock was sitting in his favourite spot, away from TV monitors and loudspeakers, those clever devices that render conversation difficult if not impossible, thereby making the increased consumption of alcohol more likely as it provides a justification for sitting in a pub in the first place. Sherlock was not counting on Bland being punctual and was in fact on his second pint of best when a somewhat flustered Bland entered Ryries. On his way to Shorrock he stopped at the counter, waved a gesture of generic apology towards the good doctor, and ordered a pint of best. When he finally sat at the small table it was as if the pleasantries of social encounters had already been taken care of and so it appeared completely natural for Shorrock to come straight to point.

"The poor woman was definitely made to suffer, but I do not think this was the doing of a Chinese gang."

"What makes you think that?"

"Well, it isn't so much a thought, more of a feeling. Not something I could put down in the autopsy report. It's torture by numbers, as it were," Shorrock carried on pre-emptying Bland's inevitable question, "ticking the boxes of the Chinese Gangster's Torture Handbook, no real passion, no enthusiasm, if you get my drift."

Bland remained silent for a few long seconds, ticking some boxes of his own. "So her torn tongue was stuffed into her vagina, I take it."

"That is exactly it. It wasn't. It was simply placed there. No relish, no intent to violate."

"Very interesting. Anything on the time of death?"

Shorrock sighed: "That is the other thing. I do not think a Chinese gangster, or indeed any gangster, would bother to take so much care to disguise the time of death. They drained her blood and removed her stomach and intestine, for example. And, before I forget, I must warn you."

Bland raised a quizzical eyebrow.

"Erica has prepared an ambush for you. Nothing whatsoever to do with me. I am not supposed to tell, but she may have arranged a blind date for you."

Bland sipped intently his pint of best, obviously more preoccupied with the post mortem than with the pre prandium.

"Anything else?"

"I have never met her before. One of Erica's bridge partners, I think." Shorrock quickly realized from Bland's furrowed brow that the identity of the blind date was not uppermost on his mind. "Not really, both thumbs were amputated. Post mortem, mercifully for the poor cow."

"It was unusual for Shorrock to refer to his post mortems in personal terms," thought Bland, "it must have been gruesome even for an old morgue hand like him".

Something approaching a picture was forming in Bland's head, but it was far too blurred to be of any practical use. He could not shake off the suspicion that he was being led up the garden path, but by whom and why?

He turned to more immediate concerns: "Why did you give Erica the idea that I am in need of a date?"

"And she had a very unusual tattoo," Shorrock, too, was out of synch, "Mrs Liang, not your date. Of course I didn't. Erica could work that out all by herself. Keep me out of it. Do you fancy another?"

Shorrock was not much of a drinker. Something must be bothering him – suspected Bland – was it Mrs Liang or the imminent awkward dinner?

"I'd better not. Perhaps we ought to be going. Let me get this."

Shorrock jumped out of his chair: "No way, Eric. Last drink as a free man and all that."

While Shorrock was paying the bill, Bland was tapping on his mobile and when his friend signalled from the counter that the account had been settled, he checked his watch, sighed, and put his jacket on, resigned to face the impending doom.

If Julia were American, she would refer to herself as conflicted. Thankfully she is not and is merely caught in two, if not three, minds. Should she tell Bland about Hon Chi Lin, or find first some more tangible evidence? At the moment, she had virtually nothing to report. A name on Gordon's list that coincidentally happened to be her friend's daughter's fiancée's father. How much of a coincidence could it be? Julia's mind was whizzing. After all, it was quite common for high-ranking Chinese party officials to send their offspring to British public schools and Fettes College was a popular choice. So the key question was: why would an ex party official be on Gordon's list?

Julia's online searching ability was exceptional. The arrival of Google had totally changed the nature of her job, rendering redundant overnight her vast collection of reference books on Chinese marks, ceramics, paintings, jades, and all the other sources of an experienced twentieth century orientalist. But she had taken to the web like a duck to water, and now even her teenage children often turned to her when they had tried and failed to find an elusive song or picture or anything. So it took her less than ten minutes to find Hon Chi Lin's online footprint. And, by golly, did he tread lightly! Even his inflatable doll company was in his wife's name and the little she could find in Chinese about him was rendered incomprehensible by the combined power of Chinese Communist Party rhetoric and Google Translate's very rudimentary appreciation of the subtleties of Mandarin.

Why would an up-and-coming party official resign without any apparent reason? No scandals, popular in the party, always backing the right horses.

Plenty of party people have business interests on the side, usually setting up shell companies. But why resign? It made no sense. Google can give information, not knowledge. Julia decided that more research was needed and then, perhaps, she would tell Bland.

CHAPTER 27

GUESS WHO IS COMING TO DINNER?

The Shorrocks' apartment was not as Bland remembered. It must have been over three years since he had been there and the contrast with his memory of the place could not have been more violent. Where there had been dressers, three-legged side tables, Chesterfield sofas, display cabinets, all the accoutrements of a middle-class Edinburgh couple living in the New Town, now there was, well, nothing. The decor was not so much minimalist as non-existent. There was a vague Japanese theme running through the very sparse items of furniture that now stood where once there had been glorious chaos, the accretion of several generations of several households.

Erica seemed to read Bland's thoughts:

"Welcome to our changed abode, Eric. Shame on you for turning down so many invitations. Come in as I want to introduce you to a very good friend of mine." And with that she stared at her husband with an intensity that spoke a thousand words, mainly along the lines "I will kill you if you have breathed a single word to Eric about this".

While walking the interminably long walk to the drawing room, Bland could not help thinking that if this interior decor gained favour Julia would soon find herself out of a job.

"Priscilla, this is Eric Bland. Eric, Priscilla Brown."

An awkward pause ensued, each member of the intended couple quickly re-adjusting their expectations to the reality facing them. Inevitably, they both spoke simultaneously, Bland regretting at once his stilted "How do you do?" to Priscilla's spontaneous "Nice to meet you, Eric". The awkwardness was broken by Priscilla bursting out in a genuine laugh, followed by Bland's equally genuine embarrassed smile.

Niceties over, the foursome sat down on what to Bland's untrained eye appeared to be wooden logs unadorned by any material that would soften the intended impact with the sitter's arse. Surprisingly, the delicately carved cedar blocks proved to be rather soothing, if not exactly comfortable.

"David, why don't you fix us some drinks. Eric would certainly do with a stiff one." Erica chuckled, looking at Priscilla knowingly.

After having taken orders, white wine for the couple, tomato juice for the hostess, Shorrock disappeared to the kitchen.

"Do not look so surprised, Eric. It is possible to come to a fork in one's life and decide, what the heck, I am going to change path. New start, and all that."

Bland was astonished and worried at the prospect of how personal the evening was going to be, when Erica carried on.

"And all thanks to that wonderful woman, what's her name, Jillian Flowers."

Bland must have looked transfixed, so Erica felt obliged to explain.

"The apartment downstairs had been burgled, you see."

Now even Priscilla seemed to be puzzled by the turn of the story.

Erica continued undeterred.

"So we had our contents valued. For insurance. In case of a burglary. Anyway, to cut a long story short, this Mrs Flowers, cool as they come, drops the bombshell."

Had it not been for the discreet lip on Bland's carved cedar seat, he would have fallen off his log.

"The awful pair of cups that had been in my family forever turned out to be libation cups, whatever they are, carved out of rhino horns, would you believe it and worth a quarter of a million. Yes, 245,000 pounds net of commission, as it happens. So we decided. Clear everything out and start afresh. And we love it, now."

Judging from Shorrock's expression the love was rather one-sided, but as he put the tray of drinks down on the floor, he conceded: "I find it rather calming."

Priscilla thought best to make a contribution to the conversation: "I love the tatami. Is it original? Where did you get it?"

Thankfully, Erica proceeded to explain, as Bland had no idea that tatami was the traditional Japanese woven grass floor covering.

After the prolonged explanation, it was Bland's turn to say something and he thought to ask Priscilla what she did. Erica jumped in: "House rules. No shop talk. But I suppose Priscilla can answer you."

"I am the manager of a cashmere shop in Princes Street. But I do other things," she did not want to be defined by her job, thought Bland, "I run a small charity to help orphan migrant children."

"And she is a very mean bridge player," intervened Erica somewhat incongruously.

"Shall we have dinner?" Shorrock was impatient to change tack, "I am starving. And I should tell you that Erica prepared the sushi herself."

Bland's life and diet had improved enormously since he had discovered sushi, delicious and vastly healthier than the pork pies and curries that had been his staple food since Bianca's death. And he had to admit that he would not mind finding out more about the rather fabulous Priscilla.

When both Shorrock and Erica repaired to the kitchen, leaving the intended couple seated at a very sparsely set up dinner table, Bland addressed Priscilla directly. "I don't know what Erica may have told you about me, but I find the situation rather awkward …"

"… so do I, Eric. Let us just enjoy this Japanese meal. We can always go for a quiet drink afterwards." Priscilla seemed to have the knack of finding the right words at the right time.

Erica and Shorrock came back with a nice tureen and proceeded to serve out some kind of soup.

Had Bland been a connoisseur of Miso soups he would have realised that it was a pretty good effort on Erica's part, but he was not and in fact he found himself constantly trying to catch Priscilla's eye, just to exchange a private look. And when he did, he felt that Priscilla, too, had turned a potentially cringing occasion into a juvenile game of stolen gazes and hidden smiles.

It was a shame that Bland, and Priscilla, too, were not paying attention to the conversation started by Erica on the Scottish independence referendum as she had an interesting and unorthodox take on the issue.

"I pro independence, you see, and that is why I voted No," Erica's apparently contradictory statement required explanation and it duly arrived.

"This was a unique opportunity of reviving and updating the Scottish Enlightenment project. Building on the French and the American constitutions and creating a secular, progressive, imaginative charter, unleashing the creativity of us Scots, using our education and legal systems to foster a more equal and tolerant society and instead ..." Erica was in full flow and there was no stopping her, "... the parochial vision of third-rate politicians like Salmond was all about cash in your pocket and setting our own taxes. What a waste."

Bland was about to make a comment about Salmond's subservience to both the Protestant and Catholic religious hierarchy, when he felt for a split second Priscilla's leg brushing his. A shiver ran up his spine and exploded at the back of his neck, a feeling he had long since forgotten. It was a thrill he had been missing for too long. Priscilla looked at him and seemed to acknowledge silently, in the intangible and inexplicable way of the first signs of mutual attraction, that she had felt the same jolt.

When his mobile rang out, interrupting Erica's rant, Bland thought that the insurance call he had arranged with DS Peng while Shorrock was paying for their pints had turned out to be unnecessary. But when Shorrock's mobile also rang out a few seconds later, he knew that his little soiree was over.

Erica, too, knew the score; you are not married for years to a forensic pathologist and not know that a call in the late evening is always bad news.

Only Priscilla was lost and taken aback by the sudden change of tone, with both Bland and Shorrock mumbling into their mobiles and Erica raising her eyes skyward in a resigned stare. She proceeded to explain: "See Priscilla, this is what happens when you are married to a pathologist and invite a DCI for dinner. Something awful happens in some god-forsaken place and off they go into the night."

"I am truly sorry about this, Priscilla, but something awful has in fact happened and David and I have to go as soon as our police car arrives. Perhaps we can re-arrange?"

Priscilla dug out a card from her purse bag. "Yes, sure. Give me a ring." It felt as if they had known each other for ages.

Bland took the card with the look of someone flattered at the prospect of a rescheduled date with a woman like Priscilla and was about to mumble something, when Shorrock asked his wife if they could take some sushi with them. From the look on Erica's face he realized that he should never have asked the question and was saved by the bell announcing the arrival of the police car.

CHAPTER 28

SILENCED?

Although the call from the station was really gruesome news, Bland could not stop thinking about the aborted dinner date. He was still cringing from his various faux pas, but two overwhelming feelings were stirring inside him, one warm and exhilarating, the other dark and upsetting.

For the first time in nearly four years he had felt a strong sexual attraction. While half-listening to Erica's interior decoration tribulations, somewhere in the deeper recesses of his brain, a voice was asking "I wonder what it's like kissing Priscilla's body. Don't you wish you could feel her naked body against yours?" He had found her instantly attractive, especially her big dark brown eyes. He had been braced for a semi-matronly Edinburgh well-meaning spinster and instead there she was, a gorgeous Jamaican manageress, plaited hair framing an intense face, wide forehead, high cheekbones, a thin mouth shielding the most luminous smile he had ever seen.

But was his bedazzlement a genuine re-awakening of long-dormant feelings or was it a putrid form of racism?

Bland could not honestly say that any of his, admittedly few, friends and acquaintances were black. The closest he had come to a black woman was as a fresh-faced constable arresting a Nigerian prostitute in Glasgow, off her head on crack, discarding what few clothes she had on her, in a vain attempt to get a glimpse of sunshine in the unrelenting Glaswegian rain. He regarded himself as race-neutral and impartial, but had he ever fancied a girl simply because she was white?

Bland's inner discourse was interrupted by Shorrock's observation: "Obviously this guy must have been a VIP if both of us are required to make an unscheduled appearance."

"There is a stench of Special Branch all over this case. We'd better tread carefully, David. I have a bad feeling about this business."

"We are talking about the Gordon case, right? I, too, have been asked politely to 'proceed with caution', as Corstorphine put it."

The car stopped in a quiet side street in Merchiston. The usual show was being played, "Do not cross" bunting liberally displayed, young constables keeping at bay nosey people with nothing better to do than gawp at officers getting in and out of the elegant detached house that until a few hours earlier had been the not so modest abode of one Mr Alan Patterson.

Bland and Shorrock were met by an eager WPC Corby who summarised the key points with her usual efficiency: "A 999 call was logged at 18.50. A neighbour called at Mr Alan Patterson's house at 18.45 as arranged with Mr Patterson to collect his cat. The neighbour, Mr Dillon Spence, was surprised to find the front door unlocked and ajar. Went in, found the crime scene, and rang 999. A word of warning, Sir, the crime scene is not pretty."

Donning the light blue plastic onesies of Police Scotland, Bland and Shorrock entered what originally must have been the scullery next to the large stone-floored kitchen and now had been transformed into a schoolboy's wet dream of a sex dungeon. "Skulduggery in the scullery" thought Bland, but luckily he stopped short of vocalizing his bad pun. Corby had not been wrong: Patterson was dangling from handcuffs bolted on to the wall, his t-shirt soaked with the blood still dripping from his throat, slit clean open. His testicles and cock were lying on the carpeted floor, in a puddle of blood, again cut clean from his crotch with a very sharp instrument, the barber's razor next to the meat and two veg a very strong candidate. Patterson's ankles were also handcuffed to the wall. Bland could not help noticing the Vitruvian Man's arrangement of Patterson's body. Hardly the Renaissance ideal of symmetrical perfection. Perhaps, being pinned to a wall with his arms and legs well apart, wearing only a t-shirt was Patterson's idea of a sex game. A game he had lost. Badly.

"Throat first, before you ask." Shorrock was examining the wounds with his usual precision and detachment. "Cock and balls later. Possible post mortem."

"Why cut off his crown jewels when he was already dead or dying?" Bland asked rhetorically, addressing no one in particular.

"Not my area of expertise, Bland. The wielder of the razor is not an expert in throat-slitting. Used far too much force. Nearly cut off his head. Very unsubtle."

Bland was perturbed at the thought that Shorrock was clearly visualizing the most efficient way of slitting someone's throat and comparing it to the clumsy job in front of him.

"Clearly a left hander. At least one metre seventy-five tall, or wearing heels, of course," continued Shorrock.

Bland seemed to have lost interest in the mutilated body and suddenly turned to Corby: "Is there a Mrs Patterson?"

"There was, Sir. Until two years ago. Separated. According to the neighbour. Will try to get her name and address." Corby was already busy on her iPad.

Bland was trying to imagine who would marry a sleazebag like Patterson. Possibly a gold digger or a catalogue bride. Neither would have the hatred required to perform the mutilations inflicted on his sweaty body.

While Shorrock was still examining the hanging body, Bland started looking around the room. All the fittings seemed very new, out of a catalogue for bored kinky housewives. Lot of red velvet, sex harness swinging from the ceiling, feather dusters and riding crops neatly displayed, range of dildos arranged by size, from the frankly miserable to the anatomically impossible. Everything was paraded too neatly, a job lot from an Ann Summers clearance. Bland turned again to Corby: "Mobile phone? Diary? Photo albums?"

"Nothing, Sir. House seems to have been swept clean of all personal effects. Forensics may still find some fingerprints and DNA. Xu Lin. Chinese national. Current address in Shanghai." Corby did not need to specify that this was Patterson's separated wife. She knew how Bland's brain worked.

"Find who is handling the divorce, will you, Corby? Presumably this street is too genteel for CCTV cameras. Better check access to this area, just in case."

Bland decided to meander through the house, looking for inspiration, if not clues. The style of the décor and the sweaty figure of the late Alan

Patterson did not fit together. There was a discreet display of good taste, colours matching but not in a paint catalogue sort of way, modern pieces sitting comfortably next to unostentatious antiques. Perhaps this was his wife's doing, but again Bland could not see an arrogant oik like Patterson giving carte blanche to a woman to do whatever she liked with his house. Unless, of course, it was hers. Shanghai looked suddenly very far away, almost unreachable.

Corby was right, as always, for there was no trace of Patterson ever having lived in the place. No photographs, no handwritten notes. Nothing. And still, Bland had a distinct feeling of familiarity with the house, as if he had been there before (which he knew was not the case). He slumped on a very inviting armchair and drew in a very prolonged sigh. And then it hit him. The smell. It was the smell. Like every other house in the world, this was endowed with its own unique set of chemicals, a one-off blend of body odours, habits, wood types, fabrics, making up an olfactory print as distinctive as a DNA sample, but so elusive to pinpoint, so impossible to classify.

Suddenly an image of Twig, his first dog, jumped into his brain. He must have been twelve or thirteen, awkward and uncertain, but with the constant certitude that his black lab would be always there for him. Until the day a fucking farmer named McBean decided to make full use of the law that allows landowners to shoot on sight dogs caught in the act of "bothering cattle or sheep" and shot Twig dead, no questions asked, no shooings issued, one black Labrador splatted in dark red blood. Twig would have had no problems in identifying the smell that gently suffused the house.

"Whenever convenient, DCI Bland, if you do not mind." Shorrock's voice was only half-jokingly reproaching Bland for his own private reverie. "You may want to see this."

Bland sheepishly followed Shorrock back to Patterson's idea of a sex dungeon, only to find his ankles unshackled and his left foot sitting in a very unnatural position.

"It was the broken ankle that alerted me. Just look at the left foot." Shorrock seemed pleased with himself.

145

Bland took the foot in his hands, it was soiled with dried-up blood and unnaturally cold, and examined it carefully. There was nothing remarkable about it. The kind of foot you expect a middle aged, sedentary, slightly overweight, man to be endowed with.

"And?" Bland was not enjoying the observation test that Shorrock had prepared for him.

"Between the big toe and the next." Shorrock's tone of voice was a passable imitation of a schoolmaster talking to a particularly thick pupil.

Bland slowly separated the cold big toe from its neighbour, got closer to take a better look and then turned to Shorrock: "Would you care to explain, David?"

"I do not know what it means, but it is the same tattoo I found on Mrs Liang. Curious, isn't it?"

"But you told me that Liang's tattoo was "very unusual". How could you say that if you do not know what it means?" Bland's recall of details on an ongoing investigation was still pretty good.

"What was unusual wasn't the tattoo itself, but where it was placed. Two inches above the anal orifice. Like Patterson's, you really have to know where it is in order to see it at all."

Without a hint of self-consciousness, Bland took his magnifying glass out of his pocket and proceeded to enlarge the view of the tiny speck of tattoo ink, looking for meaning. It was some kind of Oriental character, Bland could not make out whether it was Korean, Chinese, or Japanese, but he kept looking at it, as if expecting the ink strokes to re-arrange themselves into a meaningful clue. Which eventually they did: it suddenly occurred to Bland that he had seen the character before and the only set of Oriental characters he ever examined carefully was when searching with Julia for the Chinese rendition of "Anthony Gordon" on the silk scroll they had found in Gordon's piano.

Shorrock gathered from Bland's changed expression that he had found something: "Would you care to share, in case it is relevant to my post mortem, Bland?"

"It is not much, but Patterson and Liang are definitely connected with Gordon. But why hiding the tattoo? It was not tattooed post mortem, was it?"

"That is indeed an interesting question, but you will have to wait for your answer. It is not something I can tell you simply by looking at the thing. Perhaps, they were fond of both tattoos and Japanese baths."

"What are you talking about, Shorrock? What have Japanese baths got to do with anything?"

"The Japanese are very particular about tattoos. They regard them as a gangster's trait and do not allow tattooed people to join in communal baths. Very popular in Japan. Communal baths."

While Shorrock was delivering his spiel about Japanese customs, Bland busied himself taking a close-up photo of the hidden tattoo with his phone, as he did not want to wait for the official print. Julia should see it and perhaps she could find the hidden link. An idea was beginning to form in his head, but he did not want to elaborate not only because more evidence needed collecting and assessing, but mainly because he wanted to let it run, crazy as it was. Nothing useful was to be found at the crime scene, so he bid goodbye to Shorrock, left a few more instructions for Corby and walked into a tepid Edinburgh late evening.

CHAPTER 29

A DAY IN THE LIFE

Julia's Wednesday morning routine had been disrupted by the events of the previous days: in addition to the small matter of finding a body, being interviewed by the police, and being told by Bland to be economical with the truth, Philip and his mysterious girlfriend were arriving on Saturday.

Normally, Wednesday was Fife day for Julia – no commuting to Edinburgh, visiting local clients, doing background research in her study, dealing with backlog of emails.

Instead, she had decided that she would try to sort things out in her own mind while potting sweet peas in her small glass greenhouse. She had just finished sipping her early morning Earl Grey and was about to go out to the greenhouse when her mobile shook and rang, demanding her attention. It was Rosita.

"Hi Rosita, how are you?"

"Hoolia, sorry. It's Francisco. He is in trouble. It could be a disaster. Please help."

Julia knew that Rosita has a penchant for the overdramatic, but her tone of voice suggested that she was truly worried, bordering on the panicky. "Calm down, Rosita. What is the problem?"

"He went to his first call early this morning to repair a chipped bath, but as he got in the flat was in a mess, furniture upside down, vases smashed, and when he got to the bathroom, there was blood, blood."

"Start at the beginning, Rosita. How did he get in? Wasn't someone in?"

"Yes, there was supposed to be someone, but instead he found a note. 'Key under doormat. Replace when finished.' So he went in."

"None of this is Francisco's fault, Rosita. Relax. Has he called the police?"

"No, he has not. He is covered in blood and does not know what to do."

"How is Francisco covered in blood?" Julia was trying to keep calm, but the image of Rosita's husband splattered in blood flashed across her mind.

"When he opened the door in the bathroom, he slipped and the floor was covered in blood."

"Okay. I see. Has Francisco called Magic Touch?" Magic Touch was the company Francisco worked for, specializing in instant repairs for both private clients and public councils.

"No, he can't. This was, how do you say? freelance. He got a call on his mobile last night. We need the money, you know. What shall we do?"

"I'll tell you what we shall do. You give me the address and ring Francisco. Tell him to wait for me. Then we shall ring the police. There is no need to worry. Francisco has not done anything illegal. What's the address?"

"Thank you, Hoolia. I am so worried. Wait and I'll find the address." After a while and a lot of background noise, Rosita returned to the phone. "It's 112 Corbiehill Road. Do you know it?"

"Yes, no problem. It's in Blackhall. I'll be there as soon as I can. Tell Francisco to be patient and not to touch anything."

"Thank you so much, Hoolia. Xavier is off school with a temperature and I am feeling useless. Thank you. I'll ring Francisco straightaway. Bye."

Francisco was a tall, muscular man but was extremely haemophobic: the mere sight of blood would trigger nausea and fainting. Probably right now he would be coiled in a ball, in a silent panic, unable to function.

Getting into her car Julia thought she should ring Bland, but perhaps first she should see Francisco's state. God knows what his reaction would have been finding himself covered in blood. His worst nightmare.

So much for a quiet time to sort her own problems out.

≈≈≈≈≈

Bland got to the police station at the start of the morning shift, 8am on the dot. There was so much he needed to do and not a minute to waste. His first call was for DS Peng.

"Peng, this is Bland. Morning. Do you have the report from Mrs Carter-Reid?"

"Sorry, Sir. She rang yesterday, saying she had to take her cat to the vet. Injured paw, I think. Anyway, she said she will ring again today as soon as she has finished."

"Thank you, Peng. Ring me as soon as you get her report, will you? Bye."

That was not a good start of the day. Bland had a feeling that Gordon's musings in shorthand were important and he was disappointed to have to wait to read them.

Next, he googled 'Polish Polish' and immediately got the contact details of the cleaning outfit.

"Hello, this is Detective Chief Inspector Bland, Police Scotland. I need to speak to the manager. Urgently." Bland could almost feel the disarray at the other end of the line, probably not all the workforce at Polish Polish were on the books, he suspected.

"Yes, this is Ivan Rosisky. How can I help you?"

"Good morning, Mr Rosisky. I understand you have a contract from Reid & McHalm for the cleaning of 13 and 15 Dean Park Mews. I need details of the rota for the last month."

"Certainly, Mr Inspector. Let me get the work flow chart." Again, Bland could feel Ivan Rosisky's sense of relief that the police were not interested in his employment practices.

"The next appointment is for 6 May and the last was 8 April. We clean every fortnight, but the appointment on 22 was cancelled."

"Why was the appointment cancelled?"

"I do not know, Inspector. You have to ask Miss Morrison."

"Who is Miss Morrison?"

"She is the client. Solicitors. Reid and Mc Something."

"Sue Mollison?"

"That's right, Inspector. Sorry. Miss Mollison. My mistake."

"Are you sure Miss Mollison herself cancelled the appointment?"

"Yes, Inspector. She spoke to me and was very clear. No cleaning on the twenty-two. I have note in front of me."

"Thank you very much, Mr Rosisky. You have been very helpful. Good day."

Bland had had enough of office work and felt the urge to see Miss Mollison, but knew she would not be at the office before nine and so called Corby for a quick report on the previous night's events.

"I have traced Alan Patterson's mobile contract. Vodafone. Will have a transcript of recent calls by midday, Sir. Still no joy with the divorce lawyers. Perhaps it was just a separation. Call transcript may help. No viable CCTV coverage, I am afraid."

"Thank you, Corby. Good work. Can I ask you a question?"

"Of course, Sir."

"When you joined the station, why did you ask to be assigned to my unit?"

"With all due respect, Sir, I did not know you were in the Specialist Crime Division. It was the SCD I wanted."

"I see. And why the CID (as we used to call it), if I may ask?"

"Not interested in anything else. For me, police work means finding murderers, Sir."

"I like your single-mindedness, Corby. May it long last."

At this point, the old Bland would go out, light a cigarette, inhale slowly and deeply, feel the smoke fill his mouth, go down his throat, reach his lungs, and, having coated each surface with tar, start the return journey, exiting from the pouted lips that were Bland's trademark when exhaling smoke. Instead, Bland walked quickly to his car, sat on the driver's seat, emitted a long sigh, releasing the tension in his shoulders, and drove away with purpose. After a while he arrived at his destination, a non-descript block of flats, rang the bell and when the voice at the other end asked who he was, he replied: "Good morning Margaret, it's Eric. Bland."

Margaret Reid-Carter's front door was identical to every other door in the building, but the interior could not have been more different. Whereas all other flats were furnished without style, theme, or taste, hers was a perfectly preserved time capsule, the early Sixties condensed in two bedrooms, a living room and a kitchen diner. Melamine, Formica, and Bakelite galore everywhere; Teasmaid in the bedroom, Bland thought.

151

"Sorry to bother you, Margaret, but you are an early-morning person, I knew you would be up."

"And I knew you could not wait for the shorthand transcript. You always wanted things to be done yesterday, didn't you? Would you like a cup of tea first?"

"I wouldn't say no. This is a really bad case. Someone is planting so many red herrings …"

"Take a seat in the lounge and I'll be back with milk and two sugars."

Bland thought best not to amend the order to "no sugar" as Margaret was not aware of the new Bland, diet-conscious and no smokes.

As he sat on a Parker-Knoll armchair, wooden armrests and velour covers, Bland thought that the piece of vintage he was sitting on would probably fail all current fire regulations, but 'current' was one thing Margaret was not.

When the very sweet cup of tea arrived, Margaret beamed at Bland: "It was nice to feel useful again, Eric. This is my transcript. It's in long hand. I do not have a printer, you see." She handed to Bland a small bundle of A4 sheets with neatly handwritten notes. "Very strange character, whoever wrote these notes. Full of regrets, remorse even. Is this the confession you were looking for?"

"I wish. He was the victim. Would you mind if I have a quick read-through now? In case I have questions for you."

"Make yourself at home, Eric. I'll be in the kitchen. Looking after Mandy, poor thing."

Bland regretted not having enquired about the cat's health. Too late now.

The notes were disjointed, stream-of-consciousness stuff, but linked by one over-riding theme: the gut-wrenching regret for something Anthony Gordon must have done to a woman, identity unknown. No hints about the "something". Was a hit-and-run accident? Something momentous that changed their lives forever. Bland could not imagine how a wet fish personality like Gordon could feel such depths of sorrow. And for a woman. The sorrowful woman.

He approached the kitchen and found Margaret watching her cat, right front leg heavily bandaged, drinking milk from a bowl. "She looks on the mend."

"Oh, yes. The worst is over. She spent eight of her lives to survive. Now she's like us. One life left."

Bland felt swaddled in a blanket of melancholy and would have hugged Margaret, had she not being holding the cat's veterinary painkillers in one hand and a cup of tea in the other, thereby rendering a hug doubly awkward.

"What do you think, Margaret, who could she be?"

"Where did you find the notes?"

Bland was stumped for a moment; Margaret and Mister Meaner lived in different worlds. "At his counsellor-analyst's, shall we say."

"I see. Hence the secret shorthand. Are you sure it's a she?" Margaret was a smart cookie.

"In the transcript all references are to a she. Why do you think it could a he?"

Margaret's next question surprised Bland completely. "Was the writer an orphan? Was there a recently deceased father or mother?"

"Yes. And no. What made you think of a son-parent connection?"

"Nothing specific, Eric. Nothing that would stand up in court. I am sure that some of the smudges are teardrops. This man had a lot on his conscience."

Bland could not erase from his mind the image of Gordon, tearful and racked with remorse, scribbling in his notebook while being sexually humiliated by the Dominator.

"Thank you for the tea, Margaret, and for your help. Hope Mandy enjoys the rest of her long life."

"Hope you catch your criminals, Eric. Of course you will."

Bland himself was not so sure. Psychological profiling was not his forte and the last thing he needed now was an emotionally tortured Dr Anthony Gordon. He was ready for the next stop.

≈≈≈≈≈

Julia would tick off the houses she had visited on business as she drove past them. "Been there. Dreadful couple. Been there. Nice netsukes." And it was the same routine as she drove up Corbiehill Road, in spite of the looming drama of Francisco's blood-splattered clothes. As she arrived at 112, she recalled her visit, years before, to the house opposite. Elderly couple in their late seventies with the most erotically charged collection of shunga she had ever seen. Unfortunately for them, most were fakes. At the thought of the irony of faking erotic art, she allowed a secret smile to dance on her lips for a brief moment.

She rang the bell, but did not wait for a reply, as Francisco was most likely to be too petrified to move. She found him in the bathroom, sitting on the toilet, in a pose not too dissimilar from Rodin's Thinker, left elbow planted on his right knee, left wrist bent inwards, chin resting on the knuckles of his left hand. He hardly moved when she appeared silhouetted by the doorframe, lit from behind by the window in the upstairs landing.

"Hi Francisco, it's me. Let's go downstairs."

Francisco slowly uncoiled himself from his Rodinesque pose, first his wrist, then his arm, and finally he rose, almost majestically, from the toilet.

The kitchen was spotlessly clean and Julia went automatically to the under-sink cabinet looking for old newspapers, for no other reasons than she kept hers there. There were none, but the ample supply of black bin-bags would serve the same purpose. She arranged a couple on a chair and ask Francisco to sit.

He had not uttered a word and was clearly in shock. Julia was not quite sure how to react and restore some kind of normality. There was only one way to go: "What about a cuppa, Francisco? Let me see if there's any milk."

She opened the fridge and found it not only well stocked but meticulously arranged. "Anally retentive" was about to spring to her mind, when, coincidentally, she noticed a large dildo incongruously placed between a bar of butter and a pot of goat cheese. Luckily, the carton of semi-skimmed was in date.

While the kettle was boiling, Julia sat next to Francisco, who seemed to be slowly defrosting from his rigid posture.

"Okay, Francisco. Let us start at the beginning. Who called you last night and what did they say exactly?" Julia tried to put on as reassuring a tone of voice as she could. It worked.

"She said she was referred to me by a friend. It was urgent as her mother was visiting. She gave me the address. And she told me to come here first thing." Francisco was talking in a staccato voice, but at least he was talking.

"Did she give you her name?"

"Miss Mo…, Miss Morrison, Miss Mollison, I did not get it clear."

"Okay, let me check." Julia was surprised at her outward coolness, because her heart was racing and, had Francisco been looking at her, he would have noticed she was suddenly sweaty and flustered.

She took out her iPhone and searched the electoral register. Yes, this was Sue Mollison's house. Julia nearly fell off her chair when she read, under "other possible current occupants" the name of one "Alan W. Patterson".

≈≈≈≈≈

In spite of the unwelcome development about Gordon's spasms of conscience, Bland was almost euphoric. He had an overwhelming sensation that the waters of the investigation were finally clearing – the mud that various parties had thrown in his pond was slowly decanting to the bottom and soon, very soon, he would be able to cut through all the deception and see the face of the murderer. He had nothing concrete to base his euphoria on, but surely it must come from somewhere, or so he thought.

He glided over the few steps leading to the offices of Reid & McHalm and addressed the receptionist with a smile: "DCI Bland. I need to see Miss Mollison. Urgently."

"I am sorry, DCI Bland. Miss Mollison sent an email last night reporting sick. She is not here."

"I see. Can I have her address, please?"

"Certainly. Just a moment." The receptionist tapped on her keyboard for a few seconds and out came the answer: "112, Corbiehill Road, EH4 5AT."

"Excellent. Do you think I can see her office for a minute? I may have left my gloves there the other day."

The receptionist hesitated, but as Bland was already on his way to Sue Mollison's office, she thought best to follow him.

Bland opened the door and went straight to the armchair facing the closed side of the heavy desk, bent down looking for an imaginary pair of gloves, rose again, his nose twitching slightly. The receptionist was guarding the door, looking somewhat bemused at Bland's strange movements. "I do not think nothing was found by the cleaners, but I can check, if you wish."

"No need, no need. I found what I was looking for. Good day."

Bland stopped for a while on the steps of the offices of Reid & McHalm, his eyes wide with excitement. He had good reasons to feel triumphant. He marvelled at the twist of fate, or unexpected connection between synapses in his brain as he preferred to call it, that had made him visit Sue Mollison's vacant office. The smell was exactly the same as in Patterson's tame sex dungeon. He was certain that she had already fled, but nevertheless an immediate inspection of her address was called for. As soon as he got to his car, he contacted the station and asked for WPC Corby to join him at 112 Corbiehill Road immediately.

He had just started the engine when his mobile rang. It was Julia Flowers. "Not now," he decided and pressed the 'Decline' red button.

The thought of Julia Flowers calling him deflated somewhat his exuberant enthusiasm: Sue Mollison had killed Patterson, of that he was certain, but how did the two fit in with the rest of the Gordon case? He would worry about the bigger picture later, now the priority was catching Sue Mollison, the dark horse he had completely failed to see trampling over his investigation.

Corbiehill Road was only a short distance from Reid & McHalm and Bland got there in double quick time. He could not believe his eyes when he saw Julia's distinctive purple Honda CRV parked bang in front of number 112. "What the fuck is she doing here?" he muttered to himself. He was not surprised to find the door unlocked. As soon as he entered into the small vestibule, he thought he should shield himself and possibly Julia under an officially-sounding announcement: "This is the police. Keep calm and do not move. I am DCI Bland and am about to enter the premises."

He proceeded cautiously into the short corridor leading to the staircase when Julia, who had taken no heed of his announcement, rushed through the kitchen door:

"Thank God you are here, Eric. Come to the kitchen quickly."

Bland was too surprised by the quick turn of events to reproach Julia for her failure to take any notice of his instructions. He did not know what to expect to see in kitchen. A tall man, with an unshaven face and staring eyes, was sitting on a chair covered with black bin-bags. His clothes, jeans and a Real Madrid strip, were heavily stained with what Bland assumed to be blood.

"This is Francisco di Tella, a friend of mine. He came here early this morning to repair a bath," Julia was interrupted by Francisco.

"I went upstairs. I slipped on the wet floor. Covered in, covered in, blood." He pointed to his stained strip, clearly in shock.

Julia whispered to Bland's ear: "He has a phobia of blood, poor guy."

"Whose blood is it?" asked Bland, somewhat untactfully.

Julia took Bland gently by the arm and escorted him out of the kitchen. "I do not know. The house is empty. This is Sue Mollison's house, by the way. Is it not an extraordinary coincidence?"

"What the heck are *you* doing here, if I may ask?"

"Francisco's wife called me in a panic early this morning. He is a very nice guy, but the mere sight of blood and he stops functioning. May I ask you why *you* are here? You did not pick up my call. How did you know I was here?"

"I didn't. I am looking for Sue Mollison, who reported sick last night."

"She is definitely not in the house. Perhaps you can ring Alan Patterson."

The name 'Alan Patterson' hit Bland square in his plexus. He gasped visibly. "What on earth makes you think that Patterson knows Sue Mollison's current whereabouts?"

"Well, it is not me thinking it. According to the electoral roll he is a registered voter at this address. So, yes, he may know of her whereabouts, wouldn't you say?"

"So much for keeping a low profile, Julia. First you find the murdered body of a poor woman wrapped in cling film and now you are found chatting to a man covered in blood at the house of a fugitive."

"Is Sue Mollison a fugitive? What has she done?"

Bland was spared the need to provide an answer by the arrival of WPC Corby.

"Corby. Excellent. There is a man covered in blood in the kitchen. No wounds. He must to be taken to the station for a statement and fresh clothes. Call forensics, please. Apparently there is blood on the bathroom floor. Also, we must issue an urgent arrest warrant for Sue Mollison, the legal secretary at Reid & McHalm."

"What about Mrs Flowers, Sir?"

"Do not worry. I'll take her to the station for a statement. But first I want to take a look round the place. Mrs Flowers, please wait here. Do not move."

Bland knew that he would not find anything remotely interesting in the house, but he wanted some time alone to reflect on his failure to spot Sue Mollison's lies. He should have followed his instinct when the wretched secretary tried to implicate Julia. Instead he followed the rule book and as a result now Sue Mollison was sunbathing with a beaming smile on her face in a country with no extradition treaty with the UK, probably Venezuela.

Bland relished the thought of having to ring Murphy with the news that his hush-hush big informer had been killed by a dreary legal secretary who had read too many Mills and Boon, but could spot a loser and reel him in, hook, line, and sinker. Gutted for breakfast, poor sweaty Patterson.

Walking down the stairs after visiting the blood stained bathroom Bland was looking on the bright side: one of the red herrings had been laid to rest, if indeed this is what happens to red herrings when they are found out.

Bland was not too surprised to see that Julia had not paid any attention to his request to stay put and in fact was chatting to WPC Corby in the kitchen.

"Please, be very careful with Francisco. He is a very nice man. I have known him for years, but blood makes him a different person. Catatonic is the best description I can give you."

Corby was about to reply, when Bland butted in: "Mrs Flowers, if you do not mind. Before you can go, we need a statement. I'll give you a ride, if that is okay with you."

"Thank you, Inspector. But I am really concerned about Francisco. Could I not accompany him to the station?"

"I am afraid that is not possible, Mrs Flowers. Separation of witnesses. Proper procedure. WPC Corby will take good care of him. Do not worry."

Julia turned to Francisco: "Everything is going to be okay, Francisco. I shall tell Rosita what is happening. Do not worry about anything and go straight back home as soon as you are done at the station. Bye, Francisco."

Francisco did not appear to have taken in what Julia was saying, but nevertheless he managed to raise a faint smile.

"Corby, have forensics examine the stuff on the bathroom floor. Some kind of lubricant, I think. I'll see you later at the station."

CHAPTER 30

MOROCCAN LAMB

On the way to the station Bland was not in the mood for conversation, so Julia broke the silence:

"I have been thinking about your question and I think I may have an answer."

"What question was that?" Bland was jolted from his morose sense of failure.

"Why Gordon would want just the carcass of a baby grand. It is rather obvious, really. It would make for a perfect way of storing and shipping antiques."

"So you think he was about to move his treasure trove somewhere else?" Bland was trying to follow Julia's train of thought.

"This is just supposition, but I think that Gordon, for some reasons we do not know yet, wanted to ship his antiques somewhere else. After he died, Patterson, who must have known where Gordon kept his stuff, moved it to his own lock-up, conveniently located next door."

"Yes, you are right. This is all supposition. Patterson's lock-up is currently empty. No antique in sight. Vanished." Actually, Bland happened to agree with Julia's theory and in fact he had a pretty good idea why Patterson had been killed and by whom. Gordon's treasure was very probably on his way to Venezuela. But he did not want to tell Julia about Patterson's emasculation. As Corstorphine would have put it, he wished to keep things on the level. For the time being.

Julia must have been reading his mind: "You are not going to tell me what Sue Mollison has done, are you?"

"My job, one of my jobs, is to keep you safe and you are not making it very easy for me, truth be told. It is in your interest if you are kept out of this investigation. Please trust me on this."

"Of course, of course. I did not mean to pry."

The rest of the journey to the station was spent in an awkward silence, Julia pondering whether to tell Bland about her suspicion about Hon Chi Lin, Bland still nursing a sense of defeat for having let Sue Mollison slip through the net.

"I hope you are not making a habit of giving statements like this," said Bland arriving at the Fettes police station in a vain attempt at humour. Julia replied with a resigned half-smile.

After settling down at the office Bland was about to take Julia's statement, when DS Peng knocked at the door.

"If I could have a word, Sir."

Bland rose from his chair and met Peng in the corridor.

"I took the liberty of showing Mr Min a photo of Sue Mollison and he positively identified her as the woman asking about Dr Gordon's memorabilia."

"Good work, Peng. That about seals it. That woman had been scheming for quite some time and now it looks as if she's got away with it."

After taking Julia's statement about her presence at 112 Corbiehill Road, Bland was still puzzled at the extraordinary coincidence of events. "Are you sure you never mentioned Magic Touch and Francisco to that woman?" Bland could not bring himself to call Sue Mollison by name.

"Not that I recall. Our conversations were always purely business, usually to do with keys or paperwork. Hang on," Julia's face brightened up, "yes, of course. I remember now. About six months ago she asked me about her mother's chipped cast iron bath and I did suggest Magic Touch and Francisco. Yes, I do remember now."

"Julia, can I ask you a personal favour? Can you please take time off work and stay at home for a few days? I do not want to alarm you, but there has been another murder and I do not want you to be next."

"You have a funny way of not alarming people, Eric. Yes, of course, I had already thought of having some time for myself. And my son is coming home on Saturday."

"Excellent. Shall I call you a taxi to get back to your car?"

"Thank you, but there is no need. I'll take a walk. Fresh air. Good bye, and good luck with your investigation."

As soon as Julia left, Bland got on to the phone to Murphy.

"Good day, Murphy. Bland here. I have news for you."

"Not keen on foreplay, are you Bland? Yes, I am fine. Thank you for asking."

"Patterson is dead. Throat slit. Cock and balls cut off."

"Bloody hell. You do a fine line in gore up there in Edinburgh."

"I am pretty sure he was killed by his mistress, a legal secretary at Reid and McHalm. Is there anything you want to tell me about that?"

"Are you sure, Bland? It seems the MO fits some kind of gangland revenge."

"Pretty sure. She took most of Gordon's antiques with her. Mercenary little bitch. Absconded. Probably to Venezuela."

"I did not see it coming. Patterson kept his private life, well, private."

"So you do not know anything about shipments of antiques or the whereabouts of Sue Mollison, do you?"

"Listen, Bland. As I told you, my relationship with Patterson was off the books and certainly I could not use police resources to keep track of his mistress."

"What about his wife? Do you have anything on her?"

"Well, I do have a file on her, but there is nothing exciting in it. I'll email it to you, if you want."

"That would be most kind of you, Patrick." Bland pronounced Murphy's first name as if it were a foreign word.

"Happy to assist. So long, Bland."

In spite of Murphy's assurances to the contrary, Bland was expecting a fallout from Patterson's murder. The slime ball had his sweaty fingers in more than one pie.

Julia, far from getting used to giving statements to the police, was feeling very uneasy, an invisible hand was gripping her stomach and her diaphragm was so tense that she found breathing difficult. Her normal, happy, predictable life was being turned upside down and apparently there was nothing she could do to stop this slide into an abyss of fear and uncertainty.

Probably she had been too laid back about the whole business, blinded by the excitement of a real-life police case, but the cold truth was that several people had been killed, that she personally had been threatened, and now someone else been added to the list of victims. Julia had an intimation that it was Patterson, but she had nothing to base her suspicion on. She just had to stop thinking about the case, stop having suspicions, stop meddling, indeed. A solitary tear welled up in her right eye, resting on Julia's long lower lashes for a long while, and finally not so much running down her cheek, but rather meandering slowly, as if looking for a secret path.

She could hear her heart pounding, and a vein in her right temple pulsating in synch. If she were the type, this could be the perfect start for a panic attack, but she wasn't the type – she said to herself. She had to start behaving normally, leaving bloody Dr Gordon where he belonged. In an unattended grave, solitary, unloved, and unlamented. Julia recoiled at her own callousness. This was not who she was. She should not let the events of the last two weeks leave a mark on her character.

Suddenly, she remembered that Philip was coming home. She liked him very much, his cherubic little face her strength when her marriage was already heading for the rocks, his progress in school a source of solitary pride, his lackadaisicalness and forgetfulness a small price to pay for a well-adjusted, independent, and resourceful young man.

She would cook his favourite dish, known in the family as 'Moroccan Lamb' but actually with very few Moroccan influences. Essentially an aromatic stew, mixing the pungency of chilli and ginger with the sweetness of honey and cinnamon. Would his girlfriend like such strong flavours? Only one way to know for sure. Julia contemplated for a brief moment the possibility of Melissa being vegetarian, but soon discarded it as Philip surely would not share all his meals with such a creature.

Julia drew a mental map of her movements: she would collect her car from Corbiehill Road, stop in Stockbridge at her favourite butchers, call at Waitrose for spices and dwarf lentils, and then return home and to normality.

≈≈≈≈≈

Bland knew the moment, the precise time when a key decision about an investigation has to be taken and the time was now. Was the Patterson murder part of the Gordon case or a related but separate development? Obviously Patterson was connected with Gordon's death via his Foreign Office/Special Branch role as informer, but was his murderer, the elusive Sue Mollison, also involved with the diplomat's murder? Bland did not think so, even though, on paper, the evidence was pointing to a direct connection. This, probably, was his last big investigation before turning Superintendent, and so there was no room for error. Fuck the theory on paper. If he were to fail, he would fail in his own way. He would follow his hunch. Sue Mollison was a distraction, a red herring. His bet was that she had become aware of the Gordon's inheritance when Reid & McHalm were handling the estate and somehow she got involved with Patterson and saw him as her ticket away from Edinburgh and to sunny South America. He did not have a shred of evidence to back his supposition, but in his heart of hearts he considered the Patterson murder as solved. Now he had to concentrate on the killer or killers who murdered Gordon, the Soho dealer and his wife.

Bland picked up the phone: "DS Peng, Bland here. Do you have a minute?"

"Yes, Sir, of course. Right now?"

"If you do not mind. Thanks."

Peng duly arrived only a couple of minutes later.

"Take a seat, Peng. Just an informal chat."

Peng accommodated his long body in the small chair as well as he could and could not deny to himself that he was uneasy. It is unusual for someone in Murder to call a DS in Vice without passing it by a superior and, moreover, Bland's reputation as a career wrecker did not exactly help.

"I like your style, Peng. And not to beat about the bush, I think you are wasted in Vice."

"That's very kind of you to say, Sir, but I am happy where I am."

"I am sure you are, but life is not about the pursuit of happiness, is it? It's about fulfilment, it's about doing the right thing. How would you like to work in serious crime, Peng?"

"I would certainly consider it, should a vacancy arise."

"But you did not when Corby applied, did you? Why?"

"Personal reasons, Sir."

Bland did not pursue the matter and moved on to the real reason why he had wanted to speak to Peng: "Talking of Corby, what's your opinion, as an occasional colleague?"

"She is very thorough, Sir. Very. You have to do your homework and do it well, otherwise she will show you up." Peng was not sure where Bland was heading with his questions.

"Over-competitive, would you say?"

"No, Sir. I meant she sets very high standards for herself and, indirectly, for others, too."

"Do you trust her, Peng?"

"I am not sure I understand you, Sir. Of course I trust her. She is a fine WPC."

"That is not what I asked you, Peng. We both agree she is a fine specimen of a police constable. But do you trust her?"

"If you could give me an example, Sir. To understand what you mean." Peng felt pushed into a corner and did not enjoy the feeling.

"When she asks you to do her a favour. On a case, I mean. Do you ever feel she may have an agenda of her own?"

"To be fair, Sir, I do not have much to do with her. Different departments, you see. But when she did ask me to do something for her, I did feel that she had already done it herself and just wanted to see if I would come up with the same answer. Kind of, checking on me."

"Thank you, Peng. Sorry for putting you on the spot, but I value your opinion and I do hope you will re-consider, personal reasons notwithstanding."

"Thank you, Sir. I surely will. Is that's all?"

"Yes, Peng. For now."

When Peng closed the door gently behind himself, Bland tried to reconstruct the sequence of subconscious thoughts that had led him to ringing DS Peng first and then asking him about WPC Corby's dependability. He himself had no complaints whatsoever about Corby's competence and dedication, so where was the question about trust coming from? Bland was still pondering about his own mental processes, when a knock on the door announced the arrival of WPC Corby in person.

"Sir. News about Sue Mollison. I thought you may want to know straightaway."

"Come in, Corby. I am all ears."

"Well, Sue Mollison flew yesterday to Caracas. One way. First class, by the way. But she can afford it now. She cleared her bank accounts in the last week."

"I thought as much. Anything else? Links to Patterson?"

"Strange that Patterson's official residence was not his own house, but Mollison's. As if council taxes are not high enough."

"I do not follow."

"Because he was a registered occupier at Mollison's address, his house in Merchiston could not be his main residence and therefore it would attract a much higher council tax, Sir."

"Of course, of course." Bland had not thought of the local tax implications of the Patterson-Mollison *ménage à deux*.

"According to her mobile call records, she was in regular contact with Patterson, whose mobile is unregistered …"

"… and missing. I presume."

"Yes, Sir. Patterson's wife in Shanghai still untraced. No divorce papers filed."

"Anything about the incident in Corbiehill Road?"

"Mr Di Tella seems to be totally unconnected. His slip in the bathroom was no accident. Floor had been covered in shower gel. And the blood he was stained with is most unlikely to be human."

"Has forensics already reported?"

"No, Sir. I checked the content of the kitchen bin and found residue of sieved liver. Pig's, I guess. Mrs Flowers also appears to be involved purely by coincidence. Family friend of Mr Di Tella."

"Why would Sue Mollison go through the trouble of smearing the bathroom floor with shower gel, make some fake blood by whizzing and straining a pig's liver, and all this while preparing to flee to South America?" Bland was thinking aloud and keen to hear Corby's own theory.

"To get Mrs Flowers to her house," duly suggested WPC Corby.

"Thank you, Sherlock. But why, that is the question." Bland regretted the sarcasm in his voice as soon as the words left his mouth.

"Perhaps all Mollison wanted was for Mrs Flowers not to be at home this morning. Sir." WPC Corby was staying professional.

"Corby, call PC Dale and ask him if anyone visited Mrs Flowers's house early this morning, please. And ask Mr Alistair Reid to come to the station to see me at his earliest convenience."

"Certainly, Sir." Corby left the office as quietly as she had entered it earlier.

≈≈≈≈≈

When Julia arrived home she had a strange dog-who-did-not-bark feeling. Nothing was out of place and yet something was not quite right. She opened the front door and walked the few paces to the shed that had become PC Dale's stake-out den for the last few days. She knocked on the door and stepped inside. No trace of PC Dale. She was not alarmed by the absence of her faithful guardian angel, but was not reassured either. She would ring Bland. Just to make sure. But the brief walk back to the house was enough for Julia to be reminded of the promise she had made to herself not to be involved in the case any longer. Anyway, was it not a good sign that security around the house had been relaxed? The menacing anonymous letter was probably some kind of sick joke. Normal life will be resumed. As a show to herself that she meant it, Julia decided to get rid of all physical reminders of the Gordon case and so she went straight to the small oak roll-top desk where she kept the list of names she had found hidden in Gordon's piano. But the list was not there.

Her tidiness was bordering on OCD – there would be no other place in the entire house where she would have put the list. One of the small drawers in the oak desk was marked in her own mind as "unusual items" and the list belonged there and nowhere else. She tried to remember whether she had taken it out, perhaps to check it, but no. She recalled distinctly that she was sitting at her desk with her laptop open trying to find an online footprint for any of the names on the list and, when she had failed to discover anything, she definitely put it back in the appropriate drawer. Could PC Dale have taken it before leaving his post? Surely his duties did not extend to unauthorized entry and to removal of personal items. "Good riddance – thought Julia. Whoever had taken the list had saved her the trouble of disposing of it. Now she would go to her sewing kit drawer and get the bamboo buttons that had finally arrived from China and use them for their true purpose that was not to make her a fool in front of DCI Bland but rather to finish off the lovely cushions she had sewn out of tartan remnants. Reassuringly, the buttons were exactly where she had placed them, in the Cath Kidson floral sewing box she had somewhat extravagantly bought herself as a treat for no particular reason.

She sat down trying to arrange the disparate off-cuts into a coherent patch-work, but she found she could not concentrate. The reason was not difficult to find: she had become accustomed to PC Dale's discreet surveillance, and she felt somewhat exposed knowing that his large presence was not there. To calm herself down and to satisfy a little guilty curiosity she had been harbouring for some time, she would take a peek at PC Dale's den.

When she arrived at the door of the shed, she was not alarmed to see it unlocked. She opened the creaking door slowly. The shed was indeed PC Dale-free and so Julia walked round the place, re-asserting her ownership of her wooden summerhouse. PC Dale was spotlessly clean and tidy, so the notebook he had left on the bench stood out and attracted Julia's attention.

Gavin Dale's handwriting was rather girlish – large rounded letters, as if a pen were too small an implement to be handled by his over-size hands.

Julia did not lift the notebook from its spot on the bench, turning the pages carefully not to disturb its position. All entries were either too mundane or cryptic to be of any interest, but when Julia reached the last page her heart seemed to engage a gear so fast that her breathing became very heavy. It read: "Alan Patterson murdered. Arrest warrant issued for Sue Mollison. Flowers in danger."

CHAPTER 31

SATURDAY, BLESSED SATURDAY

As a general rule, Bland intensely disliked weekends. They meant spending time in a Bianca-free home with occasional twinges of guilt for not visiting his elderly mother, ravaged by dementia to the point of total personality and identity change.

But this particular Saturday he was energetic, full of purpose, and looking forward to the time spent away from the station. He had decided he would call Priscilla and try to arrange a date. The question was what would be the appropriate time to appear keen but not desperate. I thought that 9.30 am was a good choice, but having waited long enough, he settled on 9.23.

"Hello, Priscilla? This is Eric. Eric Bland. I do not know if you remember me …"

"Good morning. Eric. Of course I do. How could I not, with your dramatic departure mid-supper. Did you catch the bad guy?"

"Not yet. How are you? I was really sorry to leave before I could really have a chance to talk to you. I wonder whether you fancy a coffee, or maybe a meal. I promise to switch off my mobile for the duration."

"You don't have to do that, Eric. Yes, it would be nice to meet. Are you free tomorrow lunchtime? My sister was supposed to come, but she just called to rearrange. Apparently she's come down with flu."

"That's great. I mean I am sorry for your sister." Bland cursed himself for managing to sound like a total prat, but he carried on. "Tomorrow would be ideal. Where have you booked?"

"My sister quite likes my cooking and I hope you will, too."

"Sorry. Of course. Your place. The address is on your card, right? What time?" Bland realized that since Bianca died he had never had anybody round for a meal at his home.

"Shall we say twelve-thirty for one?"

"Right. Splendid. Thank you very much, Priscilla. See you tomorrow, then." 'Splendid?' where the fuck was that coming from? He had never used the word in his entire life and now, out of nowhere, 'splendid' decides to make an appearance in his personal vocabulary.

"Thanking you for calling, Eric. See you tomorrow. Bye."

When Bland put the phone down he was not sure whether to kick himself for not having been able to string together a coherent sentence or to be pleased with himself for having succeeded in getting a date with Priscilla. And at her place. Immediately he began to worry about what to bring. Bunch of Flowers? For a lunch, no. Bottle of wine. Banal. Pair of handcuffs? Joke may be misconstrued. Scented candle? What was the matter with him? Never before he had put those two words together and now they waltz in as a pair in his head as a suitable present for a lunch invitation. Bland did not want to spoil his good mood and absolved himself, putting his several gaffes down to rustiness. Actually, he had always been pathetic at making the first move. And the second.

There was no way his Sunday lunch date was going to spoilt by a call from the station. He would pop in and check that everything was on schedule and running to plan. A potted plant. That's what he would bring on Sunday. Durable and yet suggestive of romance.

Bland was about to leave for his office, when he noticed that a pad and a pen were sitting next to the phone. He did not recall putting them there, although he must have done, probably in his lengthy preparations before picking up the courage to ring Priscilla. They looked like an invitation to sit down and jot his thoughts on the case, unhurried by timetables and deadlines. He recoiled for a moment, recalling the wasted morning inflicted by Corstorphine on to his colleagues when he had invited a police coaching consultant to give a presentation on mind maps and other such garbage as means for 'thinking outside the box'. No mind mapping for him. He would simply write down some of his hunches and half-ideas. Just in case they coalesced into something interesting.

"What was Gordon guilty about? A woman? Who? Why?" Ever since reading the shorthand transcript, Bland has formed the idea that Gordon's guilt was the key to his murder and that all the antiques, the Foreign Office,

MI6, the Chinese couple, were just a smoke screen, either by design or by coincidence. Gordon had no family. Only child orphaned at thirteen. No interest in women. And yet his notes were genuine, a cry from his innermost soul, painful to read and excruciating to commit to paper. *Cherchez la femme triste*, indeed.

"Rights for China. Why?" Gordon was an establishment man through and through. Oxford. Foreign Office. Chatham House. Why rock the boat from beyond his grave? What was he repentant for? Was this related to the mysterious woman? An idea just popped in his head: if Rights for China had a branch or office in town he would go and see them on Monday. Perhaps the sorrowful woman worked there. Worth a try.

"Why was the cling-filmed woman dumped in Gordon's lock-up?" Bland agreed with Shorrock: this was no gangland killing, gruesome as it was. But then if Chinese thugs were not responsible who would have the opportunity, motive, and means to torture the poor woman so horrifically, just to make it appear as a gangland kill? Again, was this related to his doubts about Rights for China? Was there a Chinese secret cell engaged in black ops in Great Britain? Farfetched, but not impossible.

"Check Corby's file." Was he being paranoid? There was something about Corby that he could not make out and that was bothering him. She could be of Chinese descent. A great-grandparent, perhaps? Could this be a possible link with the black ops cell? Bland smiled at the ridiculousness of his own theory, but he would pull Corby's file, just in case.

Bland sat back on his chair and looked at his scribbling with a certain degree of satisfaction. Four items and four 'actionable ideas', as the bloody police consultant would say. Yes, this Saturday was definitely a good day.

Waverley Rail Station is beautifully located at the bottom of a hill dominated by Edinburgh Castle, nestled between Princes Street and North Bridge. As a major hub, you would have thought that provision would be made by Edinburgh traffic planners for an easy way of depositing and picking up passengers travelling by car. But no. Instead it has one of the most idiotic systems ever devised to ensure maximum discomfort and minimum efficiency. Like many long-suffering passenger pick-uppers, Julia had to double park well away from the station, coordinating by mobile phone precise timing of arrival at the back exit, negotiating the perennial traffic jam round the station, and then finally she was able to pick up Philip and Melissa. The next time you alight at Waverley and wonder why so few incoming passengers get greeted by family, friends, or lovers you will know that the cretinous Edinburgh traffic planners are responsible for this diminution in displays of human warmth.

Pressed by the mounting traffic behind her car, Julia had the opportunity to take but the briefest of glimpses of Philip's girlfriend, but even just a fleeting glance was sufficient to confirm that she was tall and dark. And pretty, she had to admit, even though the occasional peeks at the rear-view mirror could not allow Julia to form a definite impression. The car journey was filled with snippets of information about messy student flats, forthcoming exams, Facebook friendships, and assorted plans for the longed-for summer holidays. Julia, on her part, did not disclose anything about the extraordinary events of the last few weeks. She was glad that PC Dale was no longer keeping watch on the house. Although Philip had been away at college for only four months since his Christmas visit, he was quite different from the carefree lad she had seen in December. Was this the effect of the impending final exams or was his girlfriend having a significant influence on his behaviour? Julia had promised herself that she would never play the interfering mother, but now that her resolve was being put to the test, she found reality not as easy to cope with as she had expected.

On Saturdays the atmosphere at Fettes Police Station was quite similar to the nearby Broughton High's: both were far too large for the tiny population scuttling around the largely empty offices and corridors. The anodyne character of both buildings reasserted itself at weekends. The uninspiring, drab, and joyless architecture, now deprived of much of its function, stood proud as the enduring legacy of town planners without the slightest sense of either beauty or functionality.

Actually, there was an unusual sense of excitement running through the semi-deserted floors at the police station, as today was the annual football match against the Scottish Fire and Rescue Service – a grudge match if ever there was one. Earlier in his career Bland had played in this very match on a couple of occasions – he was a surprisingly skilful full-back – but a torn knee ligament had cut short his soccer future in the police squad.

Bland sat down at his computer full of enthusiasm and hope and soon Google rewarded him: yes, Rights for China had an office in Edinburgh. Bland jotted down the address (not very glamorous, near Haymarket Rail Station) and visualized getting there early on Monday morning.

Next on his list was a call to Bill McIntyre. Bill was a retired Scotsman journalist, the old-fashioned type who believed in following a lead on his feet not on Facebook and chose his stories because it was the right thing to do, not because they generated clicks on the website.

"Hi Bill. Eric Bland here. I hope I am not bothering you."

"Good old Eric. It must be something important for you to call on a Saturday. How is Bianca?"

Bill's question hit Bland right in the middle of his chest. He had not realized he had not spoken to Bill for over three years. No wonder he did not know about Bianca's death. There had been no notices, no funeral. Bianca's last wish.

"I am sorry, Bill, for not getting in touch for so long. Bianca died three years ago. Cancer."

"That is dreadful, Eric. How are you?"

"Trying to get on, you know. Anyhow, I need your help."

"I am out of the loop, Eric, but if I can help I will."

"This is a very long shot, Bill, but do you think it possible that the Chinese government could authorize a black ops action on British soil. I am talking assassination."

"If I were still working I would be all over you like a rash. This sounds real big. Do you have any evidence?"

"None whatsoever, Bill. None. That's why I thought you might have come across something like this when you were researching the Fang murders."

"Funny you should mention the Fang case. Apparently Min Lai was released on parole about a month ago. Remember him?"

Bland could not forget Min Lai even if he tried. He was probably the most violent psychopathic killer Bland had ever encountered. He had had nightmares and flashbacks for months after Lai's conviction.

"What happened to his life sentence?"

"Apparently, but this is only a rumour, there was pressure from on high to grant him parole. Exemplary conduct? Bullshit." McIntyre, like Bland, did not believe in the redemption of characters like Min Lai.

"Are you suggesting that Min Lai would be the ideal candidate for, shall we say, unorthodox operations orchestrated by the Chinese?"

"Eric, who is providing the financing for HS2 and the Hinckley Point nuclear power station? Do you think that that kind of money comes with no strings attached?"

"One more question, Bill. Do you have anything on the Edinburgh staff of a charity called Rights for China?"

"Anyone working on the opposition to the Marxist-Market regime in China knows the redoubtable Miss Tingting. I suggest you meet her. Anything else you need?"

"You have been a spring of knowledge, as always, Bill. As soon as I close this case we should have a drink together."

"I should warn you that it will have to be tonic water for me. Liver cancer. And close your case quickly. Borrowed time and all that."

That was Bill McIntyre, in essence. Keen on his job, curious and inquisitive, and not an ounce of self-pity in his soul. He also liked to drop the occasional bombshell for dramatic effect, as any journalist of the old school would.

Bland was taken aback for a while: "I'll do my best, Bill. Hang on in there and we shall have soft drinks and reminiscences, very soon. Bye."

Bland felt the soft fog of melancholy and regret descend slowly upon him: a single telephone call had managed to inform Bill of the death of Eric's wife and Eric of Bill's impending passing away. We take good people for granted, permanent fixtures of our habitat, ready to be relied upon if and when needed, immovable objects in the moving orbit of our own lives. Bland deeply regretted not having been in touch before and especially after

Bianca's death: Bill was a good egg, a thoroughly decent human being, a species going extinct fast.

On the bright side – and when Bland thought those words he would always provide Eric Idle's catchy tune as musical accompaniment – now he knew that there was a key woman working in Edinburgh for Rights for China and that Min Lai had been released into the wild, possibly thanks to some gentle Chinese pressure. Now Bland had one more item to tick off his to-do list: a quick look at WPC Corby's file.

≈≈≈≈≈

Julia parked her car in its usual spot, on the street and only a short walk to the front gate to her house. Both Philip and Melissa were travelling light, each carrying a small rucksack. "Who needs books when you have a MacBook and broadband," thought Julia. She was about to open the gate, when it was opened for her by the large figure of PC Dale: "Good evening, Mrs Flowers. I am going to get some milk, if that is okay with you."

Julia took a while to re-adjust her expectations to PC Dale still being part of her domestic life: "Of course, of course. Good evening to you, too." Luckily both Philip and Melissa were out of earshot, but they could not fail to notice the 6'4" uniformed policeman getting out of the gate.

"Who was that?" asked Philip when he reached the gate.

"That is PC Gavin Dale, he is our Neighbourhood Watch liaison officer." Julia was surprised by the speed with which such a brilliant lie had cropped up in her brain.

Once in the house she showed Melissa and Philip to their room and wondered briefly at how normal it was for a young couple to share a bed even though she and Melissa had never met before and all she knew was that Melissa was Philip's "girlfriend".

"Thank you, Mother," said Philip, "would you mind if we have a shower before dinner? It was a long and sticky journey."

"Of course not. I'll get you the towels."

"I'll get them. Can I help you with anything while Melissa has a shower?" It was obvious that Philip wanted to have a word in private and so Julia suddenly required some sort of culinary assistance.

"Perhaps you can give me a hand with the veg."

When they reached the kitchen, Philip addressed his mother rather sheepishly: "I should have told you before, but there are a lot of foods Melissa does not eat."

Julia's vegetarian nightmare started to form in her mind. Philip started enumerating a long list: "Fish, shellfish, pork, lamb, most vegetables, tea, coffee …"

"… what kind of diet is Melissa on?" Julia enquired with a hint of worry in her voice.

"It's not a diet. She is just not used to them. Chicken and potatoes are fine. And rice, of course."

"But I have prepared Moroccan lamb for tonight. I suppose she can always have the rice."

"Do not worry about her. She knows her eating habits are weird. But she is really nice, isn't she?"

"Haven't had a chance to know her, of course, but yes, she seems very nice. How did you meet her?"

"We were working the same shift at Wetherspoons for a while."

"I did not know you had been working at Uni."

"Nothing too time-consuming. Mainly week-ends. Bit short of cash, you know."

Julia was pretty certain that Philip's father in spite of his very well paid job (and in Swiss Francs) had better things to do with his money than supporting his son through University, but she did not want to open that can of worms, as she knew that Philip was hurt by his father's unfatherly behaviour.

"What does Melissa study?" asked Julia. Keen to change the topic.

"International Relations, like me, but she is doing a Master's."

"She does not look older than you."

"No she isn't, but I did an extra year in Berlin, remember?"

Melissa, all of her five foot eleven, appeared in the kitchen, her boyish short hair almost completely dry without any assistance from the hairdryer.

"Philip was telling me you do not eat lamb, Melissa."

"I'll have a quick shower, then," interjected Philip, happy to miss the ensuing awkward exchange.

"It is not that I do not eat lamb as such. I have never tried it before, Mrs Flowers."

"Julia, please call me Julia. I have made Moroccan lamb because it is Philip's favourite and he had not told me about you and lamb."

"Do not worry about it, Mrs … Julia. I'll try it. Philip says you are a terrific cook. Do you need a hand?"

"Not really, but thanks. It's a slow-cooking stew and it looks after itself. I'll put the rice on. Perhaps you could set the table. Cutlery is in that drawer and the plates are underneath." Julia was pointing to the massive Welsh dresser that nearly filled one side of the kitchen.

≈≈≈≈≈

"National Graduate Leadership Development Programme". This was the somewhat grandiose name of the police recruitment scheme that Corby had entered following her graduation in Ancient and Medieval History at the University of Edinburgh.

Why would a bright student with an Upper Second degree from one of UK's top Universities want to join the police? A couple of minutes of Googling produced a possible plausible answer: the starting salary of a PC is nearly double that of medievalist graduate. Corby did not seem to Bland to be motivated by money. Were there infirm parents to support? This required a lot more digging on Bland's part, but eventually he managed to reconstruct Joyce Therese Corby's family tree as far as he could. Not much of a tree, more of a single-branch wisp. Corby's father not only had not bothered to marry her mother, but had not taken the trouble to register himself as her father. And her mother had died only six years ago, aged forty-two, when Corby was still a third-year student. Her grandmother, Heather, was still alive and living, if that is not too strong a statement, in

Livingston. Adopted, noticed Bland. That is why the family tree stopped so abruptly. Corby's police career so far had been a steady progression and she was due to sit her exams for sergeant next year and expected to pass with flying colours. A young woman dealt a bad hand by the croupier of destiny and determined to rise quickly through the ranks. What was there not to admire?

And yet Bland could not shake off the feeling that Corby was harbouring some kind of dark secret, an agenda of her own. He had tried to get photos of Heather Corby online, but apparently she was not keen on Facebook or Instagram. Bland made a mental note to himself to ring Hamish on Monday, a mate of his who worked in Livingston, and to ask him whether a picture of the woman could be obtained locally. Just in case.

Bland felt quite happy with his Saturday morning unpaid stint at the station: he had some leads to follow up and the overall picture of this damn case was becoming slightly less hazy. Now he could concentrate on his priority for the day: find the perfect potted plant.

≈≈≈≈≈

Not ever having tasted lamb before turned out to be no obstacle to Melissa enjoying Julia's Moroccan Lamb, much to Philip's delight, who could add another item to the short list of foods that now could be shared with his girlfriend. While ending the meal with generous helpings of Eating Mess (as Eton Mess was known in the Flowers' household), the conversation moved towards Melissa's Master's dissertation.

"It's a really tricky topic, but Melissa is making huge progress." Philip was proud of his girlfriend's academic achievements.

"What is it exactly that you are researching?" asked Julia.

"My working title is 'Endemic corruption as State control in Communist China: the case of foreign investment'. Basically I try to argue that market communism can only be sustained by an interlinked system of widespread corruption. But this must be so boring to you, Julia."

"Quite the opposite. As it happens I am currently working with Chinese clients and your research seems to be very relevant. Please carry on."

"Well. I am looking at public records of trials involving foreign investors and so-called corrupt Chinese party officials."

Julia interrupted: "The Chinese are rather ruthless with corrupt officials, are they not. Death penalty, I believe."

"I am trying to prove the exact opposite. The party officials who get punished are those that stray from the unwritten rules of 'proper' corruption, so that the system of state-sponsored corruption can be maintained."

"What do you mean by 'proper' corruption?"

"See, mother, it works like this: suppose you have a valuable antique and you want to sell it. To whom do you sell it? Obviously to the highest bidder. But for many government contracts there is no bidding and no market price to go by. So the contract goes to the operator who bribes the right official with the right amount. There is no other way." It was clear that Philip was personally invested in Melissa's dissertation.

"So, very often it is the official who has not been successful at getting the highest bribe or who is jealous of more enterprising colleagues who gets charged with corruption. Paradoxically not for engaging in it, but for not being good at it." Julia had never heard two twenty-two year olds arguing so passionately and knowingly about politics and was nearly overcome by a swell of pride in her son and his smart girlfriend.

Melissa was now unstoppable: "My supposition is that the system relies on mutual blackmail to survive and that the occasional corruption purges are really a smokescreen."

"I never knew that International Relations could be that exciting."

"Normally it isn't, but Melissa has a personal interest. Tell her, Melissa."

"My best friend and flatmate when I was an undergraduate was from China and she killed herself when her father was put on trial for corruption."

"How dreadful. And presumably he was not guilty. Or rather he was as guilty as his accusers."

"Well, his was a strange case. It involved the illegal shipping abroad of antiquities. Every official involved with these particular antiquities was on the make, but my friend's father had had the bad idea of selling his share of the loot to a foreigner who, when it came to reselling the jades at a big London auction house, put my friend's father's name as provenance."

"May I ask you what his name was?" asked Julia with some trepidation.

"Xu Xu. Easy to remember. Why? Have you heard of his trial?"

"Just curiosity. I work in antiques, you see." The real reason, and Julia cursed herself for breaking her own promise, was that Melissa's story seemed eerily reminiscent of the whole Dr Gordon's affair and she even thought that Xu Xu could have been one of the names in the list found in Gordon's piano.

CHAPTER 32

BLANDINGS

Bland woke up all stiff and tired: he had been tossing and turning all night and he was dreading getting up and going to the bathroom only to see a very wrinkled face staring back at him in the mirror. He had to calm down and dampen his expectation to damp squib status. Priscilla had invited him probably as a courtesy to Erica or worse still out of pity for a widower with poor social skills.

And now he was having second thoughts about the potted plant he had bought from a large out-of-town garden mega-centre. The shop assistant who had honed in on him as a clueless first-time buyer seemed very knowledgeable and knew an awful lot about juniper plants – her suggestion for an all-purpose potted plant. Now in the cold light of Sunday morning the juniper plant looked like a shrivelled-up Leylandii or a cut-price cypress and far less impressive than when he saw it on the shelves.

"Fuck the plant," thought Bland, "she will not pay the blindest bit of attention to it. It could be a luminescent traffic cone and still she would say 'How nice!'".

He would take a long relaxing bath. Bland went to the bathroom, turned on the hot-water tap and for a while enjoyed the gush of water spouting from the tap and the changing sounds of the liquid cascade as the tub started filling. It was a long bath tub and he and Bianca used to share it, legs intertwined, rinsing each other's hair, tickling each other's naughty bits. Perhaps this was the reason that since Bianca's death he had always preferred showers to baths, more efficient, more utilitarian, fewer memories.

Once the water had reached the right level and temperature, Bland climbed carefully into the long bath, trying not to wet the Saturday Scotsman that would be his companion for the next quarter of an hour or so. Bland disliked all Sunday papers and their profusion of pointless features and innovations just to fill the ludicrous number of in-paper inserts, Sunday Money here, Sunday Travel there, Weekly reviews, TV reviews, book reviews, review reviews, the fucking lot.

The Saturday edition of the Scotsman was far more relaxed. The paper had long since given up the pretence of being an investigative newspaper of note and now, apart from the occasional pompous editorial, was happily reconciled with being a provincial rag, marginally better written and researched than its very mediocre Scottish competitors.

While soaking in the bath, Bland turned the pages lazily, jumping from article to article like a literate butterfly seeking linguistic nectar. He was somewhat surprised at the lack of mention of, let alone full articles about, the murder of the much unlamented Alan Patterson. Obviously the drink-driving indiscretions of overpaid second-rate footballers or the dancing prowess of TV announcers are more likely to tickle the curiosity of your average Scottish reader, but Bland would have expected the more prurient features of the murder to have attracted the attention of the odd journalist or two. Not even the full castration and handcuffing of a middle-aged man are of interest, unless a 'celebrity' is somehow involved.

Bland folded the newspaper away and took a good look at his aging body. The inevitable signs of middle age well all there in full display: the enlarged rib cage, the plumper breasts, the sagging lower stomach, the occasional raised vein. He was not exactly overweight, but he was not fit either. And certainly he was unlikely to arouse the sexual interest of a gorgeous woman like Priscilla by the mere display of his naked body. What exactly had he to offer her as a man? He regarded himself as a decent bloke, perhaps not too perceptive to the finer emotional changes, he was good at his job. Bland stopped the mental enumeration of his potential assets, as the list made him depressed. He was overthinking this date, again. The truth was that he had found Priscilla magnetically attractive, a feeling he had not felt in his mind and body for a long time, a feeling that he wanted to last, at least for a bit longer, so that he could savour it.

≈≈≈≈≈

It was a beautiful East Neuk morning when Julia woke up. The sunlight was shimmering on the calm seawaters, but in an understated way, keeping some of the softness of the early dawn. Julia drew the curtains and opened the window and inhaled overdramatically the crisp sea air, as if auditioning for an air freshener commercial. She put on her dressing gown and tiptoed to the kitchen as she did not want to disturb Philip and Melissa. She noticed that she was nearly out of milk and took this as an excuse for an early-morning walk to the corner shop, via the harbour. She put on a t-shirt and a pair of jeans, closed the front door quietly behind her and walked the few steps to the entrance gate, but as she was closing it she saw PC Dale getting out of his stake-out shed and walking towards her.

"Good morning, PC Dale," she said cheerfully.

"Trying to sneak away undetected, Mrs Flowers?" joked the young constable.

"Out of milk, actually," replied Julia who was not quite sure whether PC Dale was joking or not.

"So am I. Do you mind if I walk with you?"

Julia suspected that PC Dale, who must have been bored stiff by the many hours of pointless surveillance, simply wanted some company and so she smiled broadly at him.

"Yesterday morning a funny thing happened to me. Mrs Flowers. Just after you left I got a text asking me to collect some papers from St Andrews police station, but when I got there, they never heard of no papers. And I thought that police phones were secure!"

Julia did not feel exactly reassured by her guardian angel being tricked into leaving his post, but reminded herself of her resolve not to get involved.

"PC Dale, if you do not mind. I have told my son that you are our Neighbourhood Watch liaison officer. Not to alarm him, you see."

"No worries, Mrs Flowers. I'll be as quiet as a mouse, but if discovered, I'll be your Neighbourhood Watch guy," said PC Dale winking at her and tilting his head sideways slightly in a semi-conspiratorial fashion.

Julia's slender figure looked positively anorexic next to PC Dale's American-football physique and she found that she had to skip a pace or two just to keep up with the young constable.

A very small cat crossed their path and disappeared behind a bush.

"I do not see the point of keeping cats as pets. Cat are just like eating couscous. Pointless," commented PC Dale.

Julia could not hide a smile at PC Dale's inconsequential remark. "I, too, prefer dogs."

"I hate dogs," erupted PC Dale, "I myself keep a Mexican redknee tarantula. You know, the really hairy one."

This time Julia had to swallow a burst of irrepressible laughter: "Unusual."

"It's a female, of course. Only an idiot would keep a male. They die before they are six and are much less fun." Given a chance, PC Dale would wax lyrical for some time.

Julia thought that five years in the company of a tarantula would provide ample opportunities for arachnid-related entertainment, but fortunately they had arrived at the corner shop and she could let the surreal conversation die a natural death.

≈≈≈≈≈

Priscilla Brown lived just off the Botanics – as everybody in Edinburgh calls the Royal Botanical Garden – and so for Bland it was just like driving to work, with the only difference that his daily short commute to the station did not raise his heartbeat to the same extent. He had to stop the car in Dundas Street and regroup. For goodness' sake – he was not a teenager on his first date. So why the throbbing heart, the sweaty palms, the dry mouth? His strategy of lowering expectations clearly was not working, so he switched on the car radio instead. The familiar voices of 'I am sorry, I haven't a clue' had a soothing effect and a particularly good line delivered by Jeremy Hardy with the deadest of pans did release the tension that had been building up all morning. He started the engine and drove to Priscilla's. Her semi-detached was built in a pleasant mix of brickwork and limestone and had that typically Edinburgh look of respectability and solidity. Before ringing the bell, Bland checked that his mobile was switched off but not before taking a quick look at the time: 12.33. Perfect.

When Priscilla opened the door and exchanged looks with Bland, they both burst out laughing, as they were wearing matching outfits: she a blue skirt with a mohair V-neck beige jumper, he blue trousers and a lambswool V-neck cardigan. Even her blouse and his shirt were a very similar hue of cream.

"I like your taste in clothes," said Priscilla, "and I am pretty sure you like mine, too. Come in, come in."

Bland entered the house and immediately his nostrils detected a subtle but pervasive smell that he could not place within his range of known aromas.

"It's lemongrass," answered Priscilla who obviously could read him like an open book, "I steam it to infuse rice with its rather lovely smell. Do you like it?"

"I must confess it is not something I have tasted before. Strange combination. Lemon and grass."

"I am sure you have come across it. It is used a lot in Thai cooking. I can show it to you if you like."

Bland wished that the potted plant that he was half-hiding behind his back would dematerialize. Again, Priscilla noticed his embarrassment.

"You should not have bothered, Eric. What have you got there?"

"I was not quite sure what to bring and I am afraid this is what I came up with," said Bland producing his juniper plant.

"A juniper plant. What a lovely thought. Is it male or female?"

"That fucking shop assistant did not bother to tell me," Bland would have liked to have said. Instead he stammered: "Does it matter? I am sorry. I have no idea."

"It's about pollination. Male plants are needed to pollinate the female plants which, otherwise, produce no berries."

"It must be nice. For the male plants, I mean. To be needed."

Suddenly it was as if a large dark cloud had streamed across Priscilla's luminous face. It was so noticeable that even Bland noticed it: "It was a stupid idea, anyway. I'll return it and get something else instead."

Priscilla took the plant in her hands and gently turned over one of the small branches. "It's a female, but it has no berries. It must have missed the pollen season. Next Spring, perhaps."

By this time, the two would-be daters had reached the kitchen diner and right on cue Bland, like every other visitor to the house, exclaimed: "What a beautiful room".

It was indeed a beautiful room: the rustic kitchen opened up into a glass-ceilinged dining area, the whitewashed walls and the birch beams adding a certain air of Provence to the oak floor and pine table and chairs.

"It took me a long time to get it right, but I think it was worth it. Would you like a glass of wine?"

Bland realized that he had made a mistake by taking his car, but he could always take a taxi back: "I am having what you are having. Everything you touch is perfect, apparently."

Bland observed Priscilla moving round the stove. It looked as if she was hovering, lifting a lid here, stirring a pot there, with the effortless synchronization of someone who knows what to do and when. Something was wrong – thought Bland – nothing and no-one can be this perfect.

Priscilla came back with a little tray and two glasses of chilled white wine: "To an uninterrupted meal," said Priscilla raising her glass.

"I have made sure of that," replied Bland, raising his. He was not surprised when he sipped the wine to find it delicious, served at the right temperature, and flowing easily from the thin-rimmed glass. Perfection, again. He turned 360 degree as if looking at a planetarium: "Everything here is just so. And, if I may say, you fit beautifully in this little display of perfection."

Priscilla sat down at the table inviting Bland to do the same: "I know what you are thinking, Eric. If everything is so perfect, how is it that she is single? What dark secret is she hiding?"

"For once you are wrong. I am genuinely bowled over by how beautiful everything is, including you. Especially you." Bland surprised himself at the forwardness of his words; they came from somewhere other than his own brain.

"I did not have you down as a flatterer, Eric."

"I am definitely not. And I do not think you hold some dark secret, either."

"Now it's you who is wrong. I do have a secret. Either I keep it to myself or it comes out by date three or four. But I do like you, Eric. So here it comes now."

Bland was struggling to take in all this information at once: she liked him? And she did have a secret?

"When I was twenty-five I had to have a total hysterectomy ..."

"... so you cannot have children. Nothing dark about that ..." interrupted Bland.

Priscilla ignored the interruption: "But an unforeseen side-effect of the operation, something to do with nerve endings, meant that I ended up not just with a total hysterectomy but also with a total loss of libido. You see, for me, now, sex truly is a spectator's sport."

Without realizing it, Bland leaned back on his chair, trying, and failing, to cope with Priscilla's intimate revelation.

"As you may know, I have not been out much since Bianca died," Bland, too, was in revelatory mode, "and I did not expect a first date to be so, ehm, intense."

"I am sorry for the frankness, Eric, but I thought you deserved the truth from the start."

The next ten seconds shocked Bland as much as they moved Priscilla: he got up his chair, leaned across the table, took Priscilla's face in both his hands, and kissed her on the lips, his tongue looking discreetly for hers.

He sat back, his heart exploding inside his chest: "I don't care. You make me feel ... wanted. And it is a wonderful feeling."

"I hope you like Thai curry, Eric. As you may be eating a few of these in the foreseeable."

≈≈≈≈≈

When Julia returned home from her errand, she found the house as silent as usual, but it was a different quality of silence. It was a silence that could be broken at any time by her son or his girlfriend waking and perambulating around the house in the unique way young people do, as if they were surprised by the sudden appearance of walls and doors. She liked it.

While sipping a solitary Earl Grey, a nebulous idea that had been slowly forming in her mind suddenly became clear and she wondered why it had not occurred to her sooner. She went into her study and picked from the shelves several issues of recent catalogues of Oriental antiques from Christie's and Sotheby's. These are lavishly produced glossy magazines with gorgeous photographs and short but very accurate descriptions of the items going to be auctioned.

She started skimming through the most recent issues working her way backwards and soon started circling in red ink several items, marking the corresponding pages with Post-It stickers. After half an hour or so of checking and double checking she sat back with a self-satisfied smile. Finally she had a piece of solid evidence to present to Bland. Well, as solid as can be expected in the ephemeral world of fine art auction houses.

Right on cue, the wooden boards somewhere in the house started creaking. Someone was up. And right enough the indiscreet noise of a toilet cistern being emptied and refilled echoed in her study – a strange occurrence she had never noticed before. When she returned to the kitchen she found Melissa milling about.

"Good morning, Melissa. Would you like a cuppa?" Before Melissa could reply Julia remembered the list of forbidden foods Philip had enumerated earlier: "Sorry, I forgot. You do not drink tea or coffee, do you?"

"Morning, Mrs … Julia. No thanks, but if I could have a glass of water, please?"

"Let me show you where everything is," Julia proceeded to give Melissa a short introduction to her storing arrangements for cutlery, crockery, pots and pans, glasses, and kitchen utensils and finally served a cool glass of water from the fridge water-and-ice dispenser.

"You have a beautiful kitchen, Julia," said Melissa who seemed to be more interested in the aesthetic features of Julia's kitchen than in the precise location of pots and plates.

"Thank you. I like it anyway. Do you cook?"

"Only when Philip lets me. He is a much better cook than me. Have you tried his chicken breasts wrapped in bacon? They are delicious!"

Julia felt a slight pang of jealousy at Melissa knowing about a side of Philip's personality she herself was completely ignorant of. While he had always been a knowledgeable eater of food, Philip had never shown any interest in the preparation of the stuff, his gastronomic practical experience being confined to scrambling eggs and frying sausages.

"Excellent. Tomorrow I am working all day in Edinburgh, but I'll make sure Philip has the ingredients for his signature dish. He can cook supper tomorrow night."

"Actually Philip and I were wondering whether we could get a lift to Edinburgh tomorrow. We would like to show our CVs to a couple of charities and NGOs. Delivering them in person creates more of an impact, you know."

"Yes, of course. So you are already looking for jobs?"

"I wish. These days you are lucky to get an internship. Unpaid. Of course. Which means, working shifts in bars and restaurants. And now the prospect of Brexit makes things even more difficult."

"In what way?" enquired Julia.

"Well, not so much for me, as China is my area, but for Philip. If we were to be so crazy to leave the EU, Philip would be …" she was about to say 'screwed', but quickly repaired to "in deep waters. His dissertation is about Europe."

"I see. I'll ask him when he gets up."

"That won't be any time soon, Julia. He was up late last night and he is not an early riser, is he?"

This time Julia felt a bond with Melissa, almost a complicity in sharing the knowledge that Philip, now a young man, was as difficult to wake up in the morning as he had always been in his school days.

≈≈≈≈≈

At the end of the meal Bland was trying to find the right words. Lunch had been a strange affair, both he and Priscilla careful to avoid any reference to the intensely personal revelations that had preceded the meal.

"You may think I am saying this out of courtesy, but this was the best Thai curry I have ever had."

Priscilla looked at him in a mildly quizzical way and before she could open her mouth, Bland continued: "Not that I have had many. What I mean it's one of the best meals I have had."

Priscilla had, in fact, intended to ask that very question and the fact that Bland anticipated her made her like him even more. She got up, collected his empty plate and landed a fleeting kiss on his right temple.

CHAPTER 33

BLAND EXPRESS

Unlike the previous morning, on Monday Bland woke up in great form, truly rested, and full of energy. Certainly this blissful state was not due to the comfort of his sleeping arrangements. The night before, as soon as he returned home, he made up his mind to dispose of the double bed he had shared with Bianca for some many years and to get a new one. In the meantime he would sleep on the sofa. The very possibility that he and Priscilla might sleep in his old bed made him cringe. After Bianca's death he had kept sleeping in the large double bed, as doing otherwise would have been a betrayal, even though, or perhaps because, that was the bed Bianca had died in.

Her death had been gentle and unforgettable – just like Bianca. After she had decided to give up all medication and return home to die, she had been very weak and confined to bed for most of the seven days from leaving hospital to dying. A nurse would come twice a day to administer increasing doses of morphine, but on the very last day Bianca had refused to take any. She was so pale and her skin almost translucent. She asked him to sit on the bed and to hold her hand. Her breathing, always very shallow, became imperceptible and her muscles, what was left of her muscles, seemed to relax completely, as if she was melting away. Suddenly she opened her eyes, looked at Bland, lifted her head very slightly from the pillow, and exhaled a long, interminable, inexorable, and irrevocable last breath.

Bland had a plan for the day and was ready to spring into action.

When he arrived at the station he saw in the rota notice that it was Corby's day off. Shame, because he had a couple for jobs for her, but today nothing was going to stop the Bland Express. First stop: Livingston.

"Hi Hamish. Bland here. How is the land of the living dead treating you?"

"Traffic can be exciting, Eric, especially when it involves Lithuanian underage girls. What do you want?"

"A picture. Woman called Heather Corby. Or indeed any information about her. I am looking for Chinese ancestors."

"You know what, Eric? You do come up with some weird questions. I assume you have already checked online, right?"

"Yes, nothing there. She is not a suspect or anything. I just need to find out any connection to China. Anything at all."

"And I suppose you want it yesterday. I'll do my best. And you will remember me when a vacancy opens up in the big city, right, Eric?"

"Of course, Hamish. Thanks a lot."

Next stop: Haymarket.

Rights for China's HQs were as drab as Bland has feared, but their security was top of the range: intercom with video, industrial strength shutters, the lot.

When finally Bland reached the first-floor office, the first thing he noticed was the profusion of colours and smells in the tiny two-desk room: vibrant posters covered the walls, banners shouted about human rights and privacy, and at least two incense burners were working at full capacity. And then there was the noise: a low bass thumping rhythm with occasional shrieks.

"DCI Bland, right? How can I help you?" the diminutive Miss Tingting had a steel wire of determination and defiance in her voice.

"Miss Tingting I am investigating the death of Dr Anthony Gordon. Did you know him?"

"Not personally. Why are you asking me, if I may ask?" Miss Tingting was very guarded.

Bland thought best to take an indirect route: "I could not help noticing the strict security. Have you had problems in the past?"

"Our website receives about 200 hacking attacks a day. The flat downstairs listens to everything we say, hence the musical accompaniment" she directed Bland's look to the two large loudspeakers aimed at the floor and beyond," probably our phones are tapped, but no, no direct physical attacks. Yet."

"What do you mean by 'not personally'? Was he in touch with someone else in this office?"

"I am the only full-timer in this office. The other desk is for volunteers who help us from time to time. I corresponded with Dr Gordon for a while, but our exchanges ended when he was killed. You have not charged anyone with his murder, have you? I doubt you ever will."

Bland understood what McIntyre meant by 'redoubtable Miss Tingting'.

"Why do you think that, Miss Tingting?"

"Do you know how much the Chinese government has invested in the UK? About 30 billion US dollars. Do you know who is funding Hinckley Point and HS2?"

"I do not need a lecture in economics, Miss Tingting. I need to know how you knew Dr Gordon."

"He wrote to the office about a potential donation. Financial details, legal status. All very proper, DCI Bland."

"Did he write back when you replied?"

"Yes, he enquired whether a donation or legacy could be earmarked to a specific project."

"Which project?"

"Do I have to answer your question?" Miss Tingting looked defiantly straight into Bland's eyes.

"I do not work for the Chinese government, Miss Tingting. And if I find that any Chinese nationals are involved in Dr Gordon's murder I will charge them. I can assure you."

Miss Tingting smiled wryly: "Of course you will. If they are low-grade criminals. Anyway, Dr Gordon was interested in our campaign to expose high-level corruption in China. And then he was murdered. What a coincidence!"

"Thank you, Miss Tingting. But are you sure he did not have any personal contacts with someone else linked to your charity?"

"I wish we were a charity, DCI Bland. We are 'too political' for the Office of the Scottish Charity Regulator. If only we campaigned to save the giant panda. No, I did not get the impression that he was, or wanted to be, personally involved with Rights for China. He stressed that he wanted the donation to be anonymous."

"Thank you very much for your help. I cannot be too specific, but you may receive good news about Dr Gordon's estate in the near future."

"No sorrowful woman here," thought Bland while slowly navigating the steep staircase. He could not help admiring people like Miss Tingting. People who take up a fight they know they will not win, but carry on regardless simply because they feel they have to. He had to squeeze past two young people going up the stairs, one very tall woman with a boyish haircut, followed by a fresh-faced man, both carrying an A4 pocket file. When he reached the heavy door and opened it he had to take a deep breath: standing next to the doorway, with her back to him, he recognized immediately the silhouette of one Julia Flowers.

"Julia! What are you doing here?"

Julia jumped visibly and quickly turned around: "Oh, it's you, Eric. Please do not scare me like this again."

"I am sorry, Julia, but this is the last place I was expecting you."

"Why? What is so special about it? I just dropped my son and his girlfriend so that they can leave their CVs with a charity or something. What is strange about it?"

"Oh, it's nothing," said Bland apologetically. He joined the dots and realized the coincidence.

"Anyway, as you are here. There is something I have to tell you. About the Gordon case. It may be important." As she uttered these words, Julia realized that they sounded over-dramatic, but now it was too late to remedy.

"Of course. Perhaps we can have a coffee now."

"Actually, I have to take Philip and Melissa to their next stop and then I am seeing a client in Stockbridge. I should be free by twelve-ish."

"Fine. Give me a ring when you are free. And keep out of trouble, will you?"

When he got back to his car and sat down, Bland sighed deeply. Everything was pointing to a Chinese involvement, and he was too scrupulous to ignore it. A call to Murphy would confirm that the 'flat downstairs' was indeed a listening station, but manned by British, not

Chinese staff. And yet deep down he was certain that the sorrowful woman was the key to the case. He was about to start the engine when his mobile whirred into action. It was McIntyre.

"Hi, Eric. Have you read the Herald this morning?"

"No, Bill. I do have a life, you know."

"You are not interested in the body found in the Clyde, then?"

"Who is he?"

"The paper does not say, but fifty pounds says it's Min Lai. It's the tattoos."

Bland knew that it was a matter of when, not if.

McIntyre took Bland's silence as an invitation to carry on: "And another fifty pounds says that now Hinckley Point nuclear power station will be duly financed by our Chinese friends."

"Thank you, Bill. I am not sure where the Chinese lead will get me, but I'll let you know first. For old times' sake."

This was another nail in his theory of the sorrowful woman. If the Gordon's murder had been a contract killing on behalf of the Chinese, the 'drowning' of Min Lai would be its natural conclusion. Perhaps Gordon's pathetic notes about a woman were just that – the ramblings of a pathetic lonely man with a tortured personality.

≈≈≈≈≈

There was no client in Stockbridge. After depositing Philip and Melissa in George Street, Julia drove the short distance to Heriot Row just to pay a surprise visit to Ruthie. And perhaps catch up on the gossip about the late Dr Gordon.

On her way she could not help noticing that the ground apartment at number 55 was now for sale. As soon as she had parked the car, she took out her iPhone and paid a visit to Savills' website. Yes, Gordon's flat was for sale at a cool £800,000 'for a quick sale'.

Ruthie was as ebullient as ever, but she was very worried by her missing cat, a beast of a creature who reserved her gentle side only for Ruthie and Rupert and was totally beastly to everybody else.

"She has been missing for two days now and she never misses her evening treat. Nobody seems to have seen her." By 'nobody' Ruthie meant her network of contacts in and around Heriot Row who, no doubt, she would have alerted about the missing cat emergency.

"Maybe she has found love in the suburbs," quipped Julia.

"Do not be ridiculous, darling. Eleanor is a cat of good taste. She may have been kidnapped, of course. Anyway, what's the news with your police man?"

There was a very meaningful gap between 'police' and 'man'.

"Brand is most definitely not my 'police man', whatever that means. I am trying to stay out of his investigation as much as I can."

"Tell me more," Ruthie was intrigued by the possibility of Julia being dragged into the case against her will.

Julia thought best to leave a full account of her adventure to a later occasion: "Oh, it's nothing, but it looks as if Dr Gordon was more than a boring ex-diplomat and part-time academic."

"Tell me about it. Christine was telling me just the other day. You know his flat is for sale for eight-hundred thousand pound? Anyway, Christine was saying that she had seen a mysterious woman visiting him a couple of times. Ginger hair. Not from round here." According to Ruthie's Book of Obvious Facts nobody with ginger hair could possibly be from the New Town.

"What's so strange about that?" asked Julia feigning ignorance.

"Well, apart from the fact that nobody ever visited Dr Gordon, this woman would go in and leave after only a few minutes," said Ruthie raising her eyebrows in not too subtle a way.

"You don't think …"

"You said it, Julia: maybe Gordon was not the 'bachelor type' after all."

"Anything else about this scarlet woman?"

"Well, according to Christine, there was something funny about her face, but she can't remember what. And when she left it looked as if she was carrying a baby. But Christine was not sure. It was a couple of years ago, after all."

"Philip is back for a few days. And his girlfriend." Julia wanted to change the topic and the mere mention of a girlfriend was enough to distract Ruthie.

After twenty minutes or so of idle conversation, Julia left Ruthie's place and, on the way to her car, rang Bland.

"Hi. It's Julia. I am just round the corner. Shall I come to the station?"

"Oh, Mrs Flowers," Bland was keen to establish that Julia was a potential witness, "yes, that would be great. You can park in the visitors' car park."

"Excellent. That would save me a small fortune. See you soon, Inspector Bland," Julia had got Bland's drift.

≈≈≈≈≈

Bland was unsettled. His personal and work lives were colliding and he found himself unable to deal with the wreckage. On one level, Bland was excited at the prospect of sharing his work troubles with Priscilla. At another level, the investigation was running away from him. Perhaps his fixation with the sorrowful woman was preventing him from putting together the jigsaw pieces that had been accumulating on his desk. But how could he ignore the burning in his stomach, the doubt that could not be dislodged from his mind?

Bland could wait no longer.

"Hi Hamish, it's Bland again. Things are moving very fast here. You have not found anything yet, have you?" There was a hint of desperation in Bland's voice.

"God, Bland. You are a hard task master. You hardly put down the phone and here you are, asking for results already. Anyway, today is your lucky day. "Old-age pensioner mugged for £2". Page three of the West Lothian Courier, no less. Any guesses who the OAP is?"

"Hamish, please do not piss about. Is Heather Corby part-Chinese?"

"Only if Chinese are ginger and pale like sheets she is."

Bland could hear Hamish's silent chuckle: "Great. Anything else?"

"Not really, there was a funeral of one Adele Corby, only daughter of Heather Corby, Warriston Crematorium, about six years ago. Nothing else. Sorry, Bland."

"Thanks all the same, Hamish. Bye."

Bland leaned back on his chair and then bent forward hitting the desk hard with both hands: "Fuck. Fuck. Fucking fuck." Where is a cigarette when you need one? The sorrowful woman trail was dead and buried. Cremated at Warriston. Perhaps, Mrs Flowers would have good news for him, but he was clutching at straws now. The case was going nowhere and that was that.

≈ ≈ ≈ ≈ ≈

Bland was waiting for Julia on the steps of the police station. He saw her distinctive car park in the visitors' space and followed her brief walk to the entrance. There was no doubt: there was a grace and an effortless elegance in the way she moved.

"Mrs Flowers. Thank you for coming. Let's go to my office," Julia followed Bland through a maze of corridors and open-plan spaces and finally arrived at the now-familiar office.

"Well, inspector Bland, "Julia broke the ice after they had taken their seats, "I found something that may be of interest to you." As she was speaking she took out of her large handbag, a bundle of catalogue cuttings and placed it on Bland's desk.

"These are items recently sold at high-profile auctions in London," Bland's puzzled expression suggested that more explanation was needed, "all are fine pieces of Chinese ceramics, exquisite quality, and none of them has any solid provenance."

It was clear that Bland was none the wiser.

"You see, for one piece of such quality to be sold at Christie's or Sotheby's without any mention of provenance would be very unusual. For many, almost unheard of."

"I am afraid I still do not see how this can be of use in our investigation, Mrs Flowers," Bland was not trying to be obtuse, he truly did not see the point.

"I think that many, if not all, of these pieces are from Dr Gordon's list. And you can force the auction houses to reveal both buyer and seller, if you have reasonable grounds."

Bland's face brightened up: "So we can put a face and an identity to the sellers and establish a link with Gordon!"

"There is another thing. I thought I recognized one of the names in the list, but when I tried to check it out, my copy of the list was gone."

Bland's face lost its short-lived cheerfulness: "This is quite serious. Why did you not tell me this before?"

"I did not think you would be interested. Do you have your list here?"

"Corby has it. Damn. She is off today. Wait. I can ask Peng. He translated it." With this, Bland raised the phone, tapped the extension number, and spoke quickly: "DS Peng? Bland here. It's urgent. Can you bring the list of Chinese names that Corby had asked you to translate, please? Thanks a lot, Peng." It was clear from the conversation that DS Peng had not had the opportunity to speak a single word.

"What do you mean 'you recognized' a name, Mrs Flowers?" Bland was processing fast all the information that had been unloaded on to his already crowded train of thought.

"It's a long shot, but one of the names is the same as my Japanese friend's daughter's boyfriend's father."

Bland tried to disentangle the links of connections, but was helped out by Julia's explanation.

"My friend's daughter's boyfriend – she and Philip were at Fettes together – is Chinese and I thought I had seen his father's name on the list. Shuin Hon Chi Lin it's rather unusual, don't you think?"

Before Bland could embarrass himself with a remark along the lines that most Chinese names sounded unusual to him, DS Peng knocked on the door.

"Ah, DS Peng. Thank you so much. Have you got the list?"

"Yes, Sir. I printed it out for you. Original Chinese list and my translation."

Bland grabbed the piece of paper and scanned it for a Shuin Hon Chi Lin. "It's not on the list," he said to Julia.

"May I see it, please?" Julia's tone of voice carried more than a hint that she was sure of her case.

She looked at both lists intently, then she raised her head slowly and even more slowly she addressed Bland: "Of course it isn't on the list. This is not the original list."

Bland felt embarrassed, but under the circumstances he had to come clean. "Well, it is not exactly the very same list. WPC Corby may have added a few names." Bland was looking at Peng, who understood the game that was being played here.

"I do not mean that. Of course, there are some strange extra names. I mean the original Chinese characters are not the same." Julia stood her ground with a firmness that surprised Bland.

"I doubt WPC Corby would make such an error, Sir." Peng was happy to contribute to the conversation.

"Wait, there is a simple way to check this out. I'll go to the evidence store and get the original. Please wait here." Bland was going to sort this mess himself.

On the way to the evidence store a thousand thoughts were whizzing in his head. Was this the breakthrough he had been praying for? But what kind of breakthrough was it? After going through the signing off of the evidence, Bland returned to his office with the delicate scroll still in its plastic bag. He took it out of the bag very carefully and placed it next to Peng's printed copy.

Peng examined the two lists and then turned to Bland: "I am afraid she is right, Sir."

"Who is right, Peng? Do you mean Corby?" burst out Bland.

"No, Sir. This lady is right. Corby did not give to me the original list to translate."

"I do not understand," said Bland in exasperation, "Corby is not the type to make mistakes like this."

"This is not a mistake, Sir. Every single set of characters has been altered very slightly to make it unrecognizable." Peng was enjoying the situation more than he should have.

"I'll ring Corby at home and ask her to come to the station." Bland was thinking aloud and in fact he proceeded to do just that, but there was no reply.

"WPC Corby has always been a brunette, has she?" asked Julia.

Bland was thrown by the incongruity of the question: "That's a very strange thing to ask, Mrs Flowers, but, yes, as long as I have known her WPC Corby has always been a brunette."

DS Peng coughed nervously: "Actually, Sir, she is not a natural brunette."

"Dare I ask how you came to know that, Peng?" Bland was increasingly uncomfortable.

"It is not what you think, Sir. WPC White happened to mention this in the cafeteria the other day. You see, apparently WPC Corby is rather, ehm, reserved, but White got a glimpse of her in the showers and she is definitely a ginge. I mean, red-haired."

"Perhaps, this is a case of too much information about nothing, Peng, but thank you for your clarification."

Julia did not like the implied rebuke: "It's just that a red-haired woman was seen visiting Dr Gordon just before he was killed. That's all."

Bland gasped. It was 2-0 to Flowers and it hurt: "And how do you know this, Mrs Flowers, and why did you not tell me before? Wait. You thought it was of no interest to me."

"Someone just told me less than an hour ago and I was going to tell you. That is why I ask about the brunette thing." Julia was not the gloating type, but she was in charge and liked it.

"Well, I suppose we'd better pay Corby a visit, to clarify this mess once and for all."

Julia was about to make her way to the door, but she was stopped by Bland. "If you do not mind coming with us, Mrs Flowers, as you may be able to assist us with our enquiries."

Julia was surprised by Bland's request, but offered no resistance.

"I'll get WPC Corby's home address, Sir. Shall I meet you in the car park?" offered Peng.

"Yes, please, Peng." Bland escorted Julia to the door and then to the car park.

"The office of a well-known auction house is on the way, inspector Bland. I am sure that they will be more than happy to cooperate. I know the Head of Oriental Artworks there. Rather pompous, but keen to keep the firm out of any kind of trouble. After the big fine for five-hundred and twelve million dollars for price-fixing any reputable auction house cannot be too careful."

Under different circumstances Bland would have been very keen to learn more about the half-billion fine story, but at the moment he had only one thought in his head: could Corby possibly be the sorrowful woman? It just did not make any sense.

DS Peng arrived: "WPC Corby lives in Pilton, Sir. Shall I drive?"

Bland nodded and Julia found herself again in the back of a police car.

Pilton is not a great place to live in. In theory its location is highly desirable: near the sea, plenty of green spaces, easy commute to the city centre. And yet, an air of dejection and dereliction hangs over it. The cash shops and the heavily armoured chemists give the game away, as do the abandoned pushchairs, the used condoms and the few discarded syringes still remaining on the ground after Edinburgh City Council's brilliant 'Pick up a Stick' initiative. Why would Corby choose to live here? Surely on her salary she could afford a more salubrious location.

When they arrived at the address, Bland asked Julia if she minded waiting in the car while they sorted things out. Reluctantly she agreed.

Peng and Bland went up the staircase, as the lift appeared to be broken, and when they reached the third floor and walked down the smelly open-air corridor they knocked on the reinforced front door. There was no response. A scruffily attired middle-aged looking woman, probably in her early thirties, walked past them and spat on the floor muttering "Fucking *pòlis*" loud enough to be heard and softly enough to be able to deny it. It could not be fun for Corby to be the only copper in the village.

"If, hypothetically, the door were unlocked, Sir, then we would have reasonable cause to believe that WPC Corby's life was in danger, wouldn't we, Sir?"

"I suppose we would. I'll go downstairs to fetch Mrs Flowers, as a witness." Bland knew the drill and so did Peng.

When Bland returned with a slightly panting Mrs Flowers she was able to confirm that the front door was indeed ajar and that there had been no response after Peng had knocked repeatedly.

"You'd better follow us at a distance, Mrs Flowers," said Bland in a concerned tone.

The flat was spotlessly clean, but the smell of damp was heavy in the air. The furniture seemed to come from an Eighties sitcom set. It did not take long to confirm that Corby was not at home. To Julia's expert eye, this had the look and feel of a flat of a recently deceased and she drifted automatically towards the bathroom – her first port of call when visiting a vacant house.

The shower curtain was perfectly clean, but the rest of the cubicle showed all the signs of workmanship typical of Edinburgh City Council – the poorly grouted tiles, the sloppily fitted seal, the dripping taps, traces of the constant and losing battle against mould.

Julia, as she normally would when checking the age of the person "living" in an empty flat, went to the medicine cupboard. It was empty. So she proceeded to open the melamine doors of the 'vanity unit' underneath the wash basin. Presbyterian vanity, judging from the drabness of the sorry piece of Eighties memorabilia. Next to the thick bleach plastic bottle, there was a large Aldi shopping bag and some bubble wrap inside it. Instinctively, Julia bent down and unwrapped the messily arranged protective shield.

"Inspector Bland, you'd better come here," she said in as calm a voice as she could manage.

Bland and Peng arrived quickly. Her voice must have sounded not overly calm.

"Look under the basin and be very careful."

Bland bent down, repeated Julia's actions and, still on his knee, turned his face up to Julia: "Are these what I think they are?"

"The very same" agreed Julia.

Then Bland turned to Peng, who had felt somewhat excluded by their private conversation: "These are Doucai bowls, worth a fortune, and belonged to Dr Gordon."

"Bloody hell … sorry … I mean … what the heck?" DS Peng was as surprised as everyone else in the tiny bathroom.

"You'd better take these as evidence. They are worth three quarters of a million, so you decide how careful you should be, DS Peng."

It was obvious from Peng's expression that he was not relishing the task. While Peng was going downstairs at an exceedingly slow pace, Bland and Julia lingered a bit longer in the flat. "I suppose you'd better have a quick look around, as you are quite good at it," suggested Bland.

Julia switched to valuer mode, starting from the kitchen, then moving to the two tiny bedrooms separated by a paper-thin wall.

"Are you sure that Corby actually lives here? It feels more like a shrine than a lived-in space." Julia could see that her words had sparked something in Bland's brain.

"We have to go back to the station, quickly. Thank you very much for your help, Julia."

"I am happy if I have helped, Eric."

CHAPTER 34

THE SORROWFUL WOMAN

After Julia had been returned to her car and Peng had resumed his services at Vice, Bland was left alone in his office. Corby's mobile was not only switched off, but probably discarded somewhere with the SIM card removed. A missing person search had been started, discreetly.

Bland knew that he had one last line of enquiry open before the whole investigation was taken over by someone else, Murphy most probably.

After a quick round of telephone calls and google searches, Bland had a target destination. It was a very long shot, but he had nothing else to throw at this case.

The Royal Infirmary complex is not bad, as far as large hospital architecture is concerned. The car park should be cordoned off as a crime scene for daylight parking fee robbery, but that is the Private-Public Funding Initiative for you.

Usually the kind of enquiries that Bland was about to undertake were the routine job of young constables and so the legal medical manager's secretary was somewhat surprised when Bland announced himself as DCI Bland. In fact she had to ask what DCI stood for. Bland was the first, and probably last, Detective Chief Inspector to have visited her office.

The Legal Medical Manager was much more jovial than his job title would suggest and he, too, was pleasantly surprised to be talking to a DCI.

"The fact that this is a police investigation and that you are enquiring about a deceased person makes my job really easy, DCI Bland. What exactly are you after?"

"All you have about one Adele Corby, who died at the Royal about six years ago. And I mean everything. This is a murder enquiry and we have a potential suspect on the run, so you can appreciate the urgency."

At the mention of 'murder' and 'on the run', the LMM's ears pricked up considerably: "Of course, of course. I'll make sure personally that we deliver your request as expeditiously as we can." And with that he disappeared into the secretary's office apparently unimpeded by the weight of his jargon. "'Delivery' indeed," thought Bland.

After a surprisingly short interval, the LMM reappeared with a broad smile on his face: "Margaret is printing the file for you, but in the meantime you may want to have a look on the screen at the data we have."

"That would be great, Mr ...?"

"Thomson, Barry Thomson."

Barry Thomson pulled the visitor's chair next to his so that both could see the large computer monitor: "Since her twenties Adele Corby had had severe kidney problems, probably due to substance abuse, and eventually she required dialysis. Things took a turn for the worse and she was due to receive a kidney transplant, but, let me see, yes, her operation was cancelled just the day before. That's unusual."

"Was the operation not rescheduled?" asked Bland.

"Kidneys cannot be frozen for later use. Someone else would have got her kidney. Unfortunately she died before a new suitable organ could be found."

"Can you tell me why the operation was cancelled at the last minute?" Bland went out on a limb, hoping for the best.

"I am not sure whether the daily care records are kept for this long, but I can certainly find out which surgeon was supposed to have carried out the transplant, if that is of any use to you."

"That would be extremely helpful, Mr Thomson."

The LMM scuttled away again and then he returned with a thick bundle of paper sheets and with a Post-It note:

"These are all the data we have on Adele Corby, and this ..." he said waving the yellow piece of sticky paper, "... is the name of the surgeon. Mr Colin Patterson. Retired. I am afraid, so we do not have a current address."

"That would not be a problem, Mr Thomson. Thank you again." For the first time since the start of the entire investigation Bland knew where this case was going and he could not help breaking into a large smile.

When he got back to his car, he radioed the station and within a couple of minutes he got the address he had requested. He was not in the least surprised to find that Mr Patterson lived in Barnton, a stone's throw from J.K. Rowling's two-million-plus house.

The surgeon's house surpassed Bland's worst expectations: it was a high security compound, all glass and modern stone work, anonymous manicured garden, it missed an open-air hot-tub, but probably it was the next planned addition to this nouveau riche horror.

Eventually, the seven-foot solid steel gate was opened remotely and Bland was welcome into the house by what he took to be an Indian or Malay maid: "Mr Patterson will see you promptly. Please follow me."

The interior was living proof that wealth does not buy good taste, but Bland was too busy working out his strategy to notice the apices of kitsch reached in the Patterson household.

"Please take a seat. Would you like anything? Tea, coffee, juice?" the maid was working to a well-rehearsed script.

"Nothing for me, thanks."

After a minute or so, Mr Patterson, all five-foot five of him, arrived on the scene: "DCI Bland, forgive me, but I was upstairs on the phone." He conveniently omitted to mention that he had hurriedly called his solicitor, but that was a small detail. "If I can be honest with you, I have been expecting a visit from the police for some time now."

"And why would that be, Mr Patterson?"

"After the death of Dr Gordon, I mean," said the retired surgeon as if that was the most obvious reason in the world, "not the most commendable act in my long career, but nothing illegal, I am assured." Patterson seemed sure of his ground, but then he was an arrogant little git.

"It would help me if you could expand, Mr Patterson."

"Well, of course we all felt bad about the poor woman, but it was really Hobson's choice, wouldn't you agree?"

Bland tried to keep his cool: "Can you be more specific about the link between Adele Corby and Dr Gordon?"

"Corby. Yes, I remember now. Poor woman. She was due to get a new kidney, wasn't she? We had to postpone the operation and operate on Dr Gordon instead. Life and death. Matter of hours." It looked as if Patterson could breathe more easily now that he had unburdened himself.

"But Gordon needed a liver, not a kidney." Bland was annoyed now.

"Of course, but Dr Gordon insisted on having a British crew assisting the surgeon performing the actual operation."

"Who was he?" asked Bland, about to lose his rag.

"I am afraid I do not know. A she, actually. A Chinese lady surgeon. Very competent, I must admit. Impressive technique. I believe she was in charge of the donated organ."

"Do you know what happened to Adele Corby after the cancelled operation, Mr Patterson?"

"I retired from the NHS soon thereafter. I am afraid I have no idea."

"She died before a new kidney could be found. But I suppose the money must have helped with the occasional pang of conscience."

Bland was on his way out before Patterson had the time to mutter some word of exculpation. As he was leaving the room, he turned suddenly: "You are not related to the recently deceased Alan Patterson, by any chance?"

"He is, was, my cousin. What a way to go." Colin Patterson was not exactly racked with sorrow for the death of his relative. More relieved than bereaved.

Bland was happy to leave the golden gated community of Barnton behind him. "Sod the lot of them," he muttered to himself.

By now everything had cleared up in his head. The case was closed. Whether a file would land on the desk of the Procurator Fiscal was a different matter altogether.

He felt no satisfaction, no exultation. Another piece of shit in the jigsaw puzzle of sewers we call life. The only reason he was really happy inside was that he could talk about the case with Priscilla, something he had not done for years – sharing his life.

On his way to the station and completely on a whim, he made a short detour on the very off chance of bumping into Corby. He parked the car, walked to the reception, asked and got the piece of information he needed, meandered slowly to his destination and waited.

After twenty minutes or so, the stocky figure of Joyce Therese Corby appeared walking purposefully along one of the many well-kept paths in

Warriston Crematorium. Bland was waiting for her next to the plaque with the ashes of Adele Corby, mother.

A gentle and warm drizzle had just began to turn the stones and graves a darker shade of grey, but neither Bland nor Corby seemed to notice it.

" 'Afternoon, Sir," said Corby in a matter-of-fact tone.

"It must have been difficult for you, Corby," answered Bland.

"Difficult? Do you know what it's like living on dialysis, Sir? Of course you don't, unless you are unlucky enough to live through it. And when I say live, I mean, vegetate. No, worse. The heart constantly racing, the unshakeable fatigue, your skin itching twenty-four seven. But she never complained. Not once, Sir. Not once, in her entire miserable life. She was the most amazing mother. She made me feel important, the centre of the universe. To this day I do not know how she managed. Primary school, middle school, birthdays, illnesses, holidays, everything was to be normal for me. And it was."

"I am really sorry for you, Corby. Really," Bland meant it.

"And then, out of the blue, a ray of hope, an once-in-a-lifetime chance of an actual, proper, ordinary life. A kidney. Not a good one, mind you. My mother was not worthy of a proper one. This was half-diseased, but good enough for a near-normal life. The day before the operation, for the first time ever, I saw what true happiness really looks like. It is your mother making plans for herself, for her own life, free. Free." It was impossible to work out if Corby was crying, because by now the drizzle had turned into steady rain.

But she continued: "And he took it all away from her, from us, and for no reason. He wanted Patterson and his crew as insurance, just in case, you see. A world-class Chicago-trained Chinese surgeon was not enough for Dr Gordon. And who cares about a single mother from Pilton? You tell me, Sir."

"How did you find out, Corby?" asked Bland. Out of professional curiosity, more than genuine interest, he was ashamed to admit to himself.

"With great difficulty, is the simple answer and I was sure only after I joined the force, Sir."

"And he tried to buy you off, didn't he?"

"So, you have found the Chinese bowls, have you, Sir?" She sounded as if they had been left for him to find. "I took them only to fool him into believing that I was this harmless little woman, grateful for a lot of money. You should have seen his face when I cracked his skull. He could not believe that a little insignificant speck of dirt from Pilton could have dared to end the respectable life of Dr Anthony Gordon. Priceless. An image worth dying for."

"Nobody else knows about your mother and Gordon, Corby. You have found the bowls in his lock-up and kept them in your flat because you were ashamed not to have spotted them during your first search."

"You are very kind, Sir. You are a decent man. There aren't many like you around, are there? But I'll be fine. Just a few more hours and my mission will have been accomplished. May I go now, Sir?"

Bland looked at Corby like he had never before, a life made and nurtured by a good woman and ruined forever by a vain, pointless, man. "Are you sure about this, Corby? There may still be time to …".

"I am afraid there is not, Sir. What is done is done. And I am fine with it. Really." Corby was a determined woman, she had to be.

"Okay, Corby. I'll leave you here. Good bye." Bland extended his right hand to shake Corby's, but instead found himself hugged for a brief moment by the little stocky girl from Pilton. And it felt so right.

≈≈≈≈≈

Later that afternoon, having collected Philip and Melissa for a ride back home, Julia drove over the congested bridge with an even more philosophical attitude than usual. It had been a very tense day, but she had the strong impression that finally Bland was on top of this case. Life was returning to normal. Philip and Melissa were arguing about the unfairness of internships, thus experiencing at first hand the tension between sticking to your principles and coping with reality, as they both were applying for the very positions they regarded as elitist and unfair. The earlier shower of rain had cleared and a beautiful clear light was simmering on the Forth.

When they reached home and were walking to the front gate they were met by a very cheerful PC Dale: "Mrs Flowers, I wanted to wait for you before returning to base. My Neighbourhood Watch stint has come to an end. And it has been a pleasure being of assistance."

Julia gave the house key to Philip and asked him to go ahead with Melissa, as she wanted to talk to PC Dale on her own. "Thank you very much for your protection, PC Dale. I understand the case is closed. What a relief for everybody."

"Yes, indeed. The station is awash with wild rumours. Apparently it was WPC Corby who sent me on that wild-goose chase to St Andrews. What a stupid joke! Anyway, I had put all your stuff back into the shed. Good bye, Mrs Flowers." PC Dale and his enormous holdall quickly disappeared down the lane to the harbour.

Before getting back into the house, Julia wanted to check the state of the shed. It was much tidier than when PC Dale had moved in. Even the instruction manuals of long discarded tools and gadgets were neatly piled on a shelf and on the very top Julia thought she recognized a familiar sheet of paper. She felt a twinge of embarrassment when it turned out to be the list of Chinese names. She suddenly recalled that she had it in her hands when she had called on PC Dale to ask him if he, too, was having problems with the broadband. She looked at the list, took it in her hands and crumpled it into a tight ball which she deposited delicately in the waste-paper basket. The case was indeed closed.

CHAPTER 35

TO BE OR NOT TO BE?

One week after Joyce Therese Corby's body had been found on the beach in Cramond, Bland summoned DS Peng to his office.

"I am flattered by your offer to join your team on the Gordon case, Sir, but there are too many loose ends I do not understand. Perhaps it is best if my name is kept out of the final report."

"There are always loose ends in a case this complicated, Peng. It goes with the territory, as Corstorphine would say."

"But why did Corby give us the wrong names?" Peng was not going to let this pass.

"I suppose she needed to buy time or perhaps she was hoping that the Chinese lead would take us nowhere and that the case would be dropped."

"What about the woman in cling film, Sir?" Peng had the bit in his mouth and wasn't letting go.

"I would not be at all surprised if the crime scene revealed plenty of evidence implicating the late Min Lai, recently released from prison. Inside for GBH, extortion with menaces, attempted murder. Typical gangland murder, wouldn't you say?"

"It seems all too neat, Sir." DS Peng was a very smart cookie.

"That is the way Corstorphine likes it, apparently." Bland was testing his new potential recruit.

"I do not like it, Sir, if I may say so."

"Neither do I, Peng. Neither do I."

After dismissing Peng, Bland took out two sheets of paper from a drawer in his desk. As Julia had correctly predicted, the auction house were only too happy to cooperate and in no time had produced a list of buyers and sellers of the no-provenance precious antiques spotted by Julia. And again she had guessed right: almost all of the sellers were related, either directly or indirectly, to the names on Gordon's list. What she did not know was that

Bland had discovered that all the names on Gordon's list were current or recently retired high-ranking officials in the Chinese Ministry of Culture, which, according to Wikipedia "is responsible for culture policy and activities in the country, including managing national museums and monuments".

Bland was fairly confident that if he had the necessary resources and political backing he could find evidence to support his theory. The MoC officials came to share an antiques loot and the mutual blackmail relationship thus established guaranteed the success of the enterprise. Somehow Dr Gordon got involved, probably as the means for smuggling the loot abroad. His diplomatic bag privileges must have come in handy when he suddenly resigned his post at the embassy in Beijing. Probably the plan was to sit on the stolen antiques for a few years before selling them discreetly. Bland suspected that something must have gone wrong when Gordon started using the antiques entrusted to him as his personal wealth, especially to fund his unorthodox liver transplant operation. Once the cat was out of the bag and the Chinese Secret Service came to know of the scheme, someone had to be made an example of. It was no coincidence that Guangyao Liang, before becoming a successful Soho art dealer, was an assistant museum curator in Beijing and a name on Gordon's list.

All this left Bland with a moral dilemma of life-changing proportions. He had wrestled with it for a couple of days and was deeply troubled by the likely consequences of his eventual decision. He needed to take a walk to Princes Street.

You do not have to be a petty architectural philistine like Prince Charles to agree that compared to its look at the turn of the century the current display of urban landscape in Princes Street is irredeemably abysmal. The once coherent solidity and understated beauty of shop fronts, office doors and hotel entrances fused into the wide thoroughfare with its traffic of people, vehicles, and trams has been replaced by town planners' bullet-list architecture. Whereas the bullets should have been reserved for the criminal vandals with clipboards who have deFlowersed old Edinburgh, its Enlightenment mission, not to mention its World Heritage status.

Bland was not paying attention to the macroscopic turpitude of Princes Street, interested as he was in locating a single shop, whose address he did not know, nor its name. After two false starts he finally found the posh cashmere shop managed by Priscilla. He knew it was Priscilla's as soon as he timidly entered it – the same effortlessly perfect design that reigned in her house was reproduced in the arrangement of shelves and display cases. The shop was busy with Russian and Chinese customers, some of the few who can afford the eye-watering prices charged for the exclusive three-ply designer styles in which the shop specialised.

Bland managed to steal a brief moment in Priscilla's life: she was not attending to anything or anyone in particular, but was tiptoeing among the displays, stroking gently a scarf here and a cardigan there, enchanted by the softness of the touch and the sheer beauty of the patterns. She must have felt Bland's indiscreet gaze, as she turned abruptly, only to smile broadly at the sight of a slightly embarrassed Bland.

"Eric, what a surprise! What are you doing here?"

"I am sorry to bother you at work, but do you think you could spare five minutes for me? It is important."

"Of course. Shall we go to my office or do you fancy a coffee somewhere near?"

"Your office would be perfect."

Priscilla's office turned out to be marginally larger than a cupboard, but, of course, she had managed to make it look attractive and inviting: two low armchairs flanked an even lower coffee table housing a posh laptop and a couple of merchandise catalogues.

Bland sat nervously on the edge of the armchair while Priscilla let the whole leather vessel embrace her body.

"Is it business or pleasure, Eric?" Priscilla was trying to ease Bland's apparent unease.

"That is one good way of putting it, I suppose. Let me ask you straight: what would you prefer? Me working nine-to-five, no night calls, no ruined weekends, bigger salary or me as I am now?" Bland blurted it all out in one breath.

"Surely there is a catch. What is it?" Priscilla was not just a pretty face.

"Principles, you might say. Justice, if that does not sound too pompous."

"You have to tell me more, if you can. Of course."

"I have two options. One: I choose the quiet life, which means effectively closing a double-murder case by placing the blame on to the hired killer, who is conveniently dead. Superintendent job is mine. Two: I send to the Procurator Fiscal the list of high-ranking corrupt Chinese officials who are behind the whole sordid affair. The file goes nowhere and I can forget about the superintendent job."

Priscilla looked intently into Bland's eyes for a very long time, or so it appeared to Bland, and then she suddenly got up, straightened down her skirt, and addressed him as a naughty schoolboy: "And for a minute I thought you were serious. You are a silly kipper, Bland. There are no two options and both you and I know it. Turning to more serious matters: do you fancy Indian tonight? There is a south Indian restaurant not far from the Festival Theatre that may be worth checking out."

Bland stood up and kissed her: "Whatever you say, Priscilla. Thank you."

Later that evening, the South Indian restaurant turned out to be a mixed bag: some of the dishes had indeed retained the vibrancy of the original cuisine, whilst others had been adapted for the Scottish palate and thus had lost any credibility. For the whole meal Bland and Priscilla had studiously avoided the issue of option one or two, but Priscilla felt that Bland was really pleased with himself and bursting to tell her something. It was only when the mildly disappointing dessert had arrived that Bland finally erupted. "I may have found a way to have my cake and eat it."

Priscilla looked at her plate unable to disguise her disappointment: "As you are at it, you can have mine, too."

"I mean, what is the point of an empty gesture. There are better ways of blowing my chances of making Superintendent. Much better ways."

CHAPTER 36

BACK TO NORMAL?

Philip and Melissa were out drinking in the quaint harbour pub that had just about adapted its ways traversing the choppy waters of changing your clientele from fishermen and sailors to tourists and estate agents. For the first time in a long while Julia was left alone to reflect on the whirlwind that had shaken her tranquil life so abruptly and so deeply. What had she learned? She had been confronted with a side of her personality that was a complete revelation. At fifty she had discovered that there was a dark corner in her psyche that thrived and revelled in extreme sensations. Yes, of course, she had been scared by the sight of the murdered woman wrapped in cling film – who wouldn't – but she had also been so excited, her heart had been beating so fast and so strongly, her mind had been racing through so many bizarre suppositions and she liked the whole experience. A lot.

Did that mean that deep down she was not satisfied with her ordinary daily life? That her sense of freedom, of self-determination, of autonomy was not as satisfying and fulfilling as she thought? She looked out of the window, hazy lights flickering, muffled sea noises. Hers was not sham happiness. She was truly proud of her life. The excitement of her recent adventure was the cherry on top of a cake made of real feelings, of true achievements, of hard-fought freedoms. Without the love for and from her children, without her passion for antiques and beauty, without the knowledge that her life was her own, the cherry of adventure would be inconsequential and unsatisfying.

But she had also learned something else from working with Bland, that shared endeavour, the common pursuit of an agreed objective, was something missing in her life. Unlike her last disastrous relationship when a control freak had taken advantage of her vulnerability and inexperience to drag her into a life that was not her own, this time she would be in control, knowing what she wanted and why.

Bland had reassured her that the anonymous letter was just a ploy to derail his investigation and that she had never been in danger. He had been less forthcoming as far as the motive behind Dr Gordon's murder was concerned. He suggested that it was a tragic case involving WPC Corby. Julia felt guilty about her less than warm feelings toward the young woman; probably behind the stern and professional exterior there was a sea of torment, if she had been led to kill Gordon first and herself later.

Bland had also been rather reticent about the Mollison-Patterson liaison, but the bottom line was that the prim legal secretary fancied herself as a femme fatale and somehow managed not only to kill Patterson, but also to flee to South America.

Julia was about to enter the part of her brain marked "People Are Not What They Seem" when she heard Philip and Melissa coming home.

"You are back early. Was the pub not to your liking?" asked Julia.

"Pub is okay-ish, but we came back because Philip forgot something, didn't you, Philip?" Melissa's tone was definitely rebukeful.

"Sorry, Mother, but when you were out a Alistair Reid called and asked for you," said Alistair sheepishly.

"What did he want?"

"He didn't say, but said it was urgent and that you should ring him ASAP," said Philip even more sheepishly.

"Do not worry. It's work. And I am off today. I'll ring him tomorrow."

"I thought you would be angry. To be honest, he sounded rather worried. Perhaps you should ring him now." Now that his mother had been so forgiving Philip felt truly sorry for his forgetfulness.

"Nope. Day off means day off."

"Are you going to tell us what is going on with the Neighbourhood Watch charade, Mother?" Philip's eyes were not going to be pulled over with wool too easily.

"A little white lie. Nothing to worry about. Storm in a teacup. Everything is back to normal now."

Next morning Julia was having breakfast alone in the kitchen: her customary cup of Earl Grey was accompanied for the occasion by two rice cakes smothered in Marmite. Julia was not sure what the occasion was; she was still off work, she had made no plans for the day, and a general feeling of end-of-term expectation was in the air.

When the phone rang in the hall, Julia automatically looked at the clock on the kitchen wall: "Who would ring her at eight thirty-five?"

"Julia Flowers. Who is calling?"

"Morning, Julia. Hope I did not wake you up. Alistair Reid here."

"Hi Alistair. No, I have been up for a wee while. My day off."

"I am sorry to bother you Julia, but this business cannot wait." Alistair Reid was his usual assertive self, but Julia was not in the mood for early-morning assertiveness.

"I think I deserve a bit of a rest after the Gordon affair, don't you?"

"That is precisely why we need you, Julia. The way you retrieved those bowls and your discretion. A perfect job well done."

"I take the compliment, Alistair. Thank you. But another job? I'd rather not."

"Having dealt so well with Dr Gordon, you are perfect to graduate to Professor Hobson-Chipwell," Alistair Reid dangled the hook deftly.

"You mean the Disappearing Don?" Julia duly took the bait.

"The very same. A death certificate is finally being issued, so we can proceed with the executry, but there are, shall we say, a few problems with the estate." Alistair Reid was about to bag his big fish and he knew it.

"Why the rush? He disappeared years ago," Julia was trying to buy time.

"I'll explain in person. Rather delicate. Shall we say tomorrow, ten a.m.?"

"I'll come, but no commitment," Julia capitulated with grace.

"Thank you, Julia. See you tomorrow and enjoy your day off."

Why had she agreed to get involved with another potentially unconventional assignment? The Hobson-Chipwell mystery would resurface occasionally in the press and online: a professor of economics cannot just disappear into thin air and not stir countless conspiracy theories. Julia knew that she would agree to whatever Alistair Reid would propose. Perhaps she should keep a record of her more interesting cases, she thought.

Out of the blue she felt an urgent need to send Maisie a food parcel. Her little girl would be revising for her first University exams and some familiar provisions would be a nice way of reminding her of home.

≈≈≈≈≈

Julia was not alone in feeling an impelling need to send stuff through the post.

The following day two packages were delivered. On opening the first one, the office of the Procurator Fiscal would in all probability agree with Bland's recommendation that, although Mr Min Lai was responsible for the murder of Mr and Mrs Liang, in view of his recent death, no proceedings should be instituted.

On opening the second one, Miss Tingting would in all probability be very surprised to see that the anonymous package contained a list of high-ranking Chinese Ministry of Culture officials who appeared to have sold stolen antiques, as shown by numerous account details apparently provided by a well-known auction house.

THE END